The Dark We Know

The Dark We Know

WEN-YI LEE

GILLIAN FLYNN BOOKS

A zando IMPRINT

NEW YORK

zando

Zando supports the right to free expression and the value of copyright. The purpose of copyright is to encourage writers and artists to produce the creative works that enrich our culture. Thank you for buying an authorized edition of this book and for complying with copyright laws by not reproducing, scanning, uploading, or distributing this book or any part of it without permission. If you would like permission to use material from the book (other than for brief quotations embodied in reviews), please contact connect@zandoprojects.com.

Gillian Flynn Books is an imprint of Zando.
zandoprojects.com

First Edition: August 2024

Text design by Aubrey Khan
Moth by Carpe Diem from Noun Project
Cover design by Karina Granda
Cover art by Røkkum

The publisher does not have control over and is not responsible for author or other third-party websites (or their content).

Library of Congress Control Number: 2023951054

978-1-63893-058-7 (Hardcover)
978-1-63893-050-1 (ebook)

10 9 8 7 6 5 4 3 2 1
Manufactured in the United States of America

To those who feel left behind,

those who left something behind,

and those searching for reasons to stay.

Tell me about the dream where we pull the bodies out of the lake
and dress them in warm clothes again.

—RICHARD SIKEN,
"SCHEHERAZADE"

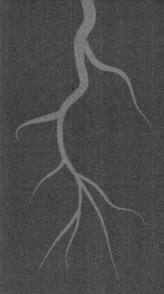

THE GIRL STANDS ON THE EDGE OF THE EARTH

and listens to the wind. On such a moonless night, the blackness of the cliffs and trees is indistinguishable from the sky.

She is smiling. Not her pageant smile, but the one she was born with, curve of teeth still unburdened by growing-up things. She was once too keen for secrets. Wandered too close to floods, kept awake by dreams of sickness and girls lost in waves. But now she is finally at ease.

She steps into the sky and falls toward the reaching water like a torn web, pieces stretched on air. For a breath she is suspended over the surface, a ballerina on black glass. Then she vanishes into the depths.

She does not emerge. All is calm, and all is well.

Elsewhere, a brother jolts awake.

Elsewhere, a boy trips over a grave.

Elsewhere, a girl picks up graphite and digs it under her nails.

The wind moves on, in search of weeping.

1

SLATER IS THE KIND OF PLACE WHERE YOU'RE born to start dying, an old mining town sunk in a crater at the end of the road with nowhere to go beyond it but down. Two years ago, death was what finally got me to leave, so of course it's what's dragged me back to this shithole now.

As Trish pulls up outside our house, I'm forced to look up from my sketchbook and see the cliffs that have swallowed the view. Trish doesn't immediately get out of the car. Instead, she taps the wheel awkwardly like there's some Big Sister speech she forgot to prepare about coming home to bury your shitty dad.

All the while, the engine hums. I rap my pencil on my knuckles, unease growing.

Trish is *usually* prepared. She's twenty-one, completely put together despite the long drive from my school in the city. Her bob is neat, and she wears nice boots with a bit of a heel, which she pressed on the brakes too often. She has more cash now that she's working with Slater's founding family, enough to send me money and pretend it isn't from her. I stopped returning it after she just re-sent it three times. Still, we don't talk about it. She's visited me once in the city and we text, but it's been a while since we spent this much time together. When she opens her mouth at last, though, her phone rings.

It's propped on the dash for GPS, so I get to see the words EMMA VANDERSTEEN pop up. Trish started tutoring the Vandersteen twins in high school. Since then she's graduated into some full-time secretarial role that apparently has no fixed work hours, since Emma tried to call three times on the drive. Trish looks like she's going to ignore this one too, but even I know Mrs. Vandersteen comes before your problematic little sister that you've been tasked with dragging home, and now that we've stopped, she has no excuse.

"Don't keep the queen waiting," I say, and take the chance to escape the car.

I grab my stuff while she takes the call. I don't carry much. It's easier to keep moving with just the same two duffel bags, hauled between the dorm and the tattoo shop I work at. When the dorms close in summer, the owner also lets me crash on the shop's couch. Usually I hate charity, but I don't have a choice, so I make up for it with all the shifts she'll let me do.

As I stand in the open for the first time in hours, Slater winter smothers me like a friend. In spring the rock irises start budding, turning the stones purple, but right now, everything's just gray. A thin wind circles the cliffs, whistling through the rock-roofed houses and coaxing their chimes into swaying. The silver tubes hang everywhere, picking up drafts from the valleys, and the melodic tinkling needles my skin in a way I wish I'd forgotten. My eyes drift to the Carvers' house next door before I snap myself out of it.

I'm not here to revisit the past, dead or alive. I've had a lot of luck since that full-ride acceptance email came in, like life realized how many debts it owed me. I ditched town two years ago without a backup plan, so I don't know what would've happened if I hadn't gotten into art school, gotten lucky hitchhiking, found the questionable hostel that would rent to an unaccompanied teen carrying a suspicious amount of cash, hadn't been kicked out of the shop when I broke in to raid the mini fridge. I've heard enough stories of kids—girls, especially—without that kind of luck, but it's done, so I don't think about it.

Or at least I didn't until about five days ago when I went and fucked it up at my portfolio showcase. Two years on an incredible scholarship put on a noose, because instead of presenting pieces on the theme of Forgotten Places, I'd presented a four-canvas argument for a child therapist. Professor Rodriguez took pity on me, assuming I'd had some sort of stress breakdown, and gave me an extension to redo my pieces. Now I somehow need to make up an entire semester's work in three weeks, so I don't fail and lose that scholarship. And I need to do it in Slater, of all places.

I didn't tell Professor Rodriguez I recognized the people in those nightmare portraits I presented.

I also didn't tell her I don't have any memory of drawing them at all.

"Isa." Phone tucked under her chin, Trish waves her keys out the window.

I'd be happy to delay going inside as long as possible, but Trish looks impatient—worried, even—at whatever's on the other end of the line. The air of trouble makes me pause, but I'm not about to get involved in the Vandersteens' business. Reluctantly, I take the keys and turn toward the house.

The two stories still don't sit together quite right, the floors sloping under their own weight. Abandoned flowerpots mound the yard and the slate shingles fleck like scabs, fissuring where the creepers grow. On the outside it's exactly like every other house, the way Dad wanted us to look. He and Mom moved to town just before Trish was born, following the digging job and leaving behind families they've never talked about. That was over twenty years ago now, but it's nothing compared to all the other families' generations.

Sometimes I think maybe he was right. Time seems to work differently here. Traps things. Stops them changing.

I scuff my thrifted Docs on the mat. Shoulder my bags against my hip. Dig my nails into my palm. Before I can insert the key, though, the door opens, and then Mom is there in the doorway.

She's so colorless in my memories that I'm surprised now to catch flushed cheeks and a pinkness in her mouth. She's all covered up as usual, stiff as a board, but she actually looks her thirty-eight years and younger than I remember.

Neither of us can say the first word, and I'm surprised, then angry, at how small it makes me feel.

Eventually it's Trish who breaks the ice. "Let's get out of the cold," she says, coming up the stairs. It's always Trish who has to mediate Mom's shit. She can't even ditch this place because Mom's got her so tied down.

Mom sounds relieved. "Yes. In the kitchen."

AS I SHUT THE DOOR behind us, Mom leans on Trish, which she never used to do. Worse, Trish lets her. Mom had Trish at seventeen, and growing up, I often felt like they were the sisters instead. Now it's like my leaving brought them even closer together.

4

There's an odd smell of vinegar inside, and the rattrap in the hallway has half a tail in it. Dad's boots are gone from their usual place by the door, soil from his ginseng-digging swept away. The mantelpiece is empty of his Bible. They've cleared him out fast. Once I've noticed, the whole house seems to shake loose, breathe.

The ground feels firmer under my feet as we pass through the living room. This bright relief will fade, like it always does, but it's a good feeling and I'll take it as long as it stays. This *is* the good part. He's gone. He's really gone. Maybe this trip won't be as bad as I worried it would be.

The feeling of lightness continues as I join Mom and Trish at the table, which surprises me again. My stomach used to knot every time I came near the kitchen. Family meals were a land mine. Any conversation could turn to shouting, and even saying no somehow meant we were raising our voices. I couldn't predict when Dad would get mad or decide I didn't deserve the food he'd paid for. I'd get nervous at how close the knives were, how easily plates and glasses could break, even if nothing was touched.

But now the spices are arranged differently; on the shelf there's a jar of peanut butter, which he was allergic to, and freshly baked cookies in airtight boxes, even though he always said they made Mom fat. She's painted her nails pink and her good porcelain plates are back out, the ones from some now-estranged friend or family member still in China. There used to be five in the set, but Dad smashed one. She's only put out three because she has hang-ups over the dead number—the kind of thing they'd always fight about too. Still, it feels like a big deal all the same, to put out breakable things because you're no longer afraid of their ruin. Every second here used to feel like it could ignite. Now Dad is dead, and the house feels for the first time like it's coming alive.

Of course, Mom spoils it when she brings the kettle over to fill my cup and nearly drops it on my lap in exaggerated shock. "What did you do to your face?"

Damn. I forgot. "Put some metal in it." It's a tiny stud in my nose. She's acting like it's a cattle ring.

"And that black thing on your mouth?"

"It's a funeral, right?"

Trish elbows me as Mom reddens.

"Your dad will—" She stops, blinking, and fills my cup. I probably shouldn't let her see my ears yet. And we won't even mention the tattoos.

I drink and pretend like she didn't bribe me to be here. When Trish, the sacrificial messenger, called me the day after the showcase, she had to reason me into coming. *Mom's willing to give you a share of the money. If you want any of it—and you need it, let's not lie—then I'm gonna come pick you up.*

I do want that money. The cash I stole ran out ages ago and the dollars the tattoo parlor pays me to sweep floors won't stretch once I graduate. Eight thousand is enough to make me grit my teeth and sit here, even if it means that I'm spending the remaining two weeks of my extension in the least conducive place in the world.

I stare out the window, down the street, hoping for inspiration. The roads in this town all run up against the cliffs at the vanishing point, sometimes running into the valleys. Only one real exit out, and a whole forest between here and anyone else. Unless I steal Trish's car or manage to hitchhike again, I'm not getting out alone.

Mom's voice interrupts my analyzing. "Trisha, they're still looking for that girl? It's been what, four days?"

"Nothing yet," Trish says warily.

A bad feeling blooms in my stomach, and so I finally feel like I'm home. I shouldn't ask, I know I shouldn't, but I suck at doing anything I'm supposed to. "What girl?"

Trish purses her lips. "Paige Vandersteen's gone missing."

Of course she is. Because this place is shit and shitty things happen to everyone here and follow you out, and God, *that* feels like coming home. Of course Emma Vandersteen was calling, if her princess has disappeared. I almost sicken myself thinking, *So it happens to good girls too.* "Just missing?" I say quietly.

Trish's voice is sharp. "Just missing."

"Officer Tai has been around all day asking everyone questions." Mom glances at me. "The police want to talk to Mason."

"Mom," Trish interrupts, but it's too late. It's the first time Mason's name has been brought up, like they were waiting for me to be stuck here. It won't be the last either. Everything here ends up involving him.

I should ask why they're looking for him. It's the obvious next question. But I don't want to know. I've done the missing girl. I've done the paralysis and grief when they find her body. Paige will turn up soon too, and it'll all be over. Just because Mason and I used to be friends, it doesn't mean I have to get involved again just because he's decided to.

Trish comes to my rescue and switches the subject. "How's Olivia?"

"They're fine." Trish thought it was cool I had a Vietnamese roommate who introduced me to even more of their Asian friends, but Olivia and I haven't talked since they tried to set me up on a date and I freaked out on their friend. "They'll collect homework for me, I guess." I can feel Mom's gaze, but she'll never ask.

That's us. We don't ask, and we don't tell. There's no fighting here. You leave or you die. I made my choice.

I'VE NEVER LIKED BEING HOME. I was always elsewhere, outdoors or being taken in by the Carvers or the Tais. As a kid that made me "social" and "adventurous." Later it started making me an "ungrateful child who treated her parents' house like it was hers to come and go from."

Art students eat up a shitty-parent backstory. You're not even an art student if you don't have some kind of trauma to mine. Here, though, my childhood stops feeling like a party trick. On the left is the bathroom, door the same rusty color Trish taught me to scrub out of my sheets the first time I woke up with blood between my legs. Opposite is Trish's room, then mine, and at the very end is the bedroom I never entered, where my parents slept. The hallway is suffocating, especially because the vinegar smell is thick here, and the air's staler than it should be. I finally let myself think *something's wrong*. But the smell seems to be coming from everywhere.

With the lock taken off a long time ago, my old door swings wide easily to reveal emptiness. My things are gone, thrown out or burned, maybe. I can imagine Dad taking out his bruised ego on whatever I left behind. I try not to think about whether that included Trish or Mom.

In here, the vinegar draws me to the window. Without thinking I tug the curtains aside to let the remaining daylight in on the sulfur yellow wallpaper, revealing the Carvers' house across the yard. The window that faces mine is open, and behind the fluttering curtains, Wren's room is hollow. I can almost see the indent of her in it, palm lifted, nose scrunched to her eyes so I can make out her dimples even from here.

I wrench myself from that image and finally figure out where the stale smell is coming from. Someone's caulked the window—not just the outside frame but the inside, too, making the pane immovable. What? I scratch at it, wondering if it was a mistake, but by the way the smell is everywhere, all the windows must have been sealed like this.

Trish wouldn't have done this. It's Mom. She's always hated opening windows and curtains, and she won't leave the house unless she has to. Now that she runs the place, she's just gone wild with it. The trapped fumes are starting to make me feel lightheaded. I almost don't realize I'm being watched until my neck prickles, directing me to Mr. Carver staring up at me from his driveway. When our eyes meet, something flickers over his brown face.

He turns sharply away and disappears into the house. I hate my immediate urge to call after him. I didn't go to Wren's funeral. Couldn't. Got the hell out of here instead with an acceptance letter and stolen cash, leave or die. I doubt I'm welcome at the Carver house anymore.

I leave him and the caulked window. No point unpacking completely, but I unzip my bag to grab fresh clothes. I brush the folder at the bottom of the bag and suddenly feel my classmates' stares all over again.

A rat scuttles overhead. They were the original tunnelers around here, until the mines sent them scurrying out. In most places in Slater, humans are the only things that breathe—other living things seem to avoid these mountains. In this house, though, there's always a few hundred heartbeats in the walls. You can't leave any food out here, or the rats will be on it the second you leave. We can't catch them fast enough.

Someone once scrawled PLAGUE EATER on my locker after one snuck into my backpack and scrambled out in the middle of the cafeteria. There was a big plague decades ago that forced the Vandersteens to close down the quarry, clogging the river with rats—before the town was saved by holy intervention, if you believe how blessed the Vandersteens supposedly are. Maybe they'll think differently now Paige is missing. Bad things only happen to sinners, isn't that right?

Trish enters with a towel and a blanket. "You okay?"

Probably what she was trying to ask me in the car, but I wouldn't have told her anyway. She doesn't need more things to worry about. "What's up with the windows?"

Trish leans against the doorframe. "It made her feel better."

So did turning a blind eye when Dad locked me out of the house. "I'm not staying if I'm going to die in my sleep from breathing in chemicals, no matter how much the inheritance is."

"I'll get a fan in here. We might sell this place soon anyway."

"Oh, so now you're a 'we'?" I sound like a whiny kid again, but I can't help myself.

Trish's mouth purses. "I ran into Mason a couple weeks ago. He asked how you were doing." She pauses. "He's always asking."

I have the renewed urge to jump out the window, sealant or not. Trish eyes me. I fill in the rest: *You should have texted him. You could have at least sent a letter; you know how he is about*

THE DARK WE KNOW

letters. You could have at least waited until his girlfriend—Our neighbor! Your best friend! The girl you were secretly pathetically in love with!—was in the ground before you ditched town.

"I didn't know you guys talked."

"I saw the four of you grow up."

"And then there were two."

Trish looks tired of me. It's such a Mom look. *How do I deal with Isa today?* Once, Trish would've known how to instantly make everything better, and part of me wants to believe that magic still exists.

But she just says, "You've had a long day, Isa. Take a shower."

"Close the door!" I yell as she exits.

She rolls her eyes but pulls it shut behind her.

I sink onto the mattress, where the pillow still has the faint dent of my head. I can't imagine this place ever selling. Every floorboard and wall is knotted with crying girls, secrets, and starving vermin. I imagine a contractor ripping down the wallpaper to find them crawling on the underside: knife-eyed rats in death throes, women on their knees clawing at the fleur-de-lis, their limbs contouring out the stripes. I used to think I heard their voices sometimes, slipping out the edges and becoming garbled. But then I realized it was probably just Mom, talking to herself in a language I don't understand.

More likely, this house will just become another abandoned building in this town, taken back over by the vines. Better that way. The rock irises might be able to give it the color we never could.

Forgotten Places. If I can focus and draw, Slater should theoretically be perfect.

. . .

WHEN I'VE SCRUBBED OFF the long drive in scalding water, I finally pull out my portfolio folder. I haven't opened it since the showcase. Now the cord bites at my fingers as I unwind it; the plastic crackles as I pull the cover open.

The canvas backs are all the same scratchy off-white, blasphemously folded into quarters, but my fingers gravitate toward one portrait that I spread out on the bed. The pallid face unfurls in the falling dusk. Air whistles—distant wind through some crack in Mom's sealant, or else breath through my teeth.

I used to take stoneworking lessons at the Vandersteens' sculpture workshop, but I started in pencils and it's still my primary medium. Graphite is cheap and dark. It can suggest entire worlds just with the contrast of negative space. Like this:

The girl is lying half-buried, roots winding through her skin. Pale skin, paler hair. She smiles vacantly at the sky, and it would be almost peaceful, if her neck wasn't slanted at a forty-five-degree angle. This was the first piece I unveiled at my showcase a few days ago, one portrait out of four that I don't remember creating at all.

It's a dead Paige Vandersteen.

Who's now missing.

Across the bare garden, Wren Carver's curtains flutter like wide lashes, and an ancient song rolls in from the valleys.

The rich dark tremor shudders softly through me, and thoughts flicker up in its echo: Wren, and then Zach—and then Mason Kane, out there somewhere at the center of them all, and the only remaining person alive outside of this house who once truly knew me.

12

I squeeze my fists. *"No."*

The song drops away, a mute button suddenly hit. My breath calms. I shove the involuntary memories away, shut out everything except what I need to do: Bury Dad. Finish my portfolio. Get my money. Get out. It's almost unsettling how easily that instinct returns.

People hear lots of things around here; the land is old and hollowed out enough to sing. For some, the mountain songs tell of the coming weather, or where the first flowers will bloom in spring. Some say it's a chorus of witches in places the ginseng doesn't grow. The really upstanding ones will say they hear holy spirits. All I've ever heard is a song that drags up my lies and transgressions from where I'd buried them, reminding me how much I shouldn't be here. Growing up, I had to learn to block it out. I've just slipped after being away for so long, and met the consequences. It's a good reminder that surviving here isn't the same as anywhere else.

Night falls. Mom and Trish bake potatoes that are already sprouting. I pull out clothes for tomorrow's funeral, draw and then throw out a few sketches, and then get into bed. I don't remember it being so small.

2

UNSURPRISINGLY I DREAM ABOUT GETTING out of town. Two years ago, I snuck onto a truck taking crates of ginseng to the city. Rattled in the carriage with the roots, watching the shadow of the cliffs fold in behind us. Back then, for the first time, I let myself hope that I could actually leave Slater behind. But today I wake up and realize I'm still here.

Fortunately, even with no sun, it's an almost beautiful day to kick your asshole dad into hell. Today a light breeze curls through the trees. The cemetery ground, stretching around the Chapel of Our Herald at the far end, is sparkling gray. Guardian angel statues usher us through the plots, roots twining through the slate chips they're made from.

"No one has this many friends," I mutter as well-wishers arrive. Trish shoots me a look that isn't exactly disagreeing but is definitely telling me to keep my mouth shut where people can hear. I don't know what I can tell her exactly. Definitely not about the drawing of Paige. I haven't even figured it out myself. Maybe I'm crazy, or maybe it's this old feeling that there's something wrong beneath my skin. All I know is that there's nothing I can do about Paige if she's already missing, and I can't afford to be distracted right now. Besides, a Vandersteen doesn't need my help. People squeeze our hands, press us with homemade jams, talk about how much of a horrible, tragic accident it was for Dad to die of a peanut allergy. Mom came back to find Dad lying swollen in his lunch, hence the closed casket. I have to stop myself from laughing every time. People actually liked Dad. It's amazing how many things you can keep shut inside a house that never opens its curtains, what the worst gossips in the world can choose to ignore.

It stops being bitterly funny when the Carvers arrive, followed by Officer Tai, bringing Slater's entire Asian population into attendance. Mom grabs my wrist like she knows I'll bolt, practically shackles me until they're too close to avoid.

I feel like a helpless kid again, surrounded by my dead friends' parents. Mrs. Carver envelops me in a warm hug and murmurs, almost in tears, "Oh, you're so big now."

I forgot she's like this. Whereas I can't remember the last time Mom hugged me, or touched me, really, other than to push or pull me somewhere, Mrs. Carver hated letting Wren go. She was always squeezing her, kissing her forehead, idly twisting her curls or running her fingers along Wren's scalp like she wasn't even doing it consciously. It was just second nature for them. Wren was like that, too—took my hand, hooked our elbows together, leaned her head on my shoulder and kissed my cheek. It meant nothing to her and too much to me.

The dread only really comes, though, when she pulls back and frowns at my face. Could be the piercings, could be the dark lipstick Mom spent the morning glaring at again, probably both. Usually the attention is the goal—to be looked at on my own terms instead of either being invisible or a monster turning heads—but Zach's and Wren's families practically helped raise me. Part of me still wants to be something they like, so they don't throw me out too.

Meanwhile, Officer Tai looks like he wants to say something to me. There aren't a lot of reasons to come across the world and end up in Slater, but one of the few things I know about Dad's family is that they were ginseng harvesters before they came and stayed harvesters in the decades after, and when he and Mom had to leave their original town, they simply found somewhere else that needed an instinct for finding the roots. Zach's mom worked with Dad—that's how Zach and I started hanging out, but Mom mentioned on the way that Mrs. Tai had since gone back to her family "somewhere out west." Zach's brother's away at college, funded by the Vandersteens, so Officer Tai is alone.

I know he's looking for Paige—for Mason—but funeral manners seem to stop him from asking questions. "Welcome home," is all he ends up saying, gruffly.

I escape as soon as I can, letting Trish take over. I'm immediately intercepted, however, by Amelia Fischer, once just another girl I saw in school and bible study; now married and pregnant, throwing her arms around me and weeping *I'm so sorry* while the husband I vaguely recognize loiters. I pat her back as she sniffles about how hard this must be for me, attention flicking instead to tracking the crowd. I can't help it. I feel on edge and need to know exactly who's around me. There's the dentist; the contractor and his wife; the ancient Cynthia who still runs the diner; Dad's former boss, Mr. Ross, plus his wife and their son, Harley—heir to the ginseng harvesting operation, general dickhead, and Zach's old team captain who didn't even attend his funeral. You can tell who in town works for whom by their hands: the stoneworkers have dust under their nails, and the Rosses' diggers have dirt.

I'm starting to think the Vandersteens aren't sending their usual single representative after all—letting the Rosses show them up—when the pale figure of Otto Vandersteen appears and makes my stomach jolt.

The last time I saw Paige's brother was also at a funeral. The whole family was there, the twins Barbie blonde and attached at the hip, round-faced and pink-cheeked in matching black dresses and crucifix necklaces made of stone. Otto's alone now, trimmed in a black coat, hair curled under his ears.

The Vandersteens supposedly all have the exact same eyes— desaturated gray with silver that twines through the iris like veins to be extracted. Like whatever deal their ancestors made when they first entered the crater of Slater demanded that every birth simply zip a new skin over ready-made insides. I've never gotten close enough to prove the story, but you don't need to get close to tell that the twins are more identical than most. Save the cropped hair, Otto has the same face as the girl that showed up dead on my canvas last week.

He's a year younger than me. We were in the same sculpting class, although we never really talked. All I remember is how incredible a sculptor he was, even at fifteen. He always had an uncanny sense for shaping the stone, like the slate chips moved themselves under his touch. Yet Paige was the one being positioned to take over the family business, because, according to Trish, the Vandersteens thought he was too fragile.

Amelia's husband mutters, "Who would have thought Paige Vandersteen would run off? Would've bet my life on it being the other one."

"You bet the Vandersteens wish it was the other one," someone else replies.

If Otto feels the attention, he doesn't reveal it. He finds Mom
right away in the crowd, says a few words to her and Officer
Tai—and then makes a beeline for me. That surprises me even
more than seeing him, enough that I don't move quick enough
to avoid him.

"I'm sorry," he begins, but I cut him off before we can do the
whole spiel again.

"*I'm* sorry. I heard about Paige."

"Oh." His expression tightens. His eyes—yes, unsettlingly
marbled—are noticeably red. He's a lot more comfortable in his
skin than I remember, though, and you couldn't mistake him for
Paige anymore. Something about the way he holds himself,
pitches his voice smoothly, wears a coat with a boxy cut. Arranged
himself like one of his own sculptures. "Have you seen Mason
Kane?"

This spell is starting to feel like a curse. The question *makes*
me see Mason, vivid and sharp with Wren and Zach beside him,
and I have to breathe deeply just to push him away. "Not since I
left." I'm still determined to avoid all the places he likes to hang
out—the grotto, Elopers' Ridge, the bare library. The only place I
plan to be is in my room working.

"Did you leave because of him?"

I'm so taken aback by the question I can only say the truth,
which is no. I must say it more fiercely than I mean to, because
Otto shakes his head. "Sorry. That wasn't appropriate."

But now I have to know. *Leave or die*, I think, but my ugly
impulse finally breaks through and picks danger. "Hang on. Why
are you looking for Mason?"

He raises his eyebrows, like he's surprised I haven't heard. "The day before my sister disappeared, they were seen heading to the Ridge. Police want to talk to him, but Mason's been hard to catch."

That sounds about right. I can't blame him for avoiding the police after they interrogated him on Wren's death and he was the last person to see Officer Tai's son, but what was he doing with Paige that he won't share with the police? People go to Elopers' Ridge to drink and hook up under the cliffs, but I can't see that being the reason.

"Are you sure she hasn't just left town?" I ask instead, even though Paige Vandersteen is the last person I'd expect to run away. Then again, everyone once thought Wren was a perfect angel, too.

Otto leans in and I remember that for all his being the quiet sibling, he's raised in the same blood that made this town. Paige Vandersteen got two hundred students to shut their mouths about her brother coming out, and now I see that Otto shares the same drill-bit stare. "She would have taken me with her," he says.

Pastor Charles clears his throat and I use the excuse to move abruptly away, rejoining Trish and Mom.

"We are gathered here today to see Jonathan Chang home to our eternal Father. Under His grace, the Son, and His angel who delivers us," Pastor Charles begins. "Jon has been a dedicated member of our community since he moved to town . . ."

I still see Otto out of the corner of my eye. There's a story about another pair of Vandersteen twins, generations ago. *Ida got lusty and sailed off with a fop; Sammy went nuts and took the drop.* The Vandersteens have tried real hard to rub out the branches of their family tree they don't like, but the tales echo. They have bad luck with twins, it seems. Emma and Pierce should've had a third, but word is that Emma could never get pregnant again.

I can't even begin to guess what Mason was doing with Paige. Like most people in Slater, I have complicated feelings about the Vandersteens—I took art classes at Mr. Vandersteen's workshop and even now I feel indebted to them. Mason, however, held a righteous dislike for the whole family, sealed away in the crumbling mansion the townspeople call the Purple House for the way the irises carpet the land. I'd believe Dad was alive again before I believed Mason was hooking up with her. But I can't think what other reason they would possibly have to be running off together.

The start of prayers distracts me. It's been a long time since I was surrounded by prayer and it makes my skin prickle, especially when Pastor Charles starts singing in tongues. But thankfully both prayers and the eulogy are short, to make time for the burial. We like the digging around here. For most of the other townspeople it's in their roots, grandparents and great-grandparents brought to Slater by treasure the ground promised. They scooped out the mountains, and now we put ourselves back in. Everyone clasps their hands for the ceremony. Dust returns to dust.

The first clump goes in. Thunk. I imagine how it must echo inside the casket. How Dad would panic if he was still alive in there because that would be it, that's six feet of earth coming down between him and life. I imagine familiar fists banging desperately on the lid, shaking the wood even as soil scatters through the cracks.

I hope he feels it.

The soil is packed and tucked. The gravediggers step away. I'm given a flat rock.

Not slate, we can't afford that since the quarry closed. But close enough, gray and striped, the size of my palm. Everyone gets one from the stack prepared, but they're waiting for us. The family. The first mourners. We'll lay our stones, and then the rest of the attendees will take turns, stacking and circling rocks into a cairn on the newly leveled earth.

We scoop out the mountains, we put ourselves back in—and then we draw the earth back on top of us. Otto strokes his stone almost thoughtfully before setting it down. All the while Pastor Charles leads the congregation in a hymn, and the voices reverberate into the growing cairn. Not too forcefully, though—to topple a cairn is to kill a loved one.

The final prayer blurs by. Then the attendees are trickling back to wherever they came from. It's back to me, Trish, and Mom. *Well*, I almost say, *let's pack it up*. But I don't think Mom would appreciate that. She's been such a perfect wife the whole ceremony, like she always has been. Always a wife, never a mother.

Then, as we're about to leave, a figure appears at the far end of the graves. A ghost or a nightmare, Mason Kane glides down the plots in a gray coat with a box cradled in his arms. He sees us across the slurried grass. He stops in his tracks, and my heart stops in my chest.

Leave, I think, but when has he ever done what anyone wants? He does not leave, and now I can't breathe. As a wind swings around the cairn, he strides across the distance and falls in alongside Mom, and I almost see two more shadows behind him.

"Mrs. Chang," he says, "I hope you're doing well." Then, to me: "Hi. You look different. Good."

In the city whenever I tried to reach for childhood memories, looking for the *authenticity* my professors kept asking me to draw, I always just came up blank. Even seeing Zach's and Wren's families brought up nothing. But Mason's voice stabs like a key and the fragments flood me now, faster than I can catch them: a cave drenched in sunlight, hand-me-down sweaters, a boat with a pirate sail, a flower chain on dark hair, glittering coins, purple pens, a fire, milkshakes, being hugged. The tide of memories feels like it's going to break me open. This is why I didn't want to see him. I can't breathe, can't stay, need to exit *now*.

When he asks, "Can we walk?" I really do break. And yet instead of shutting down, some childish feeling surges through me. I nod and follow him.

3

"SO, ART SCHOOL," MASON SAYS AS HE LEADS us through the cemetery. "I'm really happy for you."

All I can manage in reply is, "Thanks."

For all the stuff about *watching us grow up*, Trish watched us go with stormy eyes. Not trusting me to handle myself, maybe.

It'd be fair. The last time we were really together was at Zach's funeral and I didn't stick around afterward. This is a twisted way of picking up exactly where we left off two years ago, walking away from a fresh grave. Like any other regretted night, it feels impossible to talk about now that the sun's up.

Especially since the last time I saw Mason, I almost hated him. I hadn't properly talked to him—or Wren or Zach—in a long time. I'd spent months finding excuses not to spend time with them, and even more months before that so bitterly obsessed with his relationship with Wren that I almost thought I loved him before I realized I was jealous of Mason, not of her.

Objectively he's only gotten prettier: Slater's leached him away and left a beauty of a sharp husk behind. Time has carved out some devastating angles in his face, and his light brown hair is longer and swept away. Sixteen-year-old me would have thought about cutting herself open on the unfairly sharp bridge of his nose. But I'm eighteen now, and those feelings feel pathetically childish, and mostly I'm scared by how little it looks like he's been sleeping.

Start of spring semester junior year, his best friend Zachary Tai, a star track athlete, was cut from the team. He was seen running out of Mason's house, right before he shot himself by the river. Three weeks later, Wren—his girlfriend and possibly the only person who's ever made Mason Kane unsure of himself—was found floating in the pond.

She'd been missing for long enough that her parents got worried. They called all her friends and even all the girls she was even remotely friendly with, from church and class and yearbook. No one knew where she was, but during their rounds, they picked up our school rumors: Wren and Mason. Mason and Wren. People started saying she must have done something bad, to run away like that. Finally, her parents searched her room and found letters and texts from Mason, revealing the relationship they'd kept quiet for a year. They also found an unfinished letter to her mother—where she believed she was pregnant. When the Mayers' grandson stumbled on her body in their pond, Officer Tai already had Mason in custody.

Plenty of people couldn't wait to blame Wren—what did she expect, getting involved with a boy like that? But more people whispered about Mason: the rebel, the smart mouth, the unbeliever, so pretty his unknown dad must be the devil. A corruption that ruined two lives now. He'd incited his best friend to suicide. He'd killed his girlfriend to get rid of the baby. He was the last person tied to both of them. Even when the autopsy proved that she hadn't been pregnant at all and Mason was released on lack of evidence, the damage was done.

I know he didn't have anything to do with it. For most of our childhood, the four of us were inseparable. But as I drifted from them it seemed they only got closer. There was something special about the three of them that didn't include me. What the rumors didn't know was that it had always been three. Mason and Zach and Wren. Wren and Mason and Zach. And maybe, if you looked hard enough into the corner, Isadora.

But now another girl's missing. And not just any girl—a Vandersteen. Is he up to something? Or is he really just that unlucky?

"You're taking the long way," I say out loud, to cover my own thoughts. We're in an older part of the cemetery, where the original angel statues stand. One of the founding Vandersteens established their family craft of slate sculpturing to complement their quarrying business. Now the sculptors are limited to working from imported stone.

I'd forgotten how intricate the original ones were. See, you can't carve slate like other rock. Instead, you take a chisel and split a piece into thinner and thinner layers, right down the middle. Then you snap and stack all these little split chips, layering them into the shape you want. The chips pin each other down with their collective weight. These angels are made from thousands of different pieces, each feather in their wings an individual stone. The Rosses unearthing ginseng in the surrounding forest might have been the injection the town needed after the closing of the quarry, but the Vandersteens are old money. Like their sculptures, the town's built from pieces of them.

"Avoiding the view from the road," he says. "The chief came all the way to the morgue trying to find me yesterday, I'm not going to make it easy for him."

I have two questions. The first is the burning one: *What were you doing with Paige Vandersteen?* The second is the one I choose to stick to. "What were you doing at the morgue?"

He raises his eyebrows. "I work there. Teddy Dunn doesn't care about the rumors," he says, but what the old cemetery keeper does or doesn't think is lost as we stop in front of two much newer headstones: one arch and one cross.

ZACHARY TAI. LAID TO REST.

WREN AMARA CARVER. BELOVED DAUGHTER.

My tongue goes numb. I knew, of course, this is where we were going to end up. And I thought I'd been prepared, but I was wrong.

Without meaning to, I touch Wren's headstone. A violent shudder makes me jerk away, but my eyes trace the engraving anyway, the up-and-down points of the letters, the three *A*s of her middle name like arrowheads. I hadn't known they were buried next to each other.

I'm suddenly all too aware of the fact that my feet are inches away from her body. Even when I started avoiding the group, she was still the person I'd text a photo of a pretty plant, or a light in the doorway. Sometimes we'd both be in our rooms doing homework at night, and I'd text her for answers and she'd pull faces at me from the window but send them anyway. She'd leave raisin cookies in my locker with a note tucked into the bag, and I'd leave them there because I didn't dare bring them home.

A second shudder goes through me and I stumble backward, throat turning sour. I bite down on my lip until I taste blood and pull myself together, staring at the cairns marking the plots instead. Wren's is a pile like Dad's, but Zach wasn't given a proper funeral, since he shot himself and Pastor Charles wouldn't mourn him. The few of us who gathered to see his grave had to stack five stones as high as possible. It's not much, but at least one of the stones I placed there myself. I had never seen Wren's grave. None of that pile is mine.

"Isa," Mason says quietly. He's holding out a rose from his box. From what I know, he wasn't at Wren's funeral either, because everyone still thought he'd killed her. At the very least, making him a scapegoat let her parents organize a proper ceremony. A kid kills themselves, and it's all about the rules they should have followed so they didn't end up that way, and the shame on them and their family; someone disappears, and it's that the mountains take back sometimes, for all they've fed us.

I take the flower, but my fingers go clammy around the stem. When I put it on Zach's grave, a thorn pricks my skin. "You didn't miss much," Mason small talks. "New boutique opened, new bar opened, Amelia and Ben got married." *That* was his name, Ben-who-played-guitar-on-Sundays-sometimes. "Oh—*Harley and Paige* went out for a while."

"*Paige* went out with *Harley Ross*?" I'd always noticed how Zach would tense around Harley and still chase his approval like air. They were like that, the boys and their captain. Alone they were fine. Together they were a dense pack I'd feel simultaneously afraid of and drawn to whenever I passed by, and Harley was the worst of them.

"Their families are friends, remember, but she figured him out pretty quick and was planning on breaking things off. Overheard him saying some great things after about how she was probably like her brother and how they both screwed up their mom's womb; that's why she couldn't have any more kids. Mind you he hasn't stopped being a possessive dick even now; I'm avoiding him too."

I've been so caught up in the familiar banter of gossiping that I completely forgot who we were talking about. In the pause, it becomes obvious that I've realized he's baited me into the topic. He knows that I must know about Paige's disappearance by now. *Ask*, the tension chants, *ask, ask, ask.*

"So, no plans for college?" I ask instead.

Disappointment flits across his face. "No," he says carelessly. "Seems kind of far away."

"Bullshit." I'd take that answer from most other people in Slater, whose families often are born and die here, but not from him. The four of us used to imagine what we'd do after high school, which seemed so impossibly far away then. We talked about getting out and seeing the world. Zach on some sports team. Mason to some fancy college. Wren to become a famous musician. Me just because. The others were the dreamers; it took me a long time to be able to envision anything beyond Slater. It took that acceptance email to light some kind of spot in the darkness—and it took my friends dying to finally force me toward it. I can't think why he'd stay, when it's so clearly been eating away at him.

He considers me, and there's an unsettling shadow in his sleep-wrung eyes that goes beyond him. "Okay." He settles onto his haunches. "I couldn't leave their ghosts behind."

I feel a chill that has nothing to do with the wind. "Who?" I say, even though I know. He just looks at me, not entertaining the act. Wren and Zach. He's talking about seeing Wren and Zach.

Mason's mother, Sharlene, is a medium. Rumor has it that Sharlene came out of nowhere. Just appeared in Slater as a young teenager, alone and without family, moving into a house by the woods that had been abandoned by some plague-dead miner and quietly advertising her medium services to neighboring towns. While Dad had been obsessed about us blending in as much as possible, Sharlene had never tried to become part of town. Slater is not the place to be if you claim to call up ghosts. People sure believe in spirits, with the way the forests get at night, but it's against God, and the land, to drag back something that's been taken. Yet something's kept Sharlene here, and Mason along with her. At least, she's technically here—she's well-known enough that she's often out of town for hours or even days at a time for clients. He basically raised himself.

Again, though, only Mason could get away with having an outcast single mom. He managed to be so pretty and interesting that even the girls in church would giggle about him as if he were a dirty secret, ask Wren and me what we knew about him, since we were *friends*, a question that always felt like a trap somehow. Best friends forever—the three kids of color in the year and our token Lucifer. Anyway, he didn't like his mother either. They fought because he refused to let her teach him. He believed in real things, he said. Whatever crazy she had, he insisted he hadn't inherited. I've heard Mason conspire about the church, our teachers, all the things we were and weren't being told, but to him, both God and ghosts were for people with no other convictions.

Sometime in the past two years, however, he's apparently turned around and committed to his sixth sense.

I couldn't leave their ghosts.

He remains completely serious. "I saw them the night of Wren's funeral. Here. I called, and they appeared."

"Here?" With a flash of hate, I suddenly have an image of him spending nights here with them over the past two years, talking, laughing. I'm almost afraid to ask, but it comes out of me. "So you still see them?"

"Just the once," he says, and my relief makes me feel terrible. "I've been trying, because I think they were trying to tell me something, but I can't seem to break through to them anymore. The only difference is that last time, you were still in town." I don't like where this is going, but I'm rooted to the spot as he continues, righteous and rapid as ever. "Any summoning is stronger with more connections to the spirits. You, me, Zach, and Wren. I think that's the key."

"Key to what? Seeing them again? Don't spirits—I don't know, pass on? Isn't it a good thing if they're gone?"

"They're not gone, I can feel them just beyond," he insists, and it's like I don't recognize him after all. "They *were* trying to tell me something. And I know there's something wrong, because—" He hesitates. My mind fills in the pause with dread, but not enough to guess what he says next. "Paige and I were on the Ridge to do a séance at the plague house. She'd found some connection to some secret bastard Vandersteen ancestor and wanted proof."

I stare at him. I'd been so focused on people going to the Ridge to hook up that I forgot what else stands there, tucked away in a shallow cave. Alongside their treasured slate, the miners dug up a plague. It killed off hundreds and started the quarry's rapid death. Supposedly, the plague only stopped because the Vandersteens had a vision and built a house on the Ridge to quarantine all the town's sick kids, where they then died—drowned in a storm, or taken in a biblical exchange for the rest of the town's survival, depending on what you believe. Mason, Zach, Wren, and I explored the Ridge once. It hadn't even occurred to me Paige would too.

"Except we couldn't reach them either; there was something blocking their spirits from coming through. It was the exact same feeling I have when I try to reach Zach and Wren. I didn't remember the first time it happened until I felt it again. I think they're connected, and if that's true, then Wren's and Zach's deaths aren't what they seem. I also don't think it's a coincidence Paige disappeared while looking into the plague deaths." He pauses.

"This town has a history of suicides, and you know exactly which graves they are, because they're unmarked. After the plague house, I've spent the last few nights trying to reach every single one of them I can find. Almost every one is blocked just like Zach and Wren and the plague kids."

"What are you saying?" I interrupt, even though I have the dawning feeling that I don't want to hear the answer.

He runs his tongue over his teeth, and *that* makes me nervous, because anything that *Mason* hesitates to say is probably the most dangerous thing I've ever heard. "I think something killed them. And I think that something is still around."

"Zach shot himself," I say roughly, letting him flinch. "And if it wasn't you, and I know it wasn't, then Wren walked into the pond herself too."

Mason points to another grave without a cairn, a few rows back. "George Mayer, ten years old, drowned in the same pond Wren did." Points another way. "Ella Williams, seventeen, overdosed on the Ridge. Tony Astin, fourteen, missing and presumed dead.

Laurie Falkner, thirteen, missing and presumed dead. Lucy May Brandenburg, sixteen, cut her arms." He keeps pointing and reciting like he's memorized all these names and deaths. How long did he take to wander the graveyard and search them out? How many of them can he list? How many can I listen to?

"Stop," I snap, answering my own question. "Suicides happen. Disappearances happen."

"Maybe," he says. "But why are so many of ours so young?"

"I can't go down this road."

"What road?"

"Of deluding ourselves that we can do something about it. They're dead. Whatever we believe isn't going to change that."

"What about the *why*?" he demands. "What about stopping other people from getting hurt?"

"You don't even know that's going to happen. If I felt like fighting this town I would've stayed. Okay? I'm . . . I'm glad I saw the graves. I don't want to hear anything else."

He's quiet for a moment, sagging against Wren's headstone, something as usual turning through his mind. Then his pleading expression switches off, just like that, and he holds out a hand. "It was good to see you," he says stiffly.

Fine. He can have this. "You too," I say, only half lying, and touch his hand.

The mountain song jumps in my ear, broken piano keys. I startle, dropping Mason's hand. "Did you feel something?" he demands, eyes gleaming. "Look, I was right, you *do* make this connection stronger—"

"What the fuck," I whisper, backing away. The wind winds my hair around me and I almost claw it off my face. I've never heard the song come so suddenly like that, switched right on, and the

34

stained echo it leaves behind makes my throat close up. "What did you do to me?" It's so easy to rediscover my childish hate for him, the way he can exist so *carelessly*, with so much confidence that he's right. I wasn't allowed to be careless then, and I can't afford to be careless now. "What do you *want*?"

"I told you—your help. You, me, Zach, and Wren. That's how it started, that's how we reach them. If you just let me *try*, and I can show you—"

"No." He looks taken aback, and my anger steels. "No, I'm not going to help you call ghosts because you need to make yourself feel better about being stuck here. This is kind of a dick move, actually, digging this hole and wanting to drag me down with you the second you see me again. I'm over this. I've made my peace. I'm making my own life." I'm almost chanting, I know, saying words louder and louder so they're the only things I hear. "I have a life. You don't get to ruin this for me."

He blinks at me. *Hate me*, I think, because it'll make everything easier. I can leave, properly this time, without anything on my conscience. "So say I'm wrong about there being more to their deaths, and we just manage to call them as they are." Desperation flits across his face, and it strikes me that I've never seen Mason *desperate* before. "You don't want to see them again?" he asks. "*Talk* to them? That's not enough to justify trying?"

I can't put words to the wanting storm racing through my body. If I look at it close enough to try, I won't make it another step. So I just say the word I already have. "No." It comes out breathy, unconvincing, so I say it again. "No. I don't. I'm good, thanks. They're dead. I got that. You can sit here wallowing. I've moved on."

And then I do what I do best, and I turn right around and run. Through the graves, through the cairns, out through the gates to find, to my shock, Trish waiting there in her car. She must have dropped Mom off and circled back for me, knowing I'd have to walk otherwise.

"What happened?" she demands at the sight of my face, but I just tuck myself into the passenger seat and scowl until she drives off. Through the window, I watch trees and old buildings scroll past. Her music is godawful, but I keep the window up and the synth pulsing in my ears so I don't risk hearing anything else.

When I first started hearing the song, I was young and stupid enough to tell Mom and Dad at the dinner table. "The mountains talk to the people here," Dad said sharply. "This is normal, a good thing."

"But I don't like the way it makes me feel."

"You'll learn to like it. You're just not trying hard enough."

So I tried, and when that didn't work, I tried to ignore it when the wind blew and the song played on the back of my mind like a lullaby some other mother had sung to me, dragging up everything I'd ever tried to bury. I got the message. It didn't mean I belonged—it was telling me I never would. So I simply piled more walls on top of it until I left, like I was clearly supposed to. All that healing I've supposedly been doing in the city, though, has apparently just made me vulnerable all over again.

This time my secret is obvious. *Liar, liar, liar, liar.* Seeing Wren and Zach again would break me, and I want it so badly I feel turned inside out.

I don't care. I've lied to myself and everyone else enough times. I'll do it again if that's what it takes to get out of here in one piece. If something *is* out there killing, I'm not sticking around to be a victim.

4

I CAN'T CONVINCE MYSELF THE HOUSE IS AS
light as it felt before the funeral. Mason's brought back the ghosts
in my head. The sounds of my childhood return, the scurrying
feet and phantom angry whispers through the walls as I try to
sketch ideas for new pieces. Dad's dead; we buried him. But does
that mean he's gone?

Maybe not, because I sleep and dream of the forest. I'm wearing his boots—in places they're too big, but around my heels
they're cinched so tight my skin is scraping off as I walk.

I know what I'm looking for: a small plant amidst all the other
plants in the undergrowth, three stalks with five leaves of slender
bright green, topped with a cluster of berries like welled blood.
It's not what's above ground that's valuable, but below. Four-
limbed tubers with rough brown skins. Ginseng. In Chinese, one
of the only words I know, it's called *rénshēn*. Man root.

I have the strong sense that I'm not supposed to be looking.
It's not my job. It's not my concern. And yet, here, I'm filled with
feverish purpose.

The trees duck away ahead, and on the edge of a cliff are two
of the plants. Something tells me it shouldn't be this easy. But I

hurry over before I lose sight of them, and then I'm on my knees in the dirt, digging faster and faster, ignoring the steep edge in front of me. "Isa, get the hell away from there," a familiar voice says, but I don't see them, so I keep going. The earth is cold and cracks my nails, but I bury the pain. I'm looking for them. For them.

I touch something fleshy in the earth. My prize gleams at me, yellow through the soil. I work around it, loosen the root, draw out the first tuber, and snap off the stem. Its head fits neatly in the cradle of my fingers, its arms and legs sprawling over my palm. I find the second one easier, like it was just waiting to join the first. I sit there with scattered dirt around me and under my nails, holding my two roots, not sure now what I'm supposed to do with them or why I was so intent on finding them in the first place. A distant danger sounds at the back of my head. Someone's coming who wants my harvest. Poachers, I think, but that doesn't make sense.

"Isa," someone says in shock.

I turn around. Mason is standing there, in his coat, wearing a strange necklace. His eyes widen at my harvest and he holds out his hands. "I've been looking for them." My heart pounds. I feel like I'm not supposed to do this either—that someone should be stopping me—that I should be stopping me—but I close my hands over his, handing over the roots I just dug up.

When they touch him, they turn to fingers.

I WAKE TO ROUND WHITE EYES blinking at me from the ceiling and loudly swear. A second later, though, I see the out-line of wings and realize it's just a moth.

I collapse back onto my pillow, damp with sweat. Before me, the darkness seems to coil into roots, draping over the doorway, down the side of the desk. The last bit of the dream returns to me: Mason holding two things that looked less like ginseng and more like hands.

As if on cue, my phone buzzes. I grope for it and wake the screen, seeing the time—3:58 a.m.—and then a message from an unknown number: *Call me. Please.*

For a moment I have the delusion that it's Yara, the girl Olivia set me up with, who I actually really liked before I spilled hot coffee on her, froze up, ran away, and then couldn't explain to Olivia why I'd gone crazy and left their friend with first-degree burns. But then I remember that, no, I have both her number and Olivia's, although I doubt I'll be using them anytime soon. There's only one person in the world who would be trying to contact me, and whose number I don't have because I left my old phone behind.

A second message: *I got through.*

My thumb hovers over the screen. I think I might know what Mason means, but I don't want to open it. I told myself I wasn't going to entertain him. I don't know why he's texting me at four in the morning, expecting me to be able to call. I mean, I am. But he shouldn't think I am. How did he get my new number, anyway?

My phone pings again—what the hell is wrong with him? I turn off vibrations and put it face down, determined to get back to sleep.

But then the moth flutters, making its wings blink, and a thought unhelpfully creeps into my mind: after I started turning in sketch after sketch with moths in the shadows, one of my professors told me that in Chinese mythology, a moth is a spirit of the dead. I woke up with them everywhere—scribbled in the margins of my sketchbook, overtaking a landscape of a pond, sitting on tabletops, paint flecking my skin like the dust off their wings. Finally he pulled me aside and asked delicately if I'd lost anyone recently. The moths only stopped appearing once I got them inked on my skin.

I've never seen a moth here before. It's just another pest. But is it a coincidence that it's turned up right after the funeral? The spot beneath my ribs, where my two moth tattoos are, twinges, like calling to like.

Something creaks outside my door. Trish's footsteps pad down the corridor. I wonder for a second what she's doing up so late before remembering she sleepwalks. That's us, here, the living dead. She'll roam the whole house without leaving a trace. As long as she doesn't try to leave it, we've learned to just let her wander back to bed.

I'm about to shut my eyes when the silence bursts with shattering glass.

I'm out of bed in a second, racing into her room to see the moonlit silhouette of her raised arm swinging. The weak light catches the edge of the hammer as her arm comes down again onto the sealed window. More glass sprays outward, stars breaking into the night.

"Trish!" She can't hear me, but when she draws back for another swing, I catch her wrist.

She turns. Staring right through me, she lifts her free hand to cup my face.

I jerk back. Hand still hovering where my cheek was, she cocks her head slightly, as though listening for something. Then she turns and sweeps the hammerhead through the shards still clinging to the window frame.

They dislodge with a cascade of cracks, an ugly gritty grinding. A tooth snags onto her skin and rips a thin gash across the back of her hand.

"Trish!" This time I grab her and don't let go, prying away the hammer. In the splintered silence, everything is twice as loud: my own heartbeat in my ears, pattering feet, the floorboards creaking, the flutter as a breeze strokes the disused curtains, dragging them back to life.

Trish's head lolls toward the now-open window, eyelids fluttering. Okay. She's calm. I gently start nudging her back to bed. Once I tried to wake her, but she flailed and screamed bloody murder until she came back around, and by that time she'd woken Dad. After that I learned the best thing to do was just to guide her back into bed and sit with her until I was sure she was staying put.

I don't hear Mom now, though, so I tuck her into bed and draw the blanket over her. She settles in with a sigh, and on some impulse, I stroke her hair away from her face. "You're not going anywhere," I mutter.

Sometimes when I put her back to bed like this, I'd curl up with her and we both pretended in the morning I'd just accidentally fallen asleep next to her. I'm almost tempted to do it now.

Instead I absorb the decorations in her room, so different from mine. My dorm room back in school is covered with canvases, but everything I drew here stayed in sketchbooks I could take with me. Dad only tolerated my sketching because I was all but guaranteed a job at the Vandersteens' workshop when I graduated. He still constantly said I was wasting his money on supplies. I used to steal from the church craft bin instead, and I still work cheap now. Pencils and watercolors go a long way, especially now that I stretch my materials allowance as far as it goes.

I've always wondered if Trish hates me for leaving.

She rolls over and curls up under the blanket. Moonlight casts a filmy pool onto the floor. The curtains ripple lightly in a way that draws me out of bed and toward the shattered window.

Trish did a clean job; it's a skeleton frame hanging bare. The air is cool, inviting, like a seal finally broken. Wren's window faces me at a diagonal from here, sleeping now, the panes closed.

I feel like I shouldn't be able to reach the outside like this. Shouldn't be able to stretch and trace the fissures of streets between sleeping houses and the inescapable cage of cliffs, or reach out to Wren's bedroom and imagine her still waving back. Our houses are close. Close enough that I could hear Mrs. Carver's scream from next door when they told her they found Wren in the pond.

I'm suddenly overcome with the impulse to lean over until I tumble right out, and have to rapidly back away. My foot comes down on the hammer. Without really thinking, I pick it up.

The weight of it in my hand is strangely comforting. I could do so much damage if I wanted to. I want to tear this house down. Rip it out at the foundation so no one will ever even know it was here. Then maybe we can finally, finally start again.

The wind brushes against my cheek, and my fingers itch with the sudden urge to draw, calm myself down. Slowly I lower my arm, and the hammer feels suddenly damning. After a second's hesitation, I drop it out the window.

It lands with a thud. I jolt from the windowsill, tensed for no reason I can explain and sinking my nails deep into my palm. The curtains flutter. Suddenly the window seems to stare.

I pull the curtains shut, throwing us into full darkness. The fabric bunches in my fingers. The breath in the room hitches and sighs, and the four walls are enclosed once more. Beneath me there's a *skritch*, and the faintest movement of tiny feet. When I go back to my room, the moth is gone.

we

SLATER'S CHILDREN HAVE ALWAYS HIDDEN beneath the mountains. Light-footed, sharp-nosed, running away from homes. So, then. Pin the liquid moon between the peaks and simmer around it the stars. Bend the wind here, over the water, curling in the hollow of the cliffs. Flicker the little fire that bathes your little faces, splayed out on the sand. You drink forbidden liquor and do not think of the consequence. Drink sours the throat, turns the skin wet, scrapes out the mind, turns muscle slack. I have seen its blood enough. But children never know. You are careless and need care.

How quickly childhood ends. When a hammer and chisel are placed in the hand. When the girl opens her legs and touches blood. When dreams turn sticky, bodies alien and haunting. When the father undoes his belt. When the foreman takes volunteers. When two fall in love, and become blind to what they in turn neglect.

Blink—Wren Carver, the perfect daughter, the dreamer, helping your lover trace the shape of Andromeda.

Blink—Zachary Tai, the runner, the fool, tipping your throat back to drink.

Blink—Mason Kane, the rebel, the atheist, watching the girl in your arms.

Blink—you, you, watching the reflection of the flames in the water, the girl without a home. A rule of the crater that even rebellious children follow: light a fire in the dark only by water or within walls, to keep out the things that might be drawn to the warmth.

I have come and gone for so long, watching. Being together was easier, once. You still sit close with them in the sand, used to shared adventure, but growing up has made strangers of you all. You are now debris around the sun and her moon. Still, Wren Carver invited you on a perfect night—

—and *this* thing that hurts you, you cannot run from. It beats too hard on your ribs. So you met them in the park and followed them through the tunnel, and you try. You watch Wren and Mason name each other the stars. You are a stranger. You will never be wanted like that. Not by any but me.

So listen to this then:

Murmur the currents deep below. Slide the wind against the peaks, the answer of the old earth. The wet of a boy's mouth opening as Zachary Tai drinks heavily from stolen whiskey and says: *Gonna fucking fail all my classes.*

A frown on the other boy's face. *Don't say that.*

I'm not asking for pity, Mason. Besides, don't need the grades. Just need to run. Keep fit. Run faster.

Huh. Don't let me distract you, then.

Zach stares. You recognize the darkness that simmers, don't you? You draw closer for the first time. *What are you saying this for, Zach?* you ask, except do you say it at all, or am I the only one who hears? You are inconsequential. Your friends go on and on without you.

I'm so tired in class all the time. None of it makes any sense.

Mason exhales. *That's because you barely sleep. You're at practice all day.*

You wouldn't get it. The team is my life.

A shadow, there, flitting across Wren's face. *I think we all get that, Zach, but maybe you should put that bottle down.*

Oh my body is a goddamn temple. I drank too much that night. Aaaaa-men.

Do you remember these words? Or have you buried them too?

Initiation night, you mean? The one you guys had here. You never told us about it. There's all these rumors going around. Mason leans, tries to take the bottle from Zach, fails.

It's just team traditions. The guys pass it down. My dad did it.

You know that's bullshit.

Only when it's something I care about, right?

I didn't say that—

I'm not you!

Hear the impact of Zach's fist on the rock, the skin of his knuckles tearing, something cracking—you are pinned in place as movement bursts: Mason starting forward, Zach pushing away; darting, grappling, voices raising.

Stutter the light. Return to stillness. You are still pinned. You are still inconsequential.

Zach has Mason's collar in his fist. Heaves, heaves, heaves, knuckles bleeding down Mason's chest. Oh, the darkness in his soul. It calls me. I will know. And I will take.

This is living, you see. This is all there is.

Wren steps between them and lets Zach stumble away. But see, Mason grabs Zach's shoulders, squeezes. His mouth moves, a name over and over. Zach presses his knuckles to his lips. Blood

curves off his jaw. Now Wren Carver looks at you. She is disappointed at your stillness, your weakness. Why should they care
for you, when you are unable to care for them? You are broken.

So when those who are meant to be your friends leave,
you stay.

And I stay with you. I hear all the secrets the children whisper
when they think no one listens. You watch the water.

You stand at an edge.

You stand by a river.

You stand by a window, a hammer in your hand, and beneath
you all the small things stir. Do you remember the sand, Isadora
Chang, do you remember the cliffs? Do you remember the sound
of skin tearing, how you simply watched as blood dripped?

For now, I offer a smaller cleansing, empty your house of its
unwanted inhabitants. They have hidden for so long, but they
hear me again, now, and oh—flutter, a white-eyed little insect.
Small wings like tissue, shedding dust before it drowns. So you
return. So I will have you back. Patiently, patiently.

5

I ESCAPE THE HOUSE THE MINUTE DAWN STARTS breaking. I spent the rest of the night alternating between a few minutes of sleep and trying to scribble ideas in my sketchbook that don't look like hands dug up from the earth. What I haven't done is look at my phone. I almost even left it at home, but I know better than to wander around Slater without any way to get help in an emergency. Maybe I had a death wish once, but I actually have things to get back to now. Don't answer a voice in the woods even if you think it's a friend, goes general common sense, but make sure you have a friend on call too.

The surrounding roads come back to me easy. I only felt like I belonged to myself out of the house, so I wandered these often, where the mountains and valleys run so wild I feel like I have permission to do the same. Trails thread all over the place. This one behind the tire yard leads to a ledge that looks over the town, next to a steep slope of loose rock.

It's a good place to figure out something for my portfolio. I study the buildings below, their roofs lined with roots, slanting toward the quarry. It gapes at the top of the town, mine tunnels extending deeper north into the mountainside. Around me traces of dust shift in the wind, stubborn remains of whatever the miners once dug up.

Most of the pit is hidden by the trees that sprung up after it closed. The remaining workshop is enough to keep them going, along with the other businesses they control—a big sculpture can sell for upwards of thirty thousand—but Slater isn't what it was and the overgrown quarry is its memorial.

It's easier to look at the town this morning than at Trish. She was back to talking to Mom in low voices in the kitchen. Whatever. I've always been inconsequential in the family anyway. Getting out was my chance to actually make something that matters. Which is why I need to get my shit together.

I sketch the quarry experimentally, considering angles. My teachers have tried to get me into more abstract stuff, but I don't like feeling like I'm imagining things. I never liked drawing people, either. It feels too intimate. I've always liked scene studies instead—right now, I could play with the silhouette of the trees, do something with the yawning emptiness. There's no reason why I should have been drawing portraits at the showcase.

I used to come up here a lot, especially in that last year after Wren and Mason got together. I liked looking down on Slater and feeling like it was small enough to be safe. With my back pressed against the mountain, I feel vast, and I breathe easier with the open air. The evergreens furring the peaks are thick with possibility and I wonder if Paige Vandersteen is somewhere in them. People are out there, for the first time, looking not for roots but for a girl. Some girls get looked for. Not me and Wren.

A thin breeze curls around my ears. I tuck my boots under my thighs as I sketch. I focus on the depth of the quarry, filling in what I can't see from what I remember in pictures. The pools of shadow, ridges in the shape of cheeks, open mouths—

Wait, what?

My paper flutters. I smooth it out, taking in the screams that have started forming.

Shit. I clench my hand and then unclench it, needing to feel it's still connected to my nerves. I didn't draw that on purpose. The images just slipped into me, like they did at the showcase. *Exactly* like they did at the showcase. I've drawn these faces before.

A footstep lands behind me and I whirl around. Mason jumps back, swearing. I snatch my sketchbook off the ground, annoyed at myself. I'm usually better at sensing people near me. "Jesus."

"Me? God forbid."

It's almost funny. I notice he's wearing the same clothes as yesterday, which reminds me that he's been trying to reach me the whole morning. "Are you following me?"

He pauses.

"Oh my God, you were." I look at my phone, and sure enough, there's a few new messages. "How *did* you get my number?"

"Trish gave it to me. Look, this is important, okay? Something happened last night and I really need to talk to you. You weren't home, so I made some educated guesses—"

"I said I'm *not interested*. Don't you have anyone else to talk to?"

A long silence falls. "I'll go," he says, making to turn around.

"No," I blurt, then regret it as hope flares on his face. I don't think it's a coincidence that he says something happened the same night he appeared in my dream. *I reached them*, his text said. And in my dream, two hands in his.

In our hands.

"You came all this way," I mutter, gesturing for him to sit. He scrutinizes me, decides I'm lying well enough for it not to be his responsibility, and plops down. I flip my sketchbook before he can look at what I was drawing.

"Are you working on something?"

I suck in a breath, figure out something reasonable since I did just tell him to stay. "Makeup portfolio for school, so I don't lose my scholarship."

"What happened to the first one?"

"What happened with Paige Vandersteen?" I snap back, then regret it instantly, because while I wasn't going to tell him about my showcase portraits, he's more than happy to tell me what happened with Paige.

"Now you want to know?"

I don't, but the replicated drawing of the screaming kids is starting to pull on other pieces of my imagination. Paige lost in the woods. The gaping quarry. The terror in the kids' eyes. I imagine her trapped somewhere in the dark. If a girl screams in the forest and there's no one to hear it, is she still alive or already dead?

If a girl walks into a pond and there's no one to pull her out, was she dead before she even drowned?

The adult I thought I'd become feels very far away. Instead, I feel like the girl who had sleepovers, clipping plastic butterflies into her best friend's hair before letting her braid mine. Butterflies she was wearing when she died. I feel like the little girl hiding in her room, the girl being told the mountain song that hurt was a good thing. I'm angry, suddenly, at all the things this town's taken from me. I've never been in control here. Maybe finding its princess is the fuck-you I need.

"I want to know," I say, surprising us both. "What happened with Paige?"

He scrutinizes me again, then props his elbows on his knees. "Well, you know Ida Vandersteen, the twin, *got lusty and sailed off*, yeah? And you remember the plague doctor? Cecily Vandersteen? Paige found out that Ida had a kid from that sailor affair, and left her in Cecily's care. We've never heard about this kid, Sarai, because a few years later she gets the plague, and Cecily just sticks her in the plague house, where she drowns with the others. Paige wanted to do a séance to talk to Sarai. She was fixated on this idea of these family members who'd been covered up. She didn't want my mom's help, so I did it for her. Nothing happened. She said she'd come back to me, that there was a second grave she wanted to try, but then I heard she disappeared. I don't know what I'd even say to the police that they'd listen to."

"Do you ever think about where she is?"

"All day. But I can't even begin to guess."

I don't know what makes me do it—am I just tired? Am I still thinking about him in my dream, with some kind of answer I don't understand? Or do I owe it, at least, to offer whatever information on a missing girl I can?—but I pull my folder from my bag.

Mason stiffens when I take out the piece of Paige with her broken neck. Then comes Matthew Accetta, another boy from school, with a stretched throat and seeds sprouting from his tongue. The third at first glance is just a black canvas, until the white gaps in the scribbles clarify themselves into five faces in the dark, screaming—almost identical to the ones I started drawing a few minutes ago.

He picks up each as I put them down, but the fourth makes him stop. It's a boy in half profile. Most of his head and neck are obscured by moths and caterpillars, his left eyebrow dotted with pearly eggs, but you can make out enough of his face to recognize him.

Mason stares at his own portrait. "You drew these?"

The whole term I've been told my pieces felt flat. *You obviously have talent, Isa, but we need something more real. It feels like you're holding back.* Well, then this happened, and obviously there was also something *too* visceral. The questions from our seminars swirl in my head. How does art function in memory and preservation? In the record of history, how has art immortalized, transformed, renewed places and people that might otherwise have faded into time? How do the things we create converse with the things we inhabit?

What is my mind inhabiting, that this is what I create?

"I've been drawing weird things lately, without knowing it." After a second's hesitation, I flip my sketchbook back to the previous page, comparing the two drawings of the kids in the dark. The one in my sketchbook seems just a little larger, as though the faces are coming closer. "Those pieces were supposed to be for my showcase. The one I have to make up for."

Mason places his portrait back down. "When was the showcase?"

I was afraid he'd think I'm crazy, but I suppose he started the crazy first. "Last Friday." It feels strange to finally tell someone. Strange and strangely easy.

"You drew these before you came to Slater," he says, in slow realization. "Thursday, maybe? Around the time of my séance with Paige?"

I still. *Was* it the same time? "That's just a coincidence."

"This whole town is strange, Isa. Is it so hard to believe that you might have some kind of senses that aren't quite normal? That are tied to what happens in this town—to *our friends*?"

"I can't afford to be *not normal*," I snap. "My dad reminded us every day. I saw *not normal* every time I looked in the fucking mirror."

He has the grace to look embarrassed, and I've temporarily shut him up. I spent my whole life here being wound up just like Dad wanted, even though I knew damn well no matter how much pressure we put on ourselves we weren't going to become a *proper Slater family.* Getting out was really my first chance at not being so uptight all the time. But I never had problems with my drawing before I left, did I? What if that self-control was actually necessary?

As though to prove my point, the feeling of purpose—of *need*—that drove me in my dream resurfaces, and I can't stop myself from rooting it out. "You talked to Wren and Zach last night, didn't you?"

"So you did read my messages," he says, but it's less accusatory and more like he's leading me to something. Angling for a line of questioning.

I look at him. "It's not about the texts, is it?"

It feels like a test, both of us swapping vague sentences, trying to figure out who'll admit something first. Or else trying to test if that childhood bond is still there, between kids who were pirates together, who learned the same things about the world at the same time. In response, he reaches beneath his collar and pulls out a delicate chain.

My first thought is that he's wearing a crucifix and the world really has turned upside down, but at the end of the chain, instead of a cross, is a slim wooden chime.

It's the necklace I saw in my dream. I've never seen him wear it in my life. The only way I would have known to see it is if . . .

"You were there," we both say at the same time, and I pull my knees up to my chest. I've always had keyed-up senses. Imagining whispering in the walls, yes, but I developed an instinct for Dad's moods, for danger, like some undercurrent in the air is obvious only to me. It's helped me avoid bad situations. But this? I remember the digging, needing to find the roots buried in the soil. Roots shaped like people that turned into hands.

"I was in the cemetery last night trying to call them again; that's what the necklace is for. It wasn't really working. But then I thought I felt . . . you," he says slowly, like I'm a wounded animal who might bolt. "I called your name. I felt something touch my hands. And then they were there, after two years, right in front of me."

"Wren and Zach," I whisper.

"Whatever you did," he says, "it worked."

But I didn't do anything. At least, not on purpose. Anxiety thrums in my stomach, a paranoia that I can't control myself, and if I can't control myself then I have to accept the consequences. Look at Trish, who doesn't even know what her body gets up to in her sleep. I have no evidence that I sleepwalk, but I've been doing other things I'm not aware of. The showcase portraits. Now this.

"I think part of me always believed in ghosts," Mason continues. "But I thought it was a useless fixation, you know, a trap for people who can't find more productive ways to cope. I assumed

I wasn't going to feed into that delusion, even if the power was real. Now I know it's both real and works better with you around. Two years ago, I felt and saw them, but their voices couldn't get through. But last night Zach spoke." He watches me, careful and wary. "It wasn't much before they disappeared again, but he said, *It took us. Isa was there.*"

My shoulders lock.

"Why would he say that?" Mason presses.

I shouldn't have let him stay here. "I don't know." He must be able to tell I'm lying. "I don't know anything that everyone else doesn't already know."

"Think—Any time you saw him, spoke to him—"

"I don't know anything, okay?" I stand abruptly, stuffing my things back into my bag. "I didn't come here looking for more nightmares."

"It's not a coincidence that you managed to find them in a night when I've been failing for two years. It's not a coincidence that you drew Paige the day I did the séance with her, just before she disappeared."

"I don't care—"

"Isa!" I flinch, which makes him flinch.

He shakes his head and continues: "Look—after yesterday I tried to reach Paige, too, but I don't have anything of hers. It doesn't *work* with just me. I need your help to get through. People talk about things from the mountains, but none of what they say actually adds up. The logic—"

"So is this about figuring out what happened to them? Finding Paige? Or is it just answering your new study question?"

"Isa—" There's another word hanging there—*please*, maybe. I've never seen him in this state before, don't know what he'll do in it. Guilt rises hot in my throat, buried years deep. "I just want to *understand*."

"I need to go." I don't give him time to protest or say another thing to stop me. He's right; it doesn't add up, but it turns out that scared little sleepover girl isn't actually ready to say fuck-you after all, and so all she does is run, even from the only person in the world who wants her around.

Because there's no other way that Zach would have gone to Mason and said my name. Mason couldn't have known that he wasn't the last person to see Zach alive, that he wasn't the one who could've saved him, either from a killer or from himself.

I was.

I DON'T REMEMBER the details. I had gotten locked out of the house again, or I ran out, but either way I forgot a jacket and I was cold by the time I wandered to the river and saw Zach.

Zach was funny, a good athlete, and listened to his parents, which got him a long way, but he was also known to be temperamental, intense, and a bit stupid. When we got to high school Mason guessed he was probably dyslexic, but by then he'd already been written off as a lost cause. Sports was the only thing he really had.

He was always out on a run and we'd started accidentally meeting on the river road over the past year, when Mason and Wren became a separate being and our group started fracturing. We both liked this path because it was quiet and rivers, unlike ponds, felt like they could carry you away somewhere. I'd pretend like his obsession with his races wasn't worrying and he'd pretend I was still the little girl who'd draw birds on everyone's diner napkins. We never talked. I'd sit there and draw sometimes while he stretched.

This time was different, though. Wren had texted me that he and Mason had had a fight, and Mason was worried because he wasn't answering his messages. I yelled his name when I saw his back in the distance, and he whipped around jerkily.

I told Zach to go make up with Mason. I can picture him framed by dusk and water. We argued. I don't remember about what. Just that I'd never hated or needed him more than in that moment, but he wouldn't listen to me. So I just left him there. Sometime between then and morning, I found somewhere to sleep.

Sometime between then and morning, Zach blew his head off by the river road.

But I didn't know that when I woke up, the memory of the last night already blurry. What I remember more clearly is arriving at school and sensing something wrong. All around me, people's routines were too stiff, like windup toys running out of steam. Then, Wren at the end of the corridor. Harley murmured something to her in passing. I watched her stagger. Mason appeared at her shoulder to catch her, still bewildered.

Wren caught my gaze, and Mason followed her line of sight right to me. We somehow knew in that moment what had happened, even if we didn't know how it happened until later. Ten minutes later, Wren wrapped her arms around me, crying silently, as a teacher emptied Zach's locker into a box. Stuck inside the door was a photo of the four of us. I couldn't shake the feeling that there was something else wrong. But in that moment, and for all the moments until the one I still didn't know about, there was only Zach, and how our picture tore when they peeled it off his locker door, leaving part of his grin behind.

It was only later when I found out how he'd died that a piece of the previous evening came back to me, the only few seconds I've remembered since: When I called to him, he'd rapidly stuffed his hands into his pockets as he turned around, panic wiping quick from his face. He'd been holding the gun when I walked up on him. And then I just walked away.

MY PHONE BUZZES almost immediately after I get home. Mason:

I'm sorry.

But think about it please.

I don't click on the notification, but *I'm sorry* punches me in the gut. I should be the one saying it. I toss my phone aside instead, which is when I realize that on my lap, the bird's-eye drawing of the town I'd been shading has changed. Standing knee-deep in the quarry like an unfinished creation is Zach, looking over his shoulder directly at me, and smiling wide.

"What is it?" I whisper. "What do you want from me?" The odor from the caulk smell hasn't gone away; the air still feels acidic. I must have breathed it in, because it's coming up the back of my mouth. "What do you mean *it took us*? What else is there to know?"

Of course, the drawing just smiles.

My mind feels like a dull edge, and the last time it was sharp was when I woke up from that first dream, filled with purpose, the weight of two roots still in my hands. Ugly things inside me,

I think, want to get out. I've hidden them away so well. But now they're coming back from the grave, asking me to remember. I can't remember, not even if I wanted to. But for Zach, and this guilt I owe him, I could sleep. And maybe dreams will find me again.

6

I'M WALKING BAREFOOT AGAIN, AND MY FEET
are bleeding.

It's sundown, and I'm shivering. This road I'm on curves down
to the river, and in the distance, Zach stands by the water shooting butterflies.

That doesn't seem right. Isn't that a secret, that he had that
gun? But he's holding it out as I walk toward him, squinting at the
red insects swarming over the water. He fires, and they explode
in a flurry before settling back down again. "Zach?"

He turns to me and that seems wrong too. It's too calm, he's
smiling, and he still has the gun hanging loosely in one hand. This
wasn't how it happened. *The gun's not important*, some instinct
murmurs.

"Are you okay? Wren told me you and Mason had some sort
of fight."

His expression falters, then yanks back up into a smile. "I'm
fine, Isadora, leave me alone." Waving me off, he turns back to the
water. The butterflies drift around him, and I notice his shoulders tense. A chill goes through me. Suddenly I need him to come

with me more than anything. "Walk back to town with me. We can go back to Mason's. You can sort it out."

He winces at the sound of my voice. Fine. Sure. We had an unspoken agreement for this to be a silent space. But he doesn't need to look like I'm breaking the law by talking to him.

I give it one last try, even as the wind blows and I shiver again. "Walk back with me. Just as far as the square." And it wasn't even about him anymore; I was starting to feel how long the night was, and how lonely I felt, and how scared I was that this was the time Dad decided he'd stop letting me back in. *Be my friend*, I want to say, but I can't get the words out. *Our friends are going to grow old together and leave us behind and I need you to be my friend, still.*

But then he simply turns away, and my desperation snaps over into anger. "Fuck you, Zach." I spin around this time, before he can ignore me any longer, and in the corner of my eye see two rippling silhouettes in the water, both alone, one surrounded by butterflies. I watch as their fluttering shadows cluster around his head. I watch as his shadow pauses, then points the gun at them.

"Isa, get the hell away from there," says a familiar voice.

I wake with the sound of the shot, gasping and chest squeezed out with tears that won't come. All I can see is the gun, the spray of butterfly wings. The dream is already fading, but I remember the instinct scratching at the back of my mind. *It's not about the gun.* But what is it about, then?

I need to get out of this house.

Trish is going through some papers when I stumble downstairs, and she frowns at me. "Are you okay?"

"Yeah. Just a nightmare." I don't mention that it's the second one in a row or that this one was closer to an actual memory.

"Want to go get donuts and groceries?"

"Sure, whatever," I say.

She rolls her eyes. I let her sling her arm around me and run a hand through my tangled hair, missing being mothered.

TRISH TAKES THE LONG WAY like she doesn't think I'll notice. She seems stressed out even with her favorite bun, and I notice a braided bracelet has sprouted on her wrist, the kind she used to make as a kid before Dad decided he didn't like them.

The stones Blu-Tacked onto her dashboard catch the weak light. Even when we were kids, she was such a nerd about them, the only person I knew who actually cared about the mining exhibits in town hall. I'm not surprised she ended up working for the Vandersteens.

It's almost eight, and the sun's coming up. "Don't you have work?" Trish has never taken a break in her life, except maybe the one time she tracked me down in the city. It was a few months after I left, when I'd started staying at the tattoo shop and finally borrowed a phone to text her. Just *I'm safe* and the city, but she showed up two days later at the door sobbing. She didn't even try to bring me back with her, just made me promise to text, and when she left I found sixty dollars in my pocket.

"I'm on the search shift later. They've given me time off otherwise."

Right. The efforts to find Paige continue. "I don't need a chaperone."

"I'm watching out for you. I know it's not easy being back."

I can't say anything to that. In the quiet her electrosynth is unbearable, and I turn it down. She swats my hand off the dial without much force. "How are you feeling about Paige?" I told myself I wasn't going to ask, but I feel like I started unraveling the moment I got back whether I wanted to or not. As much as I want to not care, *care* is gnawing at me, for both Trish and the missing girl. Maybe I've gotten soft and lost some of my caution, but I let it. I won't mention Mason though, not yet. "It must be rough."

"You know her too."

I wince at the present tense, but I don't correct her. Mason has his suspicions, but that doesn't mean they're true. I need them not to be. "Barely. Her friends were kind of bitchy."

"God, *so* bitchy, they come around sometimes." Trish sucks air through her teeth. "She's really interested in town history, actually. Otto never cared; he's just holed up in the workshop all the time. He was there the whole day before we realized she was missing. But even outside of tutoring sometimes Paige comes around to the archive team and helps out. There's boxes of it, by the way, we have to stop her from carting them off."

It's the first I'm hearing this much about her job. "So you work with the Vandersteens' archives?"

"Did I not tell you that? Yeah—the Vandersteens are huge on their private collection. Town censuses, logbooks, old quarry accounting files, worker records, medical notes. We're going through the stuff in the Red House and bringing what's important back to the Vandersteens' private collection for safekeeping. Cecily Vandersteen, the plague doctor? She's got *so* much, and half of it is actually kind of creepy."

I smile, but it's got me thinking. Two brothers founded Slater. The one who started the mine built his mansion by the western peaks, where the Vandersteens currently still live. The other brother, a doctor, hid away with his treatments on the other side of the quarry, at what's now the clinic. They say the Vandersteens were threatened once by a too-smart boy and killed him in his sickbed, and the manor's walls are red because his blood wouldn't stop running.

At some point, that family branch became Cecily. She's more of a legend than anything, with campfire stories about her plague experiments, so it hadn't even occurred to me that of course she would have records and notes. That if Paige learned about one ancestor who died in the plague house, it might have been from the records of the other ancestor that put her there. Did Mason know that? I don't know how much Paige told him.

"She can't just be missing, though," Trish blurts, like she's been bottling this up. "I mean . . . She's not the type."

"The type to what?" I say sharply. "Who is the type?"

"I just *meant*—I mean, you know her. She was *Paige Vandersteen*. She had no reason to—there wouldn't be any reason—"

"To run away? Drown herself? Shoot herself on some abandoned road? For the mountains to take her?" My palm hurts and I realize I've pressed my nail into it, a red crescent that looks like a smile. "But the rest of them, that made sense?"

"I didn't say that—"

"Zach was stupid, and Wren was sleeping around, so that makes sense? Everything they say doesn't add up. You kill yourself and people are like, oh, the mountains, it's what you deserve, but the truth is it's just a convenient thing to say so they don't have to bother with what really happened." I know I'm just repeating what Mason was saying, but he's right, isn't he? I can still hear the gunshot from my dreams, and my heartbeat is just going and going. "Why is Paige Vandersteen the first person anyone is actually looking for? No one but her family looked for Wren, even when she'd been gone an entire *day*." My voice catches. I only found that out later, because I hadn't been paying enough attention to know she was missing either. "Paige isn't who you thought she was."

Trish is silent, and I wish I'd left the music up after all. I don't know where all those words came from. I'm not afraid of Trish, but still, I've said too much and I feel raw. "I think she heard things too," I mumble.

"What?"

"One time, our sculpture class ran late. When I walked out she was pressing her ear to the mouth of a bust." It was for a Saudi tycoon, or something. She jerked away when she saw me, smoothed out her shoulder braid she always threaded with iris creepers. Then Otto had come out after me and they'd gone off together without explanation. It was the first time I'd seen her homecoming princess thing drop even a little. I couldn't shake the feeling that I'd seen something no one else knew about. "It looked like she was listening to it. Otto did that too, sometimes. And she was looking for ghosts."

Trish's head cricks around. "What do you mean, ghosts?"

Do I do Mason's work for him? Or can I not pretend this latest disappearance doesn't feel personal now to me too? "She was looking for someone called Sarai."

Trish brakes sharply. We've arrived outside the grocery store, but like an echo of my first day back, she doesn't get out of the car. "Who told you that name?"

I was right. Trish does know something about Sarai. She must have come across the same records, maybe even helped Paige find them. But what do I say now? There's only one way I would have heard that name, and it comes to Trish pretty quickly.

"Mason?" She switches off the engine, yanks out the key. The car's hum snaps out. "What were he and Paige doing, Isa?"

But now her reaction has me uneasy. She's not just surprised, she's doing damage control. This isn't some random lost trivia about the Vandersteen family tree. This is an active secret they're still keeping. I don't know why, but if Trish is involved enough to be keeping that secret, I suddenly don't know if I should be telling her any of this at all. Paige clearly didn't.

So instead, I point to the store. "You need groceries. Ray will yell if we're parked out here too long."

She looks like she's thinking about dragging me out of the car, but decides against it and snatches up her purse. "We're continuing this," she says. When she's out of sight, I get out of the car and walk.

At its peak Slater had something like eight thousand people living in it or commuting in for the quarry. Now with less than half that number, it feels like it's still waiting for them to come back. There are too many defunct buildings and boarded-up windows. In farther-out places, like where Mason lives, the forest has started reclaiming abandoned houses. Outside Main Street, avoiding the car roads, I could walk for a long time without seeing anyone at all.

It's so empty I have to find thoughts to fill the silence before my imagination does it instead. Mason's right; Paige disappearing right after finding something her family is still keeping secret is too coincidental. He's also right that there was something else about meeting Zach by the river that I haven't caught on to. I sense that truth like an instinct, the way my gut could feel Dad walking into the house even from upstairs. Not the gun, don't think about the gun. But after two years of thinking about it on a loop, the bulge of the weapon in his jacket pocket more obvious every time I remember it, I can't step around it no matter how hard I try.

I end up at the fountain square. One of the Vandersteens' seraphs rises from the pool in its robes, long-limbed, proud, and androgynous. Wings drape from its shoulders, a chip forming each feather. Beneath it, the bottom of the fountain glitters with coins.

Zach, Wren, Mason, and I used to whisper our wishes into our coins—extra snacks, new bicycles, and no bedtime, and then when we were older, things like good grades, the newest game, to be liked—and on three, dropped them in a row. We could always spot where our wishes had landed, because the coins would be clustered together.

Later, I started coming by the fountain in the off-hours when no one else would pass by. There are some wishes you can only whisper alone: for Dad to stop being angry, for Trish to stop sleepwalking, for me to stop hurting, for Mom to stop acting like nothing was wrong. I didn't believe in fairy tales anymore, but I tried anyway. I miss the days when we only wished for stupid things. Now I think if I squint hard enough I can still spot clusters of four coins.

I'm jolted by a small boy scootering into the square. "Danny?"

He almost trips off and runs toward me, curls bouncing. "Isa!"

It's like a sudden burst of sunlight, the smell of baking pasta during a sleepover Pictionary game where Wren would pretend to be offended her brother wanted me on his team instead of her. He must be, what, ten now? Two years make a hell of a difference at his age and I can't resist: "You're so big now!" Wren loved him like crazy—she was the only person sometimes who could make him stop crying. Mr. Carver comes up behind him, smiling a little.

"He's going to be taller than me soon." But then his gaze hardens, and I tense. "Heard you're still hanging around with the Kane boy."

The Carvers never really liked Mason. He was charming enough, when he wanted to be, to overcome their suspicions about his mother, but as he got older his tendency to argue with pastors and teachers, plus his lack of religious *and* parental guidance, made people warier. When he and Wren got together, only Zach and I knew officially, although people suspected. I got the worst end of the deal, having to protect them while also wishing every day they'd break up.

It all came out when the texts were revealed, most specifically that they'd been sleeping together. The Carvers were convinced he'd killed her. Everyone was blaming one another. Mrs. Carver came over to our house and took me aside to ask, fiercely, if he'd touched me too. Any hope I'd had of a new normal after Zach's death imploded. Everyone I loved was being pressured to take a side.

So I left.

"We crossed paths," I say, not quite a truth and not quite a lie. I'm so tired of this. Danny looks between us. How much does he know?

"We thought he killed you too, you know. You just disappeared like that."

I bite the inside of my cheeks. I'd never thought about what happened after I left. I didn't think anyone cared enough to wonder. "I got into school. Just thought I'd leave early is all."

"Yeah, well. I can't blame you really. But we missed you at the service."

Danny's gone to sit on the lip of the fountain. "Dad, can I have a coin?"

"Not now." Mr. Carver beckons Danny over and picks up the fallen scooter. "You get back to school, Isadora, you hear?" he says, as something sparks in my mind. "Don't hang around with that boy. I'm praying for you. You find some good Christian boy instead. And you want company, our house is always open."

"Okay." I can't say much else. I do manage "Bye, Danny," as they head back to where they must have parked.

Get back to school, Isadora. I can't believe he called me *Isadora*, like I didn't half grow up in his house, like he didn't teach me to drive at thirteen, swapping the driver's seat with Wren in his car, just to the end of the street and back. Like we're strangers.

A memory scratches and scratches. *Isadora*, I think, and it doesn't sound like Mr. Carver's voice anymore. *Isadora*. Whose voice is that? Zach's? *I'm fine, Isadora, leave me alone.*

For the first time, my memory of that evening shutters out the gun. Why would he call me Isadora?

My phone rings, jolting me off the train of thought. I almost swipe to ignore out of habit, but it's Mason. Even then I almost let it ring through, not sure if I can talk to him. But just before it stops, I swipe to answer and put it to my ear.

"Matthew Accetta is dead."

It takes me a moment to register his words. "What?"

"Matthew Accetta is dead. They just brought his body into the morgue. I'm looking at it right now." Mason's voice is rough, drained of sleep. "He hung himself last night."

"Why are you telling me this?"

I say it instinctively, but it's an obvious deflection. "You know why." I showed him why yesterday. In black and white pencil on canvas, right next to the portrait of Paige Vandersteen. Suddenly he says, "Would you have come back if your dad hadn't died?"

I can't keep up with him, can barely make sense of my own thoughts. "What?"

"Even when you recognized the drawings, would you have come back? Texted, even? Or would you have just tossed them in the trash and gotten on with it?"

"I didn't have your number." It's not a lie. Dad had my old phone when I left, but my tongue is lead.

"So, no."

"I got out of this shit," I say, even as I think that when I ran away with no plan, part of me was hoping to end up a police file, too, so at least I'd be written down somewhere, so at least I could join them. *Leave or die,* my brain is screaming. I can't hear anything over it. *Leave this conversation right now.* There are too many voices, too many fragments. *I'm fine, Isadora. He said your name. Go back to school, Isadora. Matthew Accetta is dead. Paige Vandersteen's gone missing.* "I have a life. What would I come back for?"

"I haven't seen you look at your phone once. You sure about that life?"

"Fuck you."

"Are you serious?" he says, without flinching. Over the phone his footsteps echo, moving somewhere. "What was the last portrait you drew, Isa?"

"Why does that—" Oh. Four drawings: the five screaming kids, and three portraits. Paige Vandersteen. Missing. Matthew Accetta. Dead. And Mason. My mouth opens, words it should find slipping away before they can form. "They're just—" *Just drawings*. But they're not. Just like my dreams aren't dreams. Something happens to me when my mind slips like that. I always thought it was this wrongness inside me escaping when I wasn't careful enough to keep it back, but that doesn't explain how I would pull Wren's and Zach's ghosts from the ether, or somehow predict one fate after another.

"Something's coming through me," I murmur, without really knowing what I'm saying. Yet even as I do, it nestles coldly into the truth. It's never just been me. There's something I'm sensing, something beyond me.

I'm fine, Isadora.

My name distorts through the memory in a way that's almost familiar. Who said that? "I was there," I say, and it's almost shocking again how easy it is to admit it after two years. "At the river before Zach died. But I think something else was too."

7

I'M STILL STANDING IN THE FOUNTAIN SQUARE
when Mason pulls up. I get in, hold up a hand when he tries to
speak, and then we're off. I recognize the road to his house, in a
dead corner of town where miners used to live. Zach would have
run up here that day, and then run back down.

A second car is parked outside—his mother is home. We get
out of the car, but by silent agreement, we turn right from his
house, heading into the surrounding woods, toward the grotto.

There aren't a lot of school groups to join here, with a student
body so small; you were in athletics, band, workshop, yearbook,
or nothing. Mason was nothing, so he spent the time reading and
exploring, and once he found this cave. The trail leads over a
trickling stream, to a child-sized scoop out of the mountainside.
Every inch of its inside is covered with tiny irises. The first spring
day he took us there, the light hit just right and the flowers looked
like purple stars on the dark stone, and it was the most beautiful
thing I'd ever seen. That place was a castle one day, the belly of a
ship the next. There, the only rules were our own.

The intense memory of its safety pulls me through the forest.
We marked the way with loops of ribbons, and now we follow the

faded strips between the trees. I'm only half-aware of my feet moving. My mind just loops and loops with the memory of the river. Trying to remember something from two years ago is already like seeing something in the reflection of water; this is like sensing an invisible glass ball in the water and trying to find it by feeling how the currents distort around it.

But then there's the plank bridge Mr. Carver helped us saw, still flat across the creek. The crooked arch of the cave itself, revealing the hanging lantern as we duck inside.

It's a mess, books and papers and food containers everywhere, but the walls are still covered in painted flowers. Wren didn't want it to be bare when the flowers weren't in season, so we added permanent ones instead. I'd just grabbed whatever paint I could find. The acrylics have held up the best, but there are also spots done in crayon that are waxy in the lantern light. In one corner is a smudge in the shape of fingers. Someone's laughter shrieks in the hollow of my brain, followed rapidly by *Isadora*. I can't tell who it came from anymore.

"This is our lair," Zach proclaimed once, standing here at the entrance waving a stick for a sword. "Inside it is our treasure, and the fairy queen." He swung around to point at Wren, who laughed. "Attack, all ye who dare!"

Now the real world's followed us in. Our enemies dared, and they won. Mason collapses onto the floor and I join him, and we both sit there pressing our backs against the wall.

"Okay," he says, after how long I can't tell. "What do you remember?"

He's eerily calm for someone who just saw a dead body and thinks he might be next, but I see some of my own reactions mirrored in him: snapping off, filing things away, focusing on what needs to be done and the next step we need to take. It seems unfair that the two of us who are still alive are the most heartless half.

"He called me Isadora." I breathe in and out, feel my spine against the rock. No, that doesn't make any sense. "He called me Isadora, but there was something . . ." I can feel the truth of it sitting in me, but I can't put the feeling into words that make sense. I expect Mason to lose patience, but he's just watching me. "I used to hear—I mean I still do, I think, but I learned to block it off a long time ago—I used to hear this song from the mountains, when I was alone sometimes. Every time I heard it, I felt so . . . exposed. Like the worst parts of me heard it and came out to dance. The more I heard it the more I was sure everyone could tell. It made me feel *wrong*. But I *could* hear it. And that day I heard it in him, just under the surface.

"He was holding the gun when I got there," I ramble on. "I interrupted him. I feel like I heard something I wasn't supposed to."

"The song?"

He's too attentive. Did he even hear what I said about the gun? Isn't he mad? "Not just the song," I say slowly. My frustration rises. It feels like there's a simple thing I'm grasping at that I just can't quite articulate.

Everyone keeps asking me for something *deeper*, with *meaning*, to *put myself into my pieces*, and I've never been able to dig as deep as they want. *Broken*, like I thought again earlier; I can't explain myself, so how am I supposed to expect them to do anything for me? Professor Rodriguez, Olivia, Yara, even my boss at the tattoo shop who's obviously clued into me being screwed up but can't get me to open up on why. I'm afraid I'm losing their patience. I'm afraid the new starts I've found are just destined to become horrible endings again because something is fundamentally missing in me. Maybe I'm just not meant for people to see.

I keep dipping for that glass ball in my mind and coming up with just water. We've been sitting in silence for minutes now and I start doubting the extra presence was ever even there in the memory in the first place. Maybe I'm just trying to find something to blame for my own guilt.

I thought if I stuck it out and did everything right like Dad said I should, then the song would stop making me feel so horrible. When it only got worse no matter what I did, I kept it quiet and pretended I was just like everyone else. I kept it so quiet I stopped being able to really tell when it was the song pulling out my worst thoughts and when it was just me, and whether there was a difference to begin with. I just accepted I was born to feel like that.

But no—Zach told Mason to find me, that by being there, I'd come across something important. That night, I heard it not in me, but coming through *him*. I didn't recognize it at the time, since I'd done too good a job burying it. I just had the deep sense of something wrong, of needing to get him away.

And the longer I do let it settle in me now, the details of each individual current become clearer and clearer. As they do, I become more sure. The way Zach had been all jerky and oddly walled off, like he didn't know how to respond. The way he winced when I tried to talk to him. *Isadora,* he said the one time, sounding all wrong, and I thought, *Who said that?* "Not just the song," I say finally. "A singer."

Mason goes still, alert with the energy of having found a new conviction. "Something aware," he says, not even doubting me. "Something getting inside their heads."

78

It shouldn't make a difference, but somehow it does. A song in my head I can take—file away with all the other voices that otherwise blanket my thoughts. But some *thing*, a presence, the sound from its mouth to my ear, following me for years, stirring up my emotions . . .

"We should go back to the plague house. If it's true that this singer was responsible for those deaths too, that's where it might be easiest to detect them. We can use your awareness of it as an amplifier, but we'd need another anchor item—"

I feel violated. The cave suddenly feels too open. I want something to cover the entrance with. "Shit," I murmur. *"Shit."*

"Isa. What are you doing?" He catches my hands. I hadn't realized they were moving. I bring my wrists up to the light, and see what damage my nails have done.

I never cut, but I used to dig my thumbnail into my forearm or thigh and drag down hard. Not enough to break skin but deep enough to raise inflamed lines all across my body until I'd calmed down or run out of space. I sort of enjoyed tracing the bumps for hours after. I once had the idea for a morbid temporary art piece—*Portraits of Almost There but Not Quite Deranged Enough*— but I didn't think my teachers would go for it. It's a thing I'm supposed to have under control.

But now there are diamonds scratched into the surface of my left wrist, with smaller ones in the center of them—no, not diamonds. Eyes, red on my skin, just starting to bloom.

"Watched," I whisper.

He's staring at me, but I'm finally focusing on the back of the cave, where above stacks of books are photos and paper cuttings stuck to the wall. Like the memory, the photos are just blurry shapes at first. Then as I move closer they sharpen all at once into faces. Our faces. Everywhere.

There are things some spirit in me remembers even when my brain forgets, because they're the things I can't remember when I try and yet they crowd my dreams. They take over my body at some sound or smell or sight, a laugh that sounded too much like Wren making me drop a coffee cup and run away to cry. I've dreamt through their faces again and again and woken up with chasms in my chest even as the images slip away.

I left all the pictures I had behind in my old phone. Now that I'm seeing Mason's collection, the dreams seep through from wherever they're kept and engorge in my brain, filling empty spaces I hadn't even realized were there. My eyes drink them in even as I want to tear them out. Us at school, us by the fountain, us on our bikes, us at someone's birthday, and all through them:

Wren, chin like the tip of a heart, summer-brown and smiling with a dimple but only half her teeth. A blue skirt I helped her pick out after she spent an hour throwing options around her room. The white dress from the baptism, crucifix hanging over the collar. Wisps of her curls catching the golden edges of the sun, or tucked beneath a beanie. Head tilted, hair spilling over one shoulder; or peeking over her shoulder, a soda can covering most of her face.

Then Zach, sometimes beside her, sometimes not, taking up frames like he couldn't help but lean forward at the last moment. His hair's longer in some, curling around his ears; in others it's clipped away from his squared tanned face, all symmetrical except for his lopsided full grin, puckered to the right like a victory lap smirk. He's in his brother's old T-shirts or his sports jacket, that same red and yellow with silver buttons Matthew was wearing in my dream.

And Mason, of course, hair darkening as he got older, although half the time he's behind the camera. But also, me: no makeup yet, no piercings; my hair steadily growing out from a straight bob to a veil down my back. You can tell I never knew how to smile properly, always pressed lips, but sometimes the camera's caught me mid-laugh or with my tongue out, and I almost feel like I'm seeing a third ghost. I don't remember ever looking so young.

"It's just us," Mason says quietly. I'm sure he looks at this wall every day. "Somehow it's left to us."

Us clamps down on me, an offering I don't deserve. He says it so easily I wonder if he heard my confession at all. "Aren't you mad at me?"

"What?"

"Aren't you mad I didn't tell anyone I saw him?"

The pity in his expression hits like a sledgehammer. "What were you supposed to have done?"

"Stopped him. Not told him to fuck himself, I don't know. Why do I deserve to be the hero?" It's ridiculous when I say it out loud. How can a question that's eaten me up for years make so little actual sense? What *was* I supposed to have done?

It's so hard to fight the instinct that I'm responsible for every bad thing that's ever happened to me, that I'm just not quiet or good or fast or *something* enough, that I should see the bad things coming. I tried for so long to see them coming. I memorized footsteps, learned to smell the sour sharpness of anger and hear the spike of a heartbeat. But there was always some flaw I hadn't fixed.

At our first illegal dorm party on the rooftop. I wanted Olivia to think I was cool, the kind of person who could joke about her trauma, so I said, *I thought I had to fix it, you know, but I've come to the conclusion that some men just like hitting little girls.* They smirked and nudged my cup. *There you go. Growth.* But look, I fucked up with Olivia, I'm back, and of all the things I lost, I never lost the scared little girl. Bad things that are somehow my fault are happening again, and it's so hard to feel like I don't deserve them. Because I was selfish and didn't pay enough attention to save my best friends because I was too busy being heartsick. I ran away and told myself their deaths didn't have anything to do with me.

"You want to get all the guilt out in the open?" Mason says at last, running his hand over his mouth. "Fine. How's this: When you didn't show up at Wren's funeral, I thought you were dead too. I looked for your body. I spent weeks being afraid I would turn some corner and find you there."

The sick relief I feel hearing that makes the rational part of me nauseous. One more reason I should just stay here, in this pit, wasting away. "My point exactly."

"*My* point is there *is* no score. You don't have to earn the right to do the right thing. I can tell you all my sins too, but I'm also going to actually do something about them. I don't care that you left, Isa. I'm glad you got out. I'm glad you're doing better. I just care that you're willing to come back. You've proven twice now, maybe three times with the drawings, that no one else *can* do what you do." He pauses. "And no one else does what I do. No one else will do it but us."

Us again. Two years ago I would've laughed. The only things Mason and I had in common were that we loved the same person and our parents didn't raise us. But what would have happened if I'd come back to find Mason dead instead, without me even knowing? What if I'd tossed the drawings like he said, then heard months down the line that he'd died and pretended I didn't see it coming? Could I have walked away from that? Can I walk away from it now?

No, I think, so simply it shocks me. No, because Mason will chase this with or without me, even as he's withering away, and I can't imagine myself going back to my life if he dies and I could've stopped it. I can't imagine going back to my life if I'm the only one of us that's left. My thumb runs over the bumps of eyes on my wrist. Besides, I might not have a choice. Part of me knows something, and I might as well use it before it bursts out on its own.

Mason is right. No one's keeping score except me. These days I'm the judge of myself, and that judge's decision-making can go to hell. The fuck-you I need to say, apparently, is to my own twisted little brain.

I pull off one of the most recent pictures on the wall—us at Wren's fourteenth birthday, judging by the cake. She always had the same one, red velvet. This was maybe one of the last photos with all of us in it. Danny's there too, cheesing like it's his birthday instead.

"You wrote her that fucking poem in that scrapbook," I say. The notebook is in the photo, lying where the other presents are, dried flowers stuck all over the cover.

"Rip-off Keats," he admits. "I went looking for wildflowers for hours to stick on that. And then you showed me up with *hand-painted canvases of her favorite places*—"

"Well, *Zach* won that year. Wren played that record for months and he just got it for a dollar at the store after school."

He smiles, so suddenly my chest tightens. I have to pull back, remember where we are. Remember what brought us both here again. A song. A singer. Something that's taken our friends, has a girl missing—and might be coming for Mason next. But he hasn't brought up that omen again, and I follow his lead to focus on what we actually can do about it.

"What were you saying about an anchor item?"

"I've thought of where we can get one." He spreads his hands. "I'm going to take you to church, Isadora Chang."

we

YOU ARE BUILT FOR THE TRACK, ZACHARY TAI.

Your lungs are perfectly drawn to chase the finish line. This is a rule just for you: Your legs are long and must be kept strong. Muscle, never fat. You have never been good with numbers, but these you can calculate in your sleep: the necessary numbers of what your body eats, the exact scales beyond which it ceases to have worth.

You are so fearfully made.

Yet no matter how tightly you wind your body, there is something wrong with it, what it can't help wanting. The older you become, the more you slip, the more you hate. The faster you run, so no one sees. Your parents are finally proud. Your teachers make you excuses. With every race won, the other boys on the team pull you closer, the musk of sweat and sprays and drinks you will regret, the sound of pounding fists and feet. You are made of them now, their respect. The way they understand, more than your once-closest friends, what it is to run. What it is to feel alive with the rushing blood in your veins. You are one of them, one of them, one of them. The man your father wants you to be.

And still, here you are on this late fall day, sitting opposite your coach instead of out on the dirt track. For every high, there is a punishment. You never thought this one would come, but oh, you should have. For here it is: they cannot shut an eye to your studies any longer. Until you do better in your classes, you are no longer on the team.

You have always thought your coach a kind man, haven't you? You have trusted him. You have believed he cares.

Yet if he cared, he would not refuse your pleas. He would see that without this you are nothing, you deserve nothing. Perhaps, if he cared, he would not pretend he does not know what his wild boys do every harvest moon on the Ridge.

In the end, he lets you down too. So you swear at him, ugly words you cannot take back, and here you are now, turning down a familiar road. Do you know, even now, that you are about to betray yourself? Is it like the clink of a bottle against your teeth, an illicit bite of sugar that reminds you of being a child? Do you know, running toward the houses by the woods, that you will have to punish yourself after?

Mason Kane lets you in so quickly.

You cannot trust him either. But you never learn.

So trip on uneven pavement and stumble into metal. Your feet fail you too. But this you can do: kick, again and again, denting the can before it crashes. Kick it farther, crush it against a wall. Skid your fist off the metal and crack it into the brick. Stare at the blood as though you have never seen its color.

You are nothing more than what your body would do, little better than a beast. You hardly know what to do with it without instruction. Your coach has abandoned you, your best friend despises you, and your father will only see failure. But I am here, and I will show you the way.

8

WHEN MASON KANE TAKES YOU TO CHURCH, it's to find something that belonged to a dead girl. His séance needs three things: the place they died or were buried, an image of them or an object that was personal, and their name. Place, face, name. We have the place. The church has the other two.

"The alternative is grave robbing," Mason had said, "but we'd have to knock out a cairn, then it's fifty-fifty on which one of us gets killed off this time."

I don't like how serious he sounded, even for someone who talked to the dead as a hobby. But he's almost cheerful when Trish and I pull up in front of the church and see him waiting by his beat-up sedan. I feel more on edge with her around, but Trish's archive work for the Vandersteens includes their church archive, and she has keys to the cases. I didn't know how she'd react after I ditched her at the grocery store, but when I said Mason would show her what happened with Paige, all she said was, "What time?"

As she gets out of the car now, she also says, "Is that dirt on your leg?"

Mason glances down. "Oh. We dug Matthew's grave this morning."

Right. Because you can pass off a drowning as accident or murder, but not a hanging, they haven't held a funeral. They won't build him a cairn either. One more for Mason to add to his list.

I didn't know Matthew well, but Zach had been his mentor or something on the athletics team. The day after Zach was buried, Matthew shoved Mason in the school hallway. Mason smiled and called him a few choice words, and so Matthew had tried to swing, and he would've won if Wren hadn't gotten between them, yelling. I should've backed Wren up, but I just watched from the stairs. No one stopped them, because *boys have tempers; that's just how they are.* At least until they burst out on themselves, I guess. Now both he and Zach are gone. I should have tried to warn him. Should've, should've, should've. No. What matters now is trying to understand, at last, what's killing us. Before Mason's the next one in an unmarked grave.

The Chapel of Our Herald is always open. Light cuts through paneled windows onto ancient pews and stone tiles. Dust motes swirl in the faint incense. Above the altar is an angel cast in tinted glass, flute in hand, gazing down at the pews as though it can see the congregation there. The light coming through its mosaic swims on the piano. Wren used to play for service sometimes.

An image, sepia watercolor on canvas: a girl kneeling beneath the stained glass, begging. The light pools around her in rivulets, where unseeing gray faces are borne down the aisles by the current. A question round, second term:

What was the inspiration for this piece, Isadora?

A girl I saw once.

Just a girl I watched across the room, whispering every prayer she knew, hoping heaven would take enough pity to stitch her friend's skull back together.

Trish's feather-light touch on my spine pushes me along the aisles into the church's second wing, which doubles as a relic store and memorial. There's photos of the first Vandersteens, some of the quarry in the early 1900s, more of early congregations, people who flocked here for the rich stone that seemed endless. The statues, the pictures, the plinths blooming everywhere. Slater doesn't know what to do with itself now except grip onto its heyday. All while the world moves on without them anyway.

In color, there's a portrait of Theodore Vandersteen, Ida and Sammy's third sibling, the devout one who commissioned the fountain for the herald that scooped the rot from the town. They say he led cleansing and prayers, and eventually he and Cecily had a vision of an angel, who delivered the message that the town would be spared in exchange for the sick children. And so, the quarantine house—really, a sacrifice.

But it's not the pictures we've come for. There's a case of artifacts here: a rat cage, an old hammer, an old psalm book, things like that. There's also a rusty-haired doll, stitched with yarn and with mismatched buttons for eyes. The plaque says it belonged to an Anne Wheeler.

"Anne died in the plague house," he tells Trish, sliding the case open with her key.

Trish looks doubtful.

"His abilities are empathetic," I explain, the way he did to me. "It's stronger with an anchor item personal to the spirit."

"And their name," he reminds me. "Paige had an old locket, but it's disappeared with her. I'm hoping this will do the same trick."

He slips the doll into the satchel he brought and eases the case shut again.

"That's where that went?" Trish purses her mouth. "I knew that was missing."

Mason holds up a finger, frowning. "What's that sound?"

I don't hear it, at first—but then I do. A voice in the chapel outside, Pastor Charles's, I think, calling and rousing in an unknown yet familiar language. "It's tongues." As always, hearing it, I feel a shiver. It gets louder as we pause, a couple more voices joining in slightly different tongues, a babble flowing through the congregants from the divine.

"That's what that sounds like?" Mason says skeptically. "Can you do that?"

"I've tried. It's not my gift," I reply lightly. Not mentioning I always felt like something was wrong with me when the Spirit seemed to fill everyone else, or that the one time I tried to force it, something I was definitely sure wasn't the Spirit welled up in my head instead. "But shit. We forgot about the Absolution Squad."

"The what?"

"They do this every time there's a big scandal," Trish supplies. "So instead of, you know, holding a funeral for Matthew, they're praying the rest of us don't get corrupted by his influence."

"Don't even," I say, before Mason can launch into a righteous speech. "We're going to have to wait till they're gone."

"Hm," Trish says. Then: "Oh no."

"What?" But I see it too: the vessels for the Blood and Body, which they'll want to take out for communion, are standing on the shelf by the door. I then realize the tongues have faded, replaced by the sound of the doorknob turning.

"Damn it," Mason mutters, as Pastor Charles walks in and stops short.

"We're just visiting, Pastor," Trish says quickly. "I didn't mean to interrupt."

"Well, you should join us." He looks at Mason with much less enthusiasm. "Mason Kane. I don't suppose you're here to repent."

"I'd need something to repent for first, Pastor."

Oh, to have the audacity of a pretty white boy. The pastor purses his lips and tries to pivot back. "Girls. How have you been doing? We've missed you around here, Isa. You really should join us outside. I know these incidents can cause a lot of doubt and confusion."

Besides the way he says *these incidents* like he isn't talking about a boy hanging himself, his paternal care makes me stiffen. He's a little older than Dad, early fifties with shaggy graying hair that continues its wisps across his blocky jaw and the ghost of weathered dimples. He'd always been so welcoming, the pastor that jostled with the boys, remembered our birthdays, and told me my art was a gift. He got Wren playing in the band and encouraged me to join decorating committees for holidays. But he also refused to conduct Zach's funeral, the boy he'd played on Sunday soccer games. In the end, we buried Zach without a ceremony. Who knows if anyone even showed up for Matthew.

"Mason just wanted to learn about . . . Theodore," I manage. "To understand the plague."

Mason looks like he'd rather get the plague himself. Trish swoops in. "He's never really heard the story, and we thought he should."

The idea that Mason has somehow missed out on this piece of information in the eighteen years he's lived here is laughable, but

I'll play along if it gives us an excuse. Pastor Charles clearly isn't buying it either. I feel the same assessing glances at my nose, my ears, my darkened lips. I'm not the demure girl he remembers, and he's not the friendly pastor I once thought he was. Even before he cast Zach off, I started hearing the judgment in the sermons. When he came around for dinner and said what a family man Dad was, all I could think was that I had to behave so he wouldn't know, so I wouldn't end up on the wrong side of that preaching. A town this small doesn't have space for the other side, and I feel now like I'm on the edge of a cliff. I hate how much part of me still wants his approval.

"Yes," he says eventually, though he still looks suspicious. "Theodore had a vision that an angel was sent to take the sick and save the rest of Slater. A tragedy, but a necessary one for the greater good. Cut off the diseased limb to keep the rest clean."

He says it pointedly. Mason gives him a long stare. "So is it a savior or a killer?"

"The Lord giveth and taketh; it was an angel who brought Mary the blessed news of her coming child, and yet also an angel that delivered the final plague. *On that same night I will pass through Egypt and strike down every firstborn, and I will bring judgment on all the gods of Egypt,* said the Lord—"

"*And there was a loud wailing,*" Mason says quietly from the corner, arms folded, "*for there was not a house without someone dead.*"

Hearing Mason quote Exodus like an altar boy apparently comes as a surprise, because Pastor Charles is momentarily speechless. "Your memory does you credit," he says stiffly, at last. "If only you put it to better use."

"I put it to great use. I remember that those kids were people, not lambs. There's a lot in here about Theodore. Does anyone even know the names of the kids who died?"

No, we don't. Pastor Charles used to go on and on about Theodore's leadership and faith in deliverance, but the kids were only ever a note in the sermon's backdrop.

Mason sidesteps Pastor Charles to get at the door, and the pastor catches his arm. We're not Sunday schoolers anymore; they're the same height, eye to eye. "What were you doing with Paige Vandersteen?"

I should do something, say something, but as always, I'm just frozen.

"What do you think we were doing?" Mason asks. Jesus. He's just provoking him now, like he can't help himself, and Pastor Charles falls for it.

"You hardly want me to answer that."

"I want to hear what people are making up these days. Everyone's got so much imagination, suddenly, when it comes to these things. If they put that creativity into the sculptures, we'd all be rich and not living in this shitty town."

Jesus Christ. The cold anger radiating from the pastor sets all my alarm bells off. But I still can't find words, and it's Trish that hurriedly offers to usher us out.

"The chief wants to talk to you," Pastor Charles calls after Mason.

"You can tell him I stopped by, Pastor."

"The Angel will return to renew the town when it must. God knows it's overdue."

Mason turns around this time. "You can tell the Angel I stopped by, too."

The prayers start again as we reach the door, unknown languages that reach into me, that part of me still wants to be able to speak back. I used to think something was wrong with me if I didn't feel the way others were obviously feeling. So I pretended. And they all put their hands on me, loving me, and it was the closest thing to real family I'd ever had. Then I felt like I was even worse for faking it, and so everyone else was singing holy and all I had was the music of all the secrets inside me, one wrong move away from spilling out. Maybe I blocked that out so well I somehow blocked out God too.

But I was good at not letting on. You can act out a prayer if you know all the right words, can pull exactly the right verses. I know when to lift my hands and when to lay them. I memorized it all and thought that was the same as believing—it's not, but I could go back and make them think it is.

Instead, I leave and for once, it's the hardest thing to do.

I tuck my fists into my coat as we step back out into the open. A breeze curls around the church's chimes, replacing the tongues with light twinkling.

"Always nice to remember I'm not missing much," Mason remarks. It's also hard not to hate him for a second. He wouldn't understand. "So. Showtime?"

Showtime. Through the mountain, off the park, there is a tunnel. Through the tunnel, there is a ridge. On the ridge are elopers, smugglers, and kids sneaking out, lighting fires and opening bottles and exploring each other in the sand. At the end of the ridge, there is a house. In this house was locked a plague. And upon the plague came the flood that drowned Anne Wheeler. There, we'll attempt to reach her ghost—and hopefully find out what she knows about what killed her.

9

YOU CAN DRIVE ALMOST ALL THE WAY DOWN
to Elopers' Ridge, but the road stops at a rough clearing where
forest and rock cut through the path instead. We park in the
clearing and walk the rest of the way to the tunnel. It opens ahead
of our phone lights, a mouth in the rock just low enough that
Mason has to duck.

Slater's mountains don't quite sit flush against one another.
Sometimes the gaps in the rock widen out enough for a rivulet to
wind its own way in, picking up speed and forming a small river
before going under again. This tunnel leads to the bottom of a
chasm, with a crescent of gray sky just visible between the two
cliff faces, and a crumbling ridge that runs along the channel.

They say smugglers came through here once, but if the
church was Theodore Vandersteen's, this stretch now belongs
to his siblings. It's the site of rhymes: on one far end is Sammy's
Drop, a jutting rock where Samuel Vandersteen threw himself
naked into the water. The wide center of the Ridge, where the
tunnel opens, is where his twin, Ida, hooked up with a sailor
and got herself exiled. But apparently not before leaving behind
a kid.

True to Ida's legacy, rebel kids have been here recently. The remains of a firepit, an empty wine bottle, the faintest smell of weed in the air. The four of us used to come here sometimes; more often, I came alone. Sometimes older boys would try to kiss me, and I'd let them. Mason watches the channel as we walk along it, and I know he's thinking about how Zach was found with his upper half in the river, like a baptism he'd never come up from. I don't know how they found Wren exactly, but she died in the water too.

Something furry bobs in the channel. Pointy-nosed, long-tailed. Before I can identify it for sure, though, it sinks back beneath the surface again.

We pick our way over the thinner eroded stretches to the other end, around the outcrop to where the plague house sits in its cove: a long, low building gutted by time and storms. Half its shell has been stripped to beams, and it's rotting at its lower edges. Through the gaps I see the rows of molding cots. I take a quick picture for future reference.

"It's not the nicest place to die, is it?" Trish says.

Mason snorts. "You've never been here?"

"Trish is too good to be a Ridge kid." She's right, though. I can't imagine being trapped here, much less in a storm and at night. It was night the first time Mason, Wren, Zach, and I decided to sneak out to come see it. We were maybe thirteen and the older kids making out by the fire glanced at us as we ducked out from the tunnel, but they didn't harass us as we slipped past. The house, just worn out in the daylight, becomes mangled once the sun goes down and flashlights catch the ribs of beams in strange ways.

We did stuff like that all the time, egging one another on to places we weren't supposed to be. The Ridge, wooded hollows, the abandoned houses on Mason's road. A lot of people thought Mason was the bad influence, but they'd be surprised at how much of it was Wren's idea, how reckless she could be once she got swept up in an adventure. I never told anyone that, though. The debate around her death would have been twice as bad if they thought she made a habit of poor decisions. Some of us get to be more reckless than others. Sometimes I thought she was better off with Mason anyway, because he'd have adventures with her. All I would've done was force her to throw up more walls.

Still, going into the plague house to try to summon ghosts is different from just exploring. I don't know if I imagine it, but the temperature seems to drop as we approach the house.

When we step inside, the shell exhales over us. The molding boards creak under our feet, and the rows of broken cots look like tombs. I still can't imagine Paige Vandersteen here, trying to—what, reconnect with a lost ancestor? I'm surprised the Vandersteens haven't just torn the whole thing down, but then again, the whole town is full of empty buildings.

"You said Paige had a locket the last time?" Trish says. I can tell she's been waiting to say something. "Bronze, initial I, picture of Ida Vandersteen in it?"

"Yeah." Mason places Anne Wheeler's doll on the nearest cot. "How did you know that?"

"We found it in Cecily's collections at the Red House a few months ago. She had a whole set of items related to plague patients, including some recovered from the plague house kids.

Paige was around that day, and she was asking why Ida's necklace would be in the plague collection when Ida eloped years before that. I pointed her toward Cecily's own records, and Paige came back a few days later telling me that Ida had a kid."

"Sarai."

"Yeah. When I went back through the inventory a bit later, the locket was gone. I guess she brought it to you."

"Why didn't you say this in the car the other day?" I ask. "You were acting like it was this big secret."

"I think it is; I just don't know all of it. After Paige disappeared, I told her parents about it. I didn't know if it would help."

"They didn't react well," Mason guesses.

"No, they didn't. They reminded me my access to their archives was supposed to be confidential and implied if I talked about Sarai, I would lose my job. Then they implied they wouldn't be able to recommend me anywhere."

Which would effectively blacklist her, since most people in town wouldn't dare get on the Vandersteens' bad side.

"They're assholes," Mason says, in a tone of *I told you so*. He's never liked being reminded that his house was given to his mother by the Vandersteens, that they, too, live in that charity.

But I'm more focused on the fact that with Dad gone, Trish is currently supporting Mom *and* me, no matter how much I pretend not to see the cash appearing in my account. None of us can afford for her to leave this job on bad terms. "So should you be telling us this? We can't be risking your job."

"It's fine, Isa. Just don't do anything stupid and they won't know."

"We did just steal from the church in front of Pastor Charles," Mason points out.

Trish winces, like she wishes she hadn't followed us after all.

"Maybe if you hadn't pissed him off," I say, but Trish waves me aside.

"You think this will help you figure out what happened to Paige?"

Mason and I exchange looks. "That's the goal." He pulls out his chime necklace again. He shakes back his hair, then places his palm over Anne's doll, gesturing for us to copy him. Trish moves to the other side of the cot and stacks our palms. His other hand, with the chime, he gives the slightest, careful swing. "Anne Wheeler," he says, like calling an old friend.

A clear, low sound ripples through me, deeper than I expected from such a small thing. The ringing lingers in the room. One minute passes. Two. The air thickens, becoming soupy. My breath diffuses past my lips. Familiar anticipation tightens my stomach—something is coming near.

Someone.

Anne?

Before the chime's echo can entirely fade, Mason tilts his hand the other way.

Ding. The second chime is high-pitched, but the clarity is gone. It's a fractured, broken scraping of metal that spreads through the air like static. Goose bumps shoot up my neck. He shuts his eyes, frowning hard. The energy around us hums in the chime's echo, the presence we're looking for answering the call, but it's muted, like the block Mason described.

Yet I can still feel movement—the currents coming toward us but also being pulled back. They're not just being blocked. Something is sucking them back in. Like playing tug of war, I think, and Mason's losing. My mind fills in hands on the other side, wrapping around the air. The singer—and then my mind, blending plague stories together, lands on another name. The Angel.

"Isa," Mason murmurs, "don't freak out." I don't have time to ask what he means before he shifts his hand and places it on top of mine.

There's a yanking sensation in my gut, and a row of bedraggled children appear behind him, smiling in empty faces.

Trish and I scramble back as Mason whirls around with the doll. The ghosts vanish the second we lose contact with him, but a chill goes through me that has nothing to do with the winter. That humidity, the denseness pressing against my skin—it's the presence of a crowd. One large enough to fill the room.

He's still facing them, wide-eyed. "Can you hear us?" he asks, as beads of sweat appear on his forehead. The answer seems to be no; we saw them, but there's still something holding them back. The cold condenses around us. Trish's hand finds mine. "Isa," Mason says again, more urgent this time, reaching back toward me. Fuck.

I take his hand, flattening the doll between our palms. This time I'm ready for it: the children standing stiffly around us in old-fashioned clothes, damp hair, and strange, awkward poses. Some have their arms splayed; others have tilted their heads as though drifting off to sleep. Their flickering faces are blurry, eroded save for identical serene smiles.

The ghosts extend out to the water. I stare at one particular girl in twin braids and suddenly facial features press at the edge of my mind—an aquiline nose, a crooked mouth. "Anne?" I say, but how I know that I'm not sure. The girl extends a thin hand. A high, brittle voice:

That's mine.

"Anne." My fingers twitch. "What happened here?"

The ghost has no eyes, but somehow I can feel her staring, feel a pressure on me as something tries to break through. As if on cue, the farthest ghosts on the ridge lean sideways. The dust on the threshold shifts as the breeze sweeps through us, carrying with it a deep valley song.

I snatch Mason's chime, swallowing all vibrations. With a snap, the air is thin and dry once more, leaving me feeling oddly empty. "Did you hear that?" I demand.

For the first time, he looks disturbed. "I think so." His eyes flick downward to the surface of the deathbed, and I realize my twitching fingers have left a silhouette in the dust. Anne, I think at first, still seeing some of her face in my mind, but it's not her.

"An angel," Trish says, seeing the same slender shape, the two spread wings. "You asked what happened here. Is that the answer?"

Anne was trying to tell me something, wasn't she? The sensations are gone, only the faintest coolness left on my consciousness. But what Trish is saying makes sense. Something is moving my hands, producing answers to questions I didn't know I was asking. "The singer, the Vandersteens' angel. I don't think we're waiting for it to come back. I think it's already here. I think it's been here this entire time."

Mason nods slowly. "An angel, or what they called one, with a song that gets in your head. Makes you . . ."

"Wait," Trish says. "Are you saying you don't think there was a flood here at all?"

"There's still ashes in that fireplace." Mason points across the room. "Maybe the water didn't reach that far. It *was* raining that night, but I think every single one of these kids walked out and jumped into the water themselves."

"And something made them do it," I finish. A current under Zach's voice, something slipped under his skin. I look at Trish and Mason and am suddenly terrified to look away, in case something changes them when I'm not looking. *But why them*? I think, even then. What would the plague kids, Wren, Zach, Matthew, and Paige have in common that they'd invoke the same wrath? Cut off the black limb to keep the rest clean, Pastor Charles said, but that can't be it. That's not fair.

"So Paige," Trish starts, almost reading my mind.

I cut across her, unable to spend more time imagining what Paige Vandersteen looks like now. "Did Cecily and Theodore know what would happen when they sent the kids in there?"

"Cecily's books kept Sarai's secret, made Paige come here in the first place," Mason reminds us. "And she was looking for a second grave somehow related to Sarai. I have to think that whatever gave her that idea was in those books too."

"Trish," I say, "would you be able to get us to those records?" It feels strange, making the plans. Putting myself right at the center of it. But I lost Zach and Wren by keeping my distance. I ignored the warnings of Paige and Matthew that *I* drew. I can't make it up to them by locking myself away. I have to finish what was started.

Trish bites her lip, hard. She cares about Paige, but she also has a lot more to lose—our *family* has a lot more to lose—and I feel a stab of guilt. "If it's too risky—"

"They're in the Purple House now," she says at last, referring to the Vandersteens' estate. "I don't have a key, and I'm not supposed to be working this week. But I might have another solution. Give me some time. And give me the doll," she adds, taking Anne's toy back from Mason. "I'm going to put this back before you get accused of yet another crime."

10

I CAN'T SLEEP. IT'S 2 A.M. AND I'M DRAWING instead, trying to get *something* done and avoid dreaming at the same time, while holding back the prickling feeling creeping up on me just the same when I draw. My imagination has always run to the wildest places and needed to be firmly bricked up.

I grew up hearing voices in the walls, rats and Mom skulking around, people whispering and whispering, and it all turned into this paranoia I couldn't shake. I couldn't trust what I was feeling to be real.

But now I'm aware of a more specific source for that paranoia. Tonight I've been trying to draw the plague house from that photo I took, but the second I put my pencil down, I start imagining something lurking behind the lines. A shadow in the door, an angel in the broken window—no longer just a messenger from a whole host but one creature, one Angel, with a song that pulled the kids into the water. I've erased them again and again, wanting to get *one* draft right and prove to myself I can still do this. But it's like I lose it the second I drift off. What if this doesn't stop even when I go back to school? Why do these fragments keep bleeding through, and what if I'm the thing I actually need to escape from?

No, I can't think like that. I recognize that spiral. Especially that first year, I'd sit on the school roof at night and think about how I'd made it all the way there but it didn't feel like I'd run far enough still, and it would be easy to go farther by just tipping over the edge. But Trish somehow always knew when I was up there. My phone would light up with some text, a picture she'd taken that day. So instead, I'd sit there till the sun came up. I painted a lot of sunrises that year.

My hand's been moving without me again. This time Mason is standing in what's left of the plague house door. Behind him the shadows have slits, spots where my pencil missed that look like narrowed irises. And the more I look, the more Mason's face seems off. That isn't his chin, those are too broad to be his shoulders. Wren's mouth, tacked onto his jaw. Zach's shoulders squeezed into his skin.

My heart pounds. In a vicious surge, I tear off the page and rip it into quarters, into eighths, scattering the pieces across the floor. I'm sick of this sick of this sick of this. My art is supposed to be *mine*. This is *my* thing, the only thing I've had that I didn't lose. The only thing I produce that people find beautiful. It doesn't get to be hijacked.

Not for the first time in my life, I breathe into the quiet of my room and hope to hear something back. Except this isn't me praying, and I don't think this was sent by God. I don't like that the Angel could be with me at any time, and I won't know anymore because I've gone and blocked it out. That might have saved my life back then—but now I'm flinching at every creak, panicking every time my thoughts so much as drift, sitting on my bed with my sketchbook on my knees so none of the room is behind me. I opened the curtains, closed them, opened them again. Because the idea that there was something there I couldn't see was worse than something outside being able to see me.

Maybe it's already in my head. Maybe none of my thoughts are my own. But no, I know what hearing the Angel feels like. Shame from the core of me, hating this body I'm in. I don't feel any of that now, just anger. I could be doing anything else right now if not for it. Going to the city park with a cheap coffee and my sketchbook, planning outfits for monthly themed dinners at school. Making up with Olivia, even. Going to that ice cream place they showed me once.

Impulsively, I grab my phone, text them: *let me explain?* And then toss it across the room. Then I feel stupid, but when I get up to get it back, a car starts up downstairs.

Trish's, I think, though I'm not sure how I know that. The headlights bloom in the corner of my window. Dread spikes through me, and then I run.

For some reason we've always known where to find each other, and right now it's down and out. I'm skidding the stairs before I know it, jumping the last two steps. I fumble with the door locks and fall into the headlights illuminating the driveway.

The cold swallows me gleefully as I dash to her car stalled on the road, sputtering as she hits the clutch again and again. "Trish?" The handle won't give; the door's locked. I slam the window. Her eyes are glassy in the light's backwash. She's still in her pajamas. She's got no shoes on. Crumpled on her lap is the ancient national parks map Dad used to keep tacked on the fridge, places he always said he'd wanted to visit before he got stuck with all of us. Maybe I got it from him, this restlessness, this grudge. I haven't seen the map since I got back but it's in her fist now. I slam on the glass again. "Trish!"

She jerks. Her head turns. Behind the window her pupils are wide with confusion, her eyelids flickering like she's only just waking. I bang on the door again and she finally fumbles with the lock until I can pull the door open.

She covers her face, shoulders shuddering, and I realize she's crying. "I thought I knew where she was. I was going to go to her."

"Who?"

"I was going to get her out."

Paige. Of course she's worried about Paige. But I want her to be worried about herself for once. "*You* should have stayed with me. When you came to see me, you should've never gone back."

I worked for two years to scrub this place off me. I learned how I liked to dress, how to make meringues, learned that love doesn't have to hurt. I wish Trish had gotten that; I wish I didn't feel guilty about a life I liked. I wish she'd just come with me. But she stayed, and I'll always wonder why.

As though hearing my unspoken question, she says, "Mom."

"That's not a reason," I snap. "Mom can take care of herself." But then I realize she wasn't answering me. Mom is on the patio, wrapping a cardigan around herself, watching us.

Trish is still looking through her fingers. "I can't do everything, Isa," she mumbles.

TRISH SINKS AGAINST MY SHOULDER as we trudge up the stairs in silence. Mom has never talked about Trish's sleepwalking. She doesn't even ask what Trish was doing in the car.

As I nudge Trish's door open, though, Mom barges past me to the empty window frame and yanks the curtains over it like she's trying to seal it with the sheer force of her palms. "When did you do this?"

Trish pulls herself from me. "We can't keep going around with all the windows shut, Mom, that's insane." Climbing the stairs has cleared her head. But her voice is trembling, and I can taste the lie. I haven't known how to tell her what happened to her window. Only now do I imagine what must have gone through her head when she found it smashed to pieces. Terror—that someone had snuck in and done it, or worse, that she had. Because when you come from broken things, you're scared of being the one who's done the breaking.

"Don't talk to me like that." Mom's voice is trembling, too, sour and dark. She points at the window. "I close them for a *reason*. I told you not to open them!"

Trish hisses through her teeth, but she'll never confront Mom. This tarot boy in my illustration class said my avoidance of conflict was very Pisces of me. It's probably more abusive dad of me, but I said he was right anyway. Still, I'm bigger now. And if Trish won't ask the questions, then I will. I'm tired of living in a house with no fresh air just because of some obsessive super-stition she has.

"Why can't we open the windows, Mom?"

"I don't need to explain it to you. You do what I say."

"But you don't say anything! *Why can't we open the damn windows?*"

"It will come for us!"

I stop short. Trish has gone sheet white. "Who will come for us?"

Mom clutches her cardigan to her chest. I've never seen her like this. Not nervous, not pretending to be oblivious, but deeply, fundamentally *afraid*. "The Angel on the wind," she croaks, making me freeze. "It knows when you're dirty inside. It punishes the evil."

"Who told you that, Mom?" Trish demands.

Mom's lips part. No sound comes. I remember, suddenly, once a long time ago when she pulled me aside and asked if I was still hearing the mountain song. When I said yes, she didn't say *good* like Dad did; she grabbed me and hissed, "You don't hear it, you understand? And you don't talk about it ever again."

And I didn't, and I taught myself to block it out. But what did she actually mean by that? What does she mean now? What does she know? Trish is still trying to press. "Mom, *who told you that?*"

"She's not going to tell us," I snap.

"Just give her some space, Isa—"

"It will hear," Mom says, like a mantra. "You open the window, the Angel will hear, it will see—"

"The window isn't the problem, Mom!" I yell. Trish falls silent, and suddenly, I'm sick of her giving Mom grace. "You think there's an angel who can see all our secrets, and glass and curtains will keep you hidden? Why did you seal the windows after Dad died? What's the evil left?"

It's the closest I've ever come to confronting her about Dad, and even now it makes my mouth taste like acid. The feeling only sours as the silence drags on and on and on, and I realize I'm not getting an answer. Mom grips the hems of her cardigan, arms pressed over her chest like something will spill out. God, she's ashamed. She should be, and for years I've wished she felt guilty enough to do *something*, anything. But now that I have her shame, I don't know what to do with it. *Did you ever love him?* I want to say. *Whatever I know about love, I didn't get it from you. Do you even know what love looks like? Did you ever learn? Are we born knowing how to love, only to lose it as we go? Have I lost it all already?*

Finally she says, "You are sad. Doesn't mean you need to make other people feel bad too."

"I'm not—"

"What are they teaching you in that school?" she says. Then she's gone, door slamming behind her.

I got it from her, this silence. Inherited all the worst parts of me. I realize suddenly the thing I'm most afraid of isn't this house, isn't this town, isn't the Angel, isn't even Dad—it's ending up exactly like her. Looking at her and seeing the only way I thought I could ever turn out. I've tried so hard to get away. But how am I supposed to escape what I'm made of? There are no photos of my parents' families, nothing to prove we ever came from something beyond Slater, that we existed before all this.

Trish sinks back onto her bed. I wait for the usual—*you shouldn't have said that; she needs more time*—but instead she says, "Go back to sleep, Isa."

"Trish—"

"I'm sorry I woke you."

I wasn't asleep anyway, but I don't tell her that. I go back to my paints, tidying up the mess and laying out new sheets of paper as though that will reset my brain. I experiment with a few silhouettes, but even the most basic lines feel like they'll morph into nightmares too.

Frustrated, I walk to the window and drag open the curtain. I'm terrified and I don't understand anything and I'm so *angry* that I don't understand. I press my hand to the glass and the girl in the reflection twists her mouth, daring to be seen. "Come on. *Come on, then.*"

But there's nothing. Just me, backlit in the lights of my room— and if I squint past that, the town, asleep, unchanging; the peaks, like a closing jaw. Maybe the Angel can't hear me. Maybe it doesn't want me. Maybe I've finally done everything right, confessed all the secrets I had. Maybe it can't reach me any longer.

There's a tangible shift in the world between Slater and everywhere else, something you don't feel until you've been out and back again. A degree darker, a degree colder, the air a fraction thicker. As though a pair of wings have folded themselves over the town. A soft sound presses through the walls that sounds almost like weeping.

I still have Dad's map crumpled in my hand. I rip that up, too, but I can't find the same thrill tearing it up as I did earlier with my drawings. Everything feels hollow. Usually that emptiness is a comfortable feeling. Tonight it gnaws at me until I need to fill it.

Though it's 5 a.m., I find my phone and text Mason an invitation to get breakfast.

His reply comes in a few seconds. *See you at the court.*

I remember something about the Exodus story then, the one where the Angel brings judgment by killing the firstborns in a plague. It didn't kill all of them. The families that followed God's instructions were spared.

We

YOU KNOW WHAT THE TOWN SAYS ABOUT
your mother, because your father would repeat them: She does
not try hard enough to be part of the town. She does not care
enough to follow their rules. She holds on to too much of an old
place. There is another family, from across the ocean, and another
language, too, for reaching them.

Something you do not know, one of so many things, is that
since your mother arrived here, she has felt watched. She draws
the curtains and seals the windows, hoping a house can become
a fortress. She grew up with ghosts, but it was here she was
taught they were not to be spoken of, much less fed. She learned
this starvation, this muteness, and now you have inherited it.

The town has so many ears, and so many tongues, and so
many eyes. You can only block out so many of them. Come,
child. Stop playing your games. I can show you something better to be part of.

11

THERE WAS A JUDGE CALLED BROOKS, WHO
presided over the courthouse named after him, and now the old
building is just a café with its name shortened to The Court: the
bench turned into the counter, the wooden partitions that once
sectioned off benches now block off tables and booths. A jukebox
and stone-top billiard table occupy the old jury box. On evenings
and weekends, it's a favorite spot among teenagers, but at 8 a.m.,
the breakfast crowd consists of adults stopping by before work. I
feel their glances as they pass my booth.

Amelia Fischer walks in too, somehow looking even more
pregnant, with Ben-who-plays-guitar and her best friend, Thea,
who I'm still convinced was the one who wrote on my locker
after the cafeteria rat incident. They're followed by Harley Ross,
a new dusting of red hair along his square jaw to go with the
buzz cut.

Slater somehow feels more crowded than the city ever did.
Thankfully, Amelia and her friends only spare me a glance before
taking a table on the other end.

I sit in my window booth and nurse my coffee, sketching listlessly and remembering Mason's comment about me not having a

life because I haven't checked my phone. After the whole spilling coffee on their friend and running away to hyperventilate situation, Olivia was concerned. So concerned I flared right back up at them, knowing even while I was doing it that I was making a mistake. After that we stopped talking, and I crashed in the tattoo shop so I wouldn't have to share the room with them. I told myself it didn't matter at the time, that we were going to graduate and never see each other again, but now watching everyone come in with spouses and colleagues, greeting neighbors, I feel a dull ache. A few months ago Olivia found out I'd never celebrated Lunar New Year and said I had to come with them and their other friends. That would've been in a few weeks. That's not happening now.

I watch Amelia coo at her stomach and feel bitter about Mom again. For keeping all her secrets, acting ignorant, leaving Trish to do all the work instead. It's like whatever part of Mom got interrupted when she had Trish at seventeen just forgot to ever keep growing, and now we have to be the adults instead of her. Theoretically, she should be thrilled to find out that I also sleep with girls, so I'm less likely to get knocked up like she did.

Theoretically.

The door swings open with a tinkle of chimes and Mason steps in, morning drizzle sliding from his coat. Eyes linger as he slides into the seat opposite me. Thea leans into Harley's ear with a murmur. I know after the plague house yesterday Mason finally showed up at the police station. It's not like Mason had much to tell them, excluding our theory that there's a supernatural angel-not-angel making kids kill themselves, but apparently word's gotten around.

"You're not eating anything?" Mason says, seeing my mug.

"I've got food at home."

Mason narrows his eyes, then strides off to the counter. It's not until the waitress returns with a coffee for him and a plate for me that I find out he's gone and ordered my Court-birthday-brunch pancakes. No one can beat Cynthia's uptown for milkshakes, but The Court makes pancakes so criminal they would've been sentenced here back in the day.

"I'm not letting you pay for this," I say.

He sips his coffee, which I'll guess is still black with about fifty sugars. I scowl, weigh my deep need not to owe debts against the way my mouth is already watering and my willingness to take favors from Mason Kane in particular, and grudgingly cut a single bite of the pancakes.

That's all it takes; I basically inhale half the stack. I try to force Mason to share, but he just plucks off a strawberry. Hypocrite. As he does, I notice the dirt under his nails. "Where did you come from?"

"The cemetery." He raises his eyebrows. "My shift paid for that plate, if you remember. What were you doing up that early anyway?"

"Me? When was the last time you slept?"

He waves this away and I start wondering if he actually is part demon. "Trish's sleepwalking is getting worse." I hesitate to say it, after keeping that secret for years, but if there's a time to share I guess it's now.

The expected pause, both accusing and concerned. "It's 'getting worse'? When did it start?"

"When we were kids. But she smashed a window the other night, and last night she tried taking the car to go find Paige. Then Mom freaked out about it and started going on about letting the Angel in to punish us. She *said* 'the Angel.' I've never seen her like this before. Someone must have told her that. But who, why? I can't help thinking there's something that happened to make her like this. Maybe make them both like this."

For a while Mason's thoughtfully quiet. "Did you see your dad's body?"

I pause. "Did *you*?"

"I work at the morgue, remember? I helped put him in the coffin."

For some reason it hadn't occurred to me. "What about it?" I say warily, wondering what this has to do with Mom.

"The corpse had bites all over it, like animal bites, chewed off. He was missing a finger. You know I'm not easily spooked—but seeing that body fresh in my kitchen might have done it."

I put down my fork. Suddenly the strawberry stains on my plate don't seem appetizing.

Trish said Mom found him in the kitchen, but she didn't mention after how long. A dead body left in a house that makes you lock away your meals, because of the dozens of other residents running in the walls. Are there pieces of my father rotting beneath the floorboards? What chunk of him would I find if I went and looked under my bed?

"Sorry," Mason says, as I push what's left of my plate toward him. "But do you think your mom and the pastor are right? That the Angel is a punisher? Cleansing our sins? You said when you heard the song, it felt like your secrets were exposed."

I think hell would freeze over before Mason admitted Pastor Charles was right about anything, but I actually don't think he is. "If the Angel was just a punisher, why would all its victims be kids? Why would it go after Zach or Wren instead of adults who actually needed to be stopped?" I glance away from him, so I don't have to see in his eyes that he's known damn well for years what Dad was like. "It's too convenient."

He nods, draining his coffee. "I agree. So is it that some people just can't hear the Angel?"

"Or that the Angel doesn't want them to." Maybe I'm projecting, but the difference is important. I have too much experience with monsters that can hide in plain sight. Decide exactly who sees what side of them, until you can't prove you're not just making things up. "It's *choosing*."

Mason nods slowly, troubled. "So the question is—"

"Hey, Kane."

A shadow falls over us, illuminated by red hair. Mason just shuts his eyes. "I don't know where Paige is, Harley."

Harley's mouth is ugly, and I clench my fists in an effort not to bolt. A lot of Zach's teammates sucked—product of macho guys bonding in a small place, I guess, working one another like muscles—but Harley's been especially cruel since we were kids. The boys never talked about the yearly team initiation nights on the Ridge, but the rumors around the year he became captain were ugly. I want to get out of this seat right now. Mason, however, stands. He's taller than Harley, but it doesn't reassure me. He's always had a bit of a martyr complex, but he feels straight-up self-destructive now. I can't help but remember that the final portrait I drew was him.

"You were quick with that answer," Harley says, dangerous.

"You're not hard to predict."

"I don't know what you're telling the police to let you off again, but the whole town is watching you now. We'll find her."

"Tell me when you do." Mason sounds almost bored, but his knuckles whiten on the edge of the table. "Is this actually about her safety? Or is it just the fact you think we hooked up?"

Harley goes as red as his hair. "You shouldn't have touched her. Zach was one thing; he probably would have shot himself anyway if you asked him to, probably sucked your—"

Before Mason can move, I find myself at Harley's throat with my fork. "Shut the fuck up, Harley."

He startles, like he forgot I was there. I used to do a great job of being as invisible as possible. It also might be a bad idea to be threatening bodily harm to someone whose family used to provide for mine, but Dad's dead and the rest of us don't work for them, so fuck him. For once, I have the incredible privilege of being able to not give a shit.

In the end it's Amelia who breaks us up, hissing at Harley not to make a scene. She latches on to me with a bright, nervous smile, while Thea tugs Harley away. "How have you been, Isa?"

"Uh, fine." I lower the fork, barely able to hear my own voice over my heartbeat. I force myself to focus on her glossy cheeks, her tight ponytail. We were in the same activity group sometimes, with Wren, but we're not friends. I grip the fork tighter.

"How long are you planning to be in town?"

"Another week. I need to get back to school." *Ba-dum. Ba-dum.* I'm still holding the fork. I'm surprised by how good it felt to do *something*.

"Art school, right? Sounds perfect for you." Is she genuinely trying to make conversation? "If you want any company, we'd love to see you at group, or get dinner, or something. Just us girls. It's more important than ever now, you know, to keep track of one another. Have you stopped by the Jumping Tractor?"

Besides the fact that I'd rather do anything other than that, I'm missing something. "No, not yet." She's too perky, and I've never been good at being mean to perky girls. "I'll think about it."

Unexpectedly, she leans in and murmurs: "Be careful, Isa. I don't want to see something happen to you too."

Oh. There it is. As she pulls away, I think that diversion or not, she sounded genuinely worried about me, and the worst part of me wants to fall for it. At sixteen, I probably would have done anything for this feeling of being one of them, someone they'd protect. Except I can't fall for it, because eventually they'll remember that I'm the kind of person they want to protect their kids from.

I wish Amelia had told me I was going to hell. I wish I'd gone for Harley after all, and that he'd hit me, here in the open, so I finally have an undeniable reason to leave. So I stop feeling like I brought this unending grief upon myself. I didn't just lose Zach and Wren when I left. I left the fundamental faith that connects everyone in town. I hate them. I miss them. I'm angry that even now part of me still wants them to want me. I'd watch Dad joke around with all the kids he was mentoring and think he knew how to love everyone but me. Felt like it had to mean it was just me. But I was right, before. It's not that I was doing anything that made me unlovable. It's that he was choosing, every time, who he could take it out on.

Mason scrubs his mouth and drops back into his seat. "As I was saying," he says roughly, "our priority should be figuring out how the Angel chooses its victims. We also shouldn't risk another séance for a while until we have a clearer idea of what we're dealing with."

"Trish will come through with the archives."

"She better." He checks a shoulder against the window. There's a grimy film over it that scrubs over the mountains, turning them hazy and streaked. My fingers twitch. To pick up a pencil or a hammer, I'm not sure. Either might reveal what lies behind the glass.

"Would you leave town, if we solved this?" I ask.

"Where would I go?"

"Literally anywhere."

"Can't see it," he says humorlessly. Then, more wry: "I once asked my mom why she stayed when she hates this place. She told me running away is hardly the answer. I used to think it was an excuse. But now I get it, you know. I'm so made of this place, it feels like if I cross that border, I'd just fall into nothing."

"Don't be stupid. It's not that hard. You are so much more than—"

"Not everyone forgets as easily as you do."

I stop. He sits back, sips his coffee, looking around listlessly as though his sheer audacity hasn't knocked proper words out of my mouth. "I *did not*—"

"Danny?" Mason's out of his seat before I even see Wren's brother scampering away from the window. I snatch up Mason's forgotten coat and chase out after him to where he's caught up with the kid, who's toeing at a clump of soil.

"Hi, Isa," Danny says when I come up to them. He sounds guilty, and I realize what time it is. He's also wearing his purple backpack, and I recognize some of the iron-on patches Wren and I helped him pick out.

"Did you skip school?"

"No skipping allowed." Mason takes his coat from me, speaking very boldly for someone who ditched every morning devotion and Wednesday chapel since second grade.

Danny scrunches his eyes. "Mom and Dad say I shouldn't listen to you."

"That's convenient."

"Well, *I* say you shouldn't skip," I say, stuffing my hands into my pockets. Which, honestly, is also bold of me considering I skipped half a year of school. But Danny is *ten*, and he shouldn't be wandering around alone. "What about your friends? Aren't they gonna miss you? Where are you even going?"

He chews on the inside of his cheeks. I sigh. "Okay, we're bringing you back to school."

"You go ahead," Mason says. "I need to stop by the cemetery, anyway. I left something at my shift last night."

After that exchange with Harley, it's not hard to imagine why he'd prefer not to go back. "So I guess I'm bringing you to school again," I tell Danny, but he's looking at Mason.

"My parents said you made Wren do things. And hurt her."

Mason's mouth tightens. "I did hurt her. But not in the way they're telling you."

Danny nods slowly. "I didn't think you would."

"I didn't think I would either."

I glance at him, but this isn't a conversation for Danny.

"I'll text you when Trish has something," I tell him. "Come on, Danny. You can still make most of class."

12

DANNY KICKS AT THE GROUND AS WE WALK.
He's obviously mad about being sent back and honestly, I can't
blame him. It's been a long time since I babysat. "Stop that," I say,
when he kicks at another pile of leaves. "You're gonna twist
something."

Possibly the point, but I'm not taking him to the clinic and
explaining *that* to his parents. He sticks his hands in his pockets.
I try to find something to say, but it doesn't come. The Carvers
were like my second family, and now they feel like strangers.

It's taken me a while to admit it, but I didn't go to Wren's
funeral because I couldn't take it. Zach's death was still so thick
in the air I was choking on it, and when the chief's car pulled up
outside the Carvers' house, I knew that if I went to that funeral—
if I stayed in Slater a second longer—I was going to stop breathing
all together.

It only hit me later, long after I'd settled into the city, full-body
sobbing at two in the afternoon on some Tuesday, hearing a song
on the radio she'd liked to play: Wren Carver was dead, and I
hadn't even gone to her funeral.

Realizing my friends were gone happened over and over again, especially that first year, especially before the moth tattoos. Less now, enough that I thought the grief was over until I came back here. But for a while it could be triggered by things I didn't even remember I remembered, until I was hyperventilating over Campbell's chicken at midnight in my dorm because we'd had soup together one random Christmas at Wren's five years ago and now they were dead, dead, dead.

"Danny," I start, then realize how small he is, how stupid it is to ask a ten-year-old to rescue me somehow. But he's already looking expectantly up at me. I stutter. "Did you—was anything wrong with Wren, before she—" I realize I don't know how her death has been explained to him.

But he's old enough to understand what I mean. "She played the piano a lot," he says. I bite my lip. I don't know why I asked. "She wouldn't go to sleep, or she'd sleep for hours and hours. She kept going to church. She felt . . ."

"Sad?"

"Angry."

We didn't see that from her often. Angry—at Zach? At Mason? "Yeah?"

He nods, and I don't doubt him. "You weren't there when we put down the stones for her," he says. "I thought you were gone too."

My heart breaks. "I'm sorry, Danny."

The school comes up in its cove of now-bare trees. I used to cycle up here with Wren every morning. We'd meet Mason and Zach, usually sweating from his morning run, by the steps before going to class together. When Danny got old enough, we'd bring him along too. We were always a little late because he couldn't cycle as fast, but Wren would kiss him on the nose anyway before dropping him off, even as he squirmed.

No kisses now. He walks up the path to the school, looking back just once to see if I'm still watching, and then he's gone.

AT HOME, Trish is in the kitchen surrounded by boxes and junk I instantly recognize as Dad's. Stacks of clothes, cookbooks, a tarnished plaque, a radio, reading glasses, a harmonica, boat figurines. Typical fifty-year-old-man debris, but the collection of his presence overwhelms me.

"What are you doing?"

"Mom went to go visit someone. I'm figuring out what to toss." She pushes her bracelets up to her elbows so they don't snag on her wrists. "I might be able to get you into the Vandersteens' library today, but I'm waiting on the time. You're not busy, are you?" She smirks at the look I give her. "Okay, well. Help me sort some of this."

Reluctantly I sit and help sort things into piles—clothes, junk, possible donations, et cetera. It's weirdly satisfying sending most of it into *junk*. As we work, I feel like filling the silence.

"How are you feeling?"

She doesn't immediately give any indication of having heard me. "You want to know something, Isa? We didn't always have this rat problem, or Mom's obsession with closing the windows."

"Feels like we did." Sure, I don't remember my first few years, but I don't remember it ever *starting*. The rats have been quiet the past couple days, though, now that I think about it. The trap in the corner is empty.

"For you. All this started after I was born. Dad told me that once and I don't think he was lying. I know the sleepwalking freaks you out. I'm sorry. I'm a one-girl haunted house, apparently. Ooooh," she jokes sarcastically, wiggling her fingers.

I don't laugh. "He told you that?"

She gives me a look, like *Don't push it*, but maybe I want to. Maybe this should get stabbed with a fork too. The rats caused half of Dad's flare-ups. Teeth marks in our shoes, or brown pellets in the rice bin. We set traps, left bait, stuffed up every hole we could find, but they just kept breeding. Once I saw him catch a rat, slosh it in cooking oil, and set it on fire. Its squeals kept me up for nights. It would be just like him to make it Trish's fault somehow.

Now I'm mad she's sorting Dad's stuff. "Mom's making you do this while she goes off? That's fucked." A familiar look at my tone, and my own familiar wave of frustration. "Who's she going to see anyway?"

"Mrs. Carver. She offered Mom a part-time at the post office."

"A part-time *job*?" I didn't even know she and Mrs. Carver still talked to each other, but I guess years of playdates don't go away too easily. And I didn't know she wanted a job, since Trish has one. Dad used to take it as a personal insult if anyone implied he couldn't provide, and Mom had still been in school when they got married, so I always just figured her staying home with us was her preferred arrangement. Come to think of it though, she's been out of the house just as often as I have the past few days. I realize I don't know who she is without Dad. Maybe she's finally unfreezing after twenty-one years.

"Here." Trish tosses me an old cassette.

"What's this for?"

"You want to take it out on something, take it out on that."

"Very funny." But I pry open the case and yank out the tape. It is kind of satisfying, something of his unraveling with a tug. "Why are you acting like we'd want to keep anything from this piece of shit? Just chuck it all on a fire."

She studies the model boat she's holding too carefully. "Mom's not there yet."

"What does that have to do with you?"

Her jaw twitches.

I can't stand the silence. What's wrong with me today? The morning's caught up to me, Harley and Mason and Amelia and Danny. Slater's too crowded, too few places for everyone to go. I miss talking to Trish.

"I saw Danny Carver just now, he kept talking about Wren playing the piano, the days before . . . I don't remember that. I guess I wasn't really around." I'm rambling.

She frowns. "The piano." But before she can elaborate, the doorbell rings and she jumps up to get it.

The cold trickles into the hallway with a tinkle of chimes, fluttering the tape ribbon in my hands. I glimpse blonde hair and a coat. Then Trish steps aside and ushers Otto Vandersteen in.

IT'S NOT OFTEN there's other people in this house, and definitely not a Vandersteen. Even as I freeze, Trish pushes junk aside, flustered. "You're early."

"Sorry."

"I just boiled water. There's tea and cookies, if you want. Isa," she says finally, "Otto wanted to talk to you first."

"Thanks." Otto takes a cookie when Trish pushes the tin at him. "Trish said you wanted to get into the family archives." I look at Trish, who folds her arms. When she said she'd find another way to get us into the house, I didn't think that meant Otto.

If I had to pick a Vandersteen to trust it would be him. Still, that doesn't mean I do. His family doesn't just run the town; they *are* the town. Their slate roofed the houses, built the tombstones and chalkboards. It makes up the fountains, the porches, and this floor we're sitting on. The whole town is gray with their old wealth, and half the residents are fed by it. If he tells his parents the wrong thing, we're screwed. But Trish seems to trust him.

"Did she tell you why?"

"I kind of wanted to hear it from you."

"Right." I wasn't prepared for this conversation. I don't even know how much I should be sharing. But I run through the facts: Paige learning about Sarai from Cecily's records, Mason's first séance with Paige and then our decision to do a second one. I hesitate there, but whatever the police know I'm sure he's heard already, and he doesn't seem fazed. "So this part is going to sound a little crazier," I say, glancing at Trish, who just nods.

Otto fiddles with the stone cross around his neck. I try my best to explain that we think the plague kids, Paige, and other kids in town were taken—I try to avoid *killed*—by the Angel using a song to get in their heads, and that we're hoping Cecily's records show us what Paige was looking at and tell us what actually happened when the Vandersteens received the Angel's vision.

Otto absorbs all this while staring into the table. "It's not crazy," he says when I'm done. "Look, I've always been . . . sensitive. Not in the way everyone else thinks, but other ways. There's always been songs in these mountains, and my whole family used to be able to hear them—that's why Jakob and William claimed this place as theirs. That's what our last name means. Vandersteens, from the stone. Supposedly it's a myth and we don't do that sort of thing anymore, but I can hear it in the rocks when I sculpt. The stones tell me when they're the right shape, and whether they're prone to snapping. But I've heard this song you're describing too, and it's different. Born from the others, sure, but twisted away into its own thing."

Otto is a bit of a cryptid. I won't pretend to understand everything he just said, but what matters is that he knows what I'm talking about. "You hear it too?" I don't know why I'm so shocked—haven't I always known the twins seemed to listen to the stone? "Did you ever tell anyone?"

"No, most people already think I'm delusional. I did tell my parents, and they brought Sharlene Kane in to try and exorcise me."

"It didn't work."

"It did not. Then I gave them something bigger to worry about than me listening to rocks." He smiles wryly and I'm suddenly sorry I never tried to talk to him in class. I think we could've been friends.

"So you think we're right? There's something out there, something that's been around since at least the plague days."

"Yes. And I think you're right that it's the same thing as the Angel, and that my family has the answer to what your Angel actually is. Every damn thing in this town is connected to my family. Paige and I talked about changing that. Doing better, you know? It was supposed to be us. But I barely saw her before she disappeared, and then she was just gone."

I realize he's switched from present to past tense, and it makes me wince. "We don't know that Paige is—"

"No, we don't. But like I said, lying's a waste of time. I know what the odds are." He scrunches his nose, blinks away. "If you want to get into the library, we can go now. My parents are out. Tell Mason to meet us there."

Now? But this might be our only opportunity. As I send the text, Otto says, "I heard you almost stabbed Harley Ross this morning."

Startled, I put my phone down too far to the left and knock the cookie jar off the table. "Damn it. I mean, yeah. I did."

Unexpectedly, he grins. "I hope it felt good."

I grin back. "It did, actually."

The jar rolls and bumps to a stop against a cabinet. In the recess under the cabinet door, something round glints at me from the dark. Slowly, I walk over and pick up the jar, flicking the small object out into the open.

I recognize it instantly as it rolls out: Dad's wedding ring, thick and silver with the wedding date engraved inside it. Or at least it used to be silver. Now part of it is stained brown like it's rusted, except when I roll it over my thumb, it leaves a bloodstain on my skin.

My heart pounds, Mason's words coming back. *He was missing a finger.*

"Isa?" Trish. I drop the ring in my pocket, shutting down the racing thoughts, and return to the table with the jar.

"Got it." Otto is watching me, and I meet his gaze with a challenge. He doesn't say anything, and holds the door open for me as we leave.

"Trish, you're not coming?"

"I have to finish up here. I'm going to need the car."

She's still surrounded by Dad's things. From the patio, I watch her pick up a music box and open the lid, tinny music floating out. She frowns, and I think I hear the faintest confused hum come between her lips before Otto shuts the door behind us.

13

OTTO CYCLED OVER, SO I BORROW TRISH'S
old bike, since mine is nowhere to be found. By the time we get to
the Purple House, Mason's already parked a short way from the
actual estate and is waiting for us with obvious wariness when
we dismount.

The looming Vandersteen estate is a steepled claw over a small
hill, one wing of the building pitching over the low side. Every
surface is clad with slate that has the faintest plum sheen. The
rock irises have rooted here, too; in warm seasons the entire
manor is wreathed in violet flowers, a blooming hollow hall
embedded with iron windows.

For now, though, the Purple House is an ornate shadow
streaked by the vines, surrounded by statues and wide gardens.
I've passed by, especially when it's in season, but I never imagined
going inside. I almost expect alarm bells to start clanging when
we follow Otto through the doors, but only our footsteps echo.

The entrance hall is lined with busts of past Vandersteens.
Right by the door is Jakob Vandersteen. Next to him is his wife,
Beatrice, the sculptor, with flowing hair, and his son, who set up
the clinic. The rest of the family tree spreads around us, although

unsurprisingly, I don't spot Sammy and Ida. The sculpting is exquisite, but the mausoleum makes me uneasy. The Vandersteen heads are heavy and pockmarked, with deep-set eyes made from a hundred shards hammered to curve inward. They make busts like this for rich people all over the world, shipped out along with dried ginseng worth hundreds a pound to Europe and Asia. It's strange sometimes to think that these things we dig up go closer to where my parents are from than I ever will.

"You guys are *really* into the whole stone-working thing," Mason remarks. He seems fascinated by the mansion's insides, almost too keenly so, like he's already looking for flaws.

"You can say it's creepy," Otto says, turning into a hallway papered in deep wine, a cream runner going over the stone floor.

"It's creepy."

"Thanks." Otto leads us farther down the corridor. The walls burn with lamps in tarnished holders that have probably been here since the house was built, and at the far end is an ornate window looking out into the bare garden. Silhouetted in the window is the statue of an angel, watching us over clasped hands. I can't take my eyes off it as we get closer. The hallways are ribbed with arches that round off the corners, and it feels like we're burrowing downward, although light still comes weakly through the windows.

"Is your statue being done?" Mason asks. Side by side, he almost looks like a shadow of Otto—elongated, slightly darker hair, slightly darker eyes, though just as pale skinned.

"I'm not planning to be around for that."

"Yeah? Where you off to?"

A pause, almost surprised. "Somewhere sunny."

"Beach boy," Mason says, amused. "I could see you surfing."

Otto blushes, but then the color drains just as quickly as it came. I hear it a second later: high-heeled footsteps, barely audible on the carpet. *"Hide,"* Otto hisses, grabbing my arm and shoving me through the nearest door, into what looks like an abandoned guest room papered in blue. Mason doesn't argue for once, slips in right after me and pulls the door shut as the *tap tap tap* comes to a stop right outside.

"What are you doing? Is that the library key?"

Emma Vandersteen, current lady of the house, speaker at school functions and town anniversaries. Her voice is clearer than I expect—the door's keyhole is huge, almost there purely for decoration. It makes the door itself feel like paper, like she could see our shadows through it if we turned on a light behind us.

"Looking for something for the genealogy project," comes Otto's reply.

"You don't care about that."

"What would you know about it?"

"My daughter is missing, would it hurt you to stop the attitude for one day?" She sounds so pained I clench my fists. "Dear God, I'll go crazy—where's Trisha?"

"You sent her home."

"Her father just passed away. I'm not always the villain,—"

The syllables come through garbled. I haven't heard that name for him in a while and it takes me a moment to realize Emma's not referring to another person. "Again, please stop calling me that," Otto says.

"It's my mother's name, and the one I gave you. Everyone else can call you whatever you want." The pause drags long enough to hurt. "We have dinner with the Rosses tonight. Dress *nicely*. If you're going to the library, switch off the lights when you leave. And tell Laney to go sweep in there."

"Yeah."

Emma's footsteps recede, then stop. "And be polite. Or just be quiet. We don't need any more drama."

Mason and I wait a few extra seconds before ducking back out. Otto is still staring after his mother with his arms tightly crossed. "Growing up they would tell us everything in this town belonged to us," he says, almost distantly. "She'll let me own everything except myself. Isn't that ironic?" Then his expression snaps together and he pivots roughly on his heel to march down the hallway. "It's just down there."

The change in topic is obvious, and I search for some way to help. "So what are all these rooms *for*?"

He's too quick to answer, sounding almost relieved and brushing hair from his face too deliberately. "Used to be for other family members. They're mostly just locked now, but they open sometimes. You can play hide and seek anywhere but in them. Paige made a game called peekaboo when we were kids, though. You put your eye right up to the keyhole and then run away before anything can look back." He says this casually as he descends another short flight of steps, and I remember that of all the strange places in Slater, the Purple House is the one that only one family knows. The twins, although miles better than their parents, still live here. I wouldn't be surprised if some of their strangeness came from it.

Otto flips a light switch, revealing a windowless alcove lined with shelves, a neat stack of boxes in one corner. This is the room that drove Paige Vandersteen to a possibly fatal obsession with her missing ancestor. The floor is more stone covered by velvet rugs, and on the mantelpiece are slabs of slate in display cases. They've got a few different variants—red, green, purple, red—but that black piece in the center I know for sure was dug straight out from Slater. It has a different weight to it, like it's being pulled toward the earth even now, and I would recognize its ashy shade anywhere. It's the same color as the floor. Cut raw like this, you can see the layers striping its side like scars.

"Slate is metamorphic," Otto remarks. "It's formed by mud rock being compressed deep in the earth. The pressure literally squishes it into another rock entirely."

"More weight!" Mason quips, then sees our blank looks. He pitches his voice down dramatically. "I saw Goody Vandersteen with the Angel." More blank looks. "It's from—never mind."

"You're both nerds," I say. "I'm guessing these boxes are Cecily's collection."

"Yeah, Trish said they hadn't been unpacked yet."

"You guys start with Cecily's stuff," Mason says, already scanning one of the other shelves. "I'm going to look for anything else from the plague period, immediately after and maybe immediately before." He tugs a folio off the shelf and opens it to finely drawn maps. Topographic sketches, survey of the quarry, early town planning. The linework is incredible. It's strange to imagine Slater in the old days. "We're looking for anything about Sarai, anything about the plague house deaths, anything about Theodore and Cecily's angel vision."

"We don't even know what Paige was looking at exactly. There's so much in here."

Mason doesn't respond, lost somewhere behind the shelves. Great. I've given Mason Kane free rein in the Vandersteens' private collection. I'm sure he won't abuse that at all.

I pick up a couple sheafs of brittle old paper, tied together with new string, probably by Trish's team. Cecily's handwriting covers them in tight, intricate calligraphy. It's gorgeous, but there's no way I'm scanning all these boxes today. I can't even remember the last time I read something that wasn't for school. I look up at Otto hopelessly. "Paige didn't tell you *anything*?"

"No. Which I should have been more worried about. I was too busy with this sculpture."

"You couldn't have known."

"Couldn't I?" He folds his arms and, clearly uncomfortable, makes a show of looking around.

But then he stops, straightens, leans forward with scrunched brows. I put down the set of anatomical drawings I was flipping through—Cecily was both a scientist *and* an artist, which is incredibly unfair. "What are you looking at?"

"This house has a lot of secrets," he says. "None of us know all of them." Otto's voice has that odd, slightly distant quality I remember from when he was really focused on something, usually the pile of rocks he was sculpting.

He wanders forward to the fireplace. It looks like it hasn't been lit in years, but after a moment I see what he's seen: faint ashy footsteps on the border, like someone stepped into the fireplace and then back out.

Happy to abandon the reading, I join him crouching under the mantelpiece and switch on my phone light as he runs his fingertips across the soot-blackened stones. I don't see anything. But Otto's hand pauses in the top corner. Without asking, he takes my phone and shines it right at a stone up there, revealing a small hole bored through the center, just big enough to hook a finger through.

"Slots," I find myself saying in surprise. A technique of Mr. Vandersteen's, where a specific stone in the whole stack could be pulled out and put back in without collapsing any of its neighbors. A trick passed down through the generations of Vandersteen sculptors—maybe even from the Vandersteens who built this house.

"There's a few of them around. Paige was better at finding them than I was." He leans forward, one foot in the fireplace, and puts an eye to the hole.

A second passes before he turns back to grin. "There's something in there."

He manages to pull the stone free; it slides loose from the cavity to reveal some notepapers scrunched inside, school-ruled. They're crumpled into balls, as though someone stuffed them in in a hurry, but they're new and could only have been put there by one person.

I pretend not to see his hands shake as he brings the papers under the light. Whatever's in them, Paige took the trouble of hiding them and went to the Kanes to call her a ghost. She didn't tell her twin any of it, when they spent their whole lives telling each other everything. She believed she'd found a missing branch of the family tree, and something about that revelation... what? Made her vulnerable? Drew the Angel's attention?

We both unfold a piece, and then stare at them. They're covered in insane scrawls. There's a few strings of random letters and numbers, and then scribbled even bigger between the lines are actual words repeated over and over: PATIENT PATIENT NUTS PATIENT KIND COMING LUSTY FOP PATIENT GRACE MUST DROP LOST FOUND FLOOD.

"Uh," I say. "Was Paige . . ." Completely out of it? Losing her mind? It could be the Angel getting in her head, the song makes me feel crazy enough, but we've never heard of anyone else doing this. They'd even gone through Wren's room and read her letters. She was unusually worried, sure, convinced she was pregnant and everything, but she wasn't writing like this.

"No, this isn't like her." Otto clenches his sheet so hard it almost tears. He points to a few of the words. "She was writing about Sammy and Ida."

Lusty, nuts, drop, fop. The rhyme. Sure. "She *was* looking for Ida's daughter. She writes *flood* there too." Though I can't guess what any of the rest of it means.

"What are you guys looking at?" Mason, with books and folders cradled in one arm, reemerges from the shelves.

"You can't read all that."

"Don't underestimate me." He sets the stack down and comes over, frowning at the notepapers. I explain how we found them, and his frown deepens. "Those are reference codes."

"What?"

He points to the strings of letters and numbers that I'd dismissed. "See? Sets of four characters. The filing system in this library uses the same one."

I look at Otto. "You didn't catch that."

"I told you I never come in here!"

"There's a few different codes," Mason says, already taking my sheet and heading for the boxes. "Let's pull them out to start."

I QUICKLY REALIZE the first book I pick up is dated after the plague, so Sarai won't be in them. But I can see why Paige might have found it so interesting—Cecily's writing is as hard to read as I expected, but she describes patients in depth, from fever and gangrene to childbirths. I never thought of the clinic as much of a historical place, but Cecily paints a picture of Slater around its residents' bodies over the months. How they change with the season, the quarry's business, the interactions with one another.

I don't recognize most names and I keep getting distracted by illustrations. I do find one mention of the Angel, in an entry about a birth where the baby survives but the mother doesn't: *I've made this unnatural exchange before, but I am still rattled by lifting a crying pink child from a fresh corpse. May the angel deliver her too.*

We swap comments out loud. Cecily rarely notes suicides, but she frequently mentions the health and morale of the quarry workers, as well as their "wild superstitions" and apparent paranoia about digging in certain places that should be "addressed." There are notes on experimental cures for black lung and tendon strains, theories of hallucinating sounds from prolonged immersion in the earth.

If I thought the Vandersteens run the town now, it was nothing compared to when the quarry was in its prime. Cecily describes the workers like numbers to be balanced and scientific problems to solve, and is more annoyed than anything about illnesses and accidents. She and Theodore clearly worked closely together. I come across some advice she wrote to him that that I instantly hate: *Considering possibility of more migrants instead, who aren't as affected by the mountains the way those born here are.*

"Here's another one," Otto says at another point, drowning in bitter sarcasm as he reads: *"Theodore's been telling the boys that there's witches in the woods they must bribe to keep them away from town. Ridiculous, but children will believe anything.* I don't even want to know who the witches actually were."

It's a while before Otto finds the first mention of Sarai in the earliest dated journal so far. Cecily describes her cousin Ida— Ides, she calls her—showing up one night with a baby in the rain, after months of absence—and simply vanishing again by the time Cecily woke, leaving the baby with only a name and a locket. The one Paige stole for the séance, still missing with her.

"But there's barely any mention of her during the plague," says Mason, who's skimming the journal for that year, 1958. "Pages on symptoms and treatments, references to biblical plagues—here, a little note, *Sarai moved to exterior wing as ill.* That's weeks before this entry, where she talks about Theodore asking her to pray together, and them deciding to round up all the sick kids for quarantine." He frowns. "It was hardly a vision. They'd already built the house, and it happened to be raining all that week. She mentions Sarai having the superstition that an angel takes children in storms, and that the girl would be able to see if it was true. It's like they didn't start their story about the vision until after it had already happened."

We flip, but the answer to that superstition comes in another journal from 1954, where Sarai must be old enough to start rebelling. She was apparently obsessed with one of Cecily's senile patients, an old man called Hawthorne Redford that Sarai called Thorn. He told her stories about the Angel that appeared in the storm when he was quarry foreman, and Sarai started becoming paranoid of rain.

I'll send her to Theodore if he wants to teach her actual Word, Cecily wrote, clearly annoyed, but the name makes Mason sit up.

"I've seen that name." He disappears into the shelves again; by the time he comes back out with a few ancient-looking books, Otto and I have found Hawthorne Redford again pages later:

Thorn dead at the near unnatural stubborn age of 93. Slipped and snapped his back, asked to be buried by the quarry. Sarai inconsolable. Sent her to Theodore, she clearly gets it from Ides. But curiosity did lead me to finding Thorn's logs from the archive. Sure enough, there was a storm-night collapse in the mine when he was foreman that had him removed. I suppose he was driven to visions, or felt God's presence, or simply wanted to add grandeur to a tragic accident. Either way, he's been spreading his delusions around. Sarai is still hysterical about even strong winds.

"Exactly the person I would want to leave my baby with," Otto comments dryly.

"Here," Mason says, handing each of us a book. It's the foreman logs Cecily just mentioned. "If he was ninety-three in . . . 1954, I figure the collapse he's talking about would be somewhere in here."

We all flip, and I'm almost afraid to handle the ancient pages, but in the end it's Mason who finds it, sitting up suddenly. "Look, July 1889, soon after they started extending the quarry into a mine. The workers digging find an existing crevasse in the rock. Thorn sends a survey team to explore it. Five kids, no older than fifteen. Small enough to fit comfortably. They're tasked with finding out what's on the other side. Some of them don't want to, claiming they get"—air quotes—"*Queer feelings* from the tunnel. He makes them go anyway. And while they're in there, the tunnel collapses."

"Before they can dig the kids out, a freak storm hits, preventing them from going in until the waters recede. When they finally get back down there—" He makes a determined exhale through his teeth. *"It was as though the stone and the waters had fused the children to the earth as one. There was no telling where one body ended and another began, and where flesh turned to stone."*

As Otto curses softly, a flash comes to me with horrible certainty: graphite shadows, screaming faces in one blackness. I know, somehow, that this is what I've been drawing. Mason glances at me, obviously having connected the same dots.

"Thorn loses it." He thumbs more pages. "The Angel's everywhere here. After the burial—doesn't say where, annoying—he starts imagining the kids in his walls. He starts rambling about repentance and atonement, freaks out about the Angel every time it rains. Here, he says he's going to take his case to the Vandersteens, convince them all the child workers should be set free. Then he must have gotten fired, since the log ends."

"Or committed," I mutter. "Cecily said he was a long-time patient." Was he crazy, though? "But he doesn't actually say anything about the Angel that night. What had him so convinced?"

Mason nods. "I think he actually saw something. If this is the first time the Angel killed, it seems to have revealed itself before it learned from its mistakes. Either way, something was different about this night." He pulls back Cecily's page about Hawthorne's death. "Hawthorne's grave by the quarry has to be where Paige wanted to take me next. She said she needed more time to find it. Maybe the Angel got to her before she could. Maybe because the old man knows something it didn't want us to. So we have to go."

Otto and I exchange looks. "To the quarry?" I say.

"It's been sectioned off for years," Otto says. "It's overgrown. The things I hear coming from that direction—"

Mason waves this off. "There'll be a way. Look at this old map, there's a descent point about twenty minutes from here—"

"I *strongly encourage*—"

"How would you even find the grave?" I ask, cutting Otto off. "Cecily doesn't say where he was buried, and there's no way we're finding it in that forest ourselves. You said you need the grave, don't you, or the site where they died? Place, face, name?"

"I need the grave," Mason agrees. "You don't. You found Zach and Wren in your sleep when I'd been trying for years. In the plague house, Anne Wheeler talked to you. You draw things you shouldn't know about."

"You want me to draw you a ghost?"

"It's not the drawing that's letting you see—you said yourself that you dream them. The art's just a tool, focusing something bigger you're catching on to. You're like a dowsing rod. You *are* the anchor object."

"Are you objectifying me?"

"Very funny. You know what I mean. I'll go myself, but like you said, I'm not going to find it."

That's when I know I don't have a choice, even if I don't like the idea of deliberately trying to find the nightmares pushing through me. Three of my portraits explained, now. Only the portrait of Mason is left. That omen picks up again, thrumming low and dark in my chest. I imagine him trying a séance alone and the Angel coming too close before he's even realized. That image knocks on a third thought, a flash of trees and Trish's face, but it's gone again before I can catch it, and I'm left only with the need to make sure Mason doesn't fulfill my cursed prophecies.

"Fine. First thing tomorrow."

"Otto?" Mason offers.

Otto doesn't seem to hear. He's still rereading Thorn's last entries. "He never calls the Angel a punishment for the kids. The only one that actually sounds punished is him. Makes you wonder how that got turned around over the years. I don't believe the Angel is a punishment anyway, because once I decided I cared about myself more than I cared about what other people say about me, I've heard the song *less*. Does it help that I'm protected by my last name? Sure. Does my mother still insist I'm just a tomboy? She probably won't stop. But this stopped." He taps his temple. "That beautiful song that wanted me to do ugly things? That's gone, mostly, and whenever I do hear it, it just seems angry that it can't reach me anymore."

"You're saying it told you to hurt yourself?" I say, my heartbeat picking up uncomfortably. "You hear a *voice*?"

He tilts his head. "More like emotions, urges . . . Do you hear a voice?"

I don't answer, not even sure myself. Otto taps the book. "Thorn wonders over and over why the Angel chose those kids. It does want something from us, I think, just not repentance."

"Shame," I say, finally putting all the feelings that respond to the song in a word. "Anger, guilt, helplessness."

"Yeah," Otto says. "That. The Angel's drawn to all of it."

"You're saying it feeds on those emotions?" Almost unconsciously, Mason touches the center of his chest; I realize after a second it's where his chime hangs under his shirt. "Must be a fucking feast here, then."

"Only one way to find out." But I'm thinking too, now, of Zach and Wren. What they were feeling when they died, how much

THE DARK WE KNOW

they must have felt to draw a monster to them, and how neither Mason nor I saw enough to stop it. We're all quiet for a moment. I'm sure Otto is thinking of Paige.

"My dad will be getting home soon," Otto says after a while. "And you should get back before it's dark. I'll try to see if there's a better way mapped to the quarry."

We exchange numbers and he watches us leave from the doorway of the library. I glance back at him over my shoulder. Standing so still, he almost looks like just another statue already.

MOM'S MADE DINNER and we sit at the table, soundlessly eating onion stew and bread. According to Mom, Trish said something about going to church. She's not back yet, so Mom and I are alone. I'm glad for the hot food, even if it reminds me of family dinners that made me feel sick. *He's dead, and it's nice to have hot food, because Mom is trying, and it's cold outside.* Considering the only thing I can usually afford outside the cafeteria is junk, I should be grateful. Still, meals here taste like salt. Fresh stuff's hard to come by, especially in the winter when the trucks seem to get lost coming down this road.

The wind promises rain tonight, and every time it howls against the window, I shudder. Mom is tense, too, glancing at the windows every time there's a particularly strong gale, as though measuring its breaking point. The kitchen clock is loud enough to hear the second hand, and it feels like our chance to fix us is rapidly ticking away as we make our way through the food. As we eat, I also remember that the rats here have had a feast.

There are so many things I want to demand she answer: about the Angel, about the state of Dad's body, about this supposed new job, about who she was before she came to Slater and why she can't bring herself to talk to me either. Shame, anger, guilt, help-lessness, I think; Mom *is*, in fact, a feast of it. Instead, as usual, all I can manage is:

"Do you need me to change the traps?"

"No need, all still empty. Maybe they're finally gone."

I don't want to know what lies beneath this house, what other pieces of us the little monsters in the walls might have tucked away. The boxes of Dad's stuff have been moved to a corner, and I can't help but think of sculptures. How enough chips, when piled on top of one another, can take on the shape of something living.

We eat. Mom is tense, but tense is better than grieving. I wouldn't know what to do if she was grieving. I don't know how to take care of her. The concept doesn't really exist in our relationship.

Except when I shift in my seat, the ring in my pocket digs into my thigh. I'd forgotten about it. Bloody. Tucked into the corner. It feels like there's one more secret left in the house, one that Mom knows something about. About the Angel? Or something else altogether?

I tear off chunks of bread. Over the sealed window, the cur-tains are still despite the trees swaying outside in the dark. Instead of the relief that hit me on the first day, the house's emp-tiness is now heavy with a deep unease. Like something is linger-ing in the space Dad left behind. I look at the window again. Shut, locked, watertight. Mom is chewing. The dark rain presses against the glass. I can almost believe she really kept something out of the house.

Or that she sealed something in.

What did those kids feel being buried alive in that tunnel with a storm raging outside? I hated school but I loved the sculpture workshop, its paints and sketchbooks and wood fires and the sounds of lightly hammered stone, the way it taught me I could make something. It's the Vandersteens' best legacy, but even that is spoiled now that I know where the rock comes from. So of course, tomorrow, like a masochist, I'm going to try to call up that nightmare.

When my phone vibrates with a call from Mason I excuse myself gladly from the table. "Hello?"

"Can you come over?" He doesn't sound like himself at all. In the background, I hear rain and wind. My pulse stutters.

"Are you okay?"

There's a long pause, during which I almost seize up. "I'm at the grotto, but . . . I don't feel like I'm alone."

Fear shoots through me. I'd only thought about him being in danger during the séance, but we don't know that's true. He sounds fine, even when I try to detect any other presence in his voice, but it's not a risk I want to take. I've been able to block it out. As far as we know, he can't. "Okay. Stay on the line. Mom—" I hesitate to ask her for help, but this is more important. "Can I borrow your car?"

"For what?"

"Just—please?"

She frowns, but nods. Fumbling with my phone, I run upstairs to snatch my coat, grab her keys from the hook, and get in the car. I have a second to realize that I'm sitting where Dad used to. Then I'm pulling out, headed for the hills, the background noise from Mason's phone just a second offbeat from the rain dashing my windows.

14

MY PHONE'S FLASHLIGHT BARELY BREAKS THE rain as I park near his house and head toward the grotto. These woods, up against the mountain, are never bright, but on a wet winter evening they're a single mass. There are rules we all learn as kids: Don't go into the trees after dark. If you hear something alive, you do not. Even if it sounds like a friend.

But the rules were made by people with homes to safely shelter in. I've accepted I am the thing looking through the church's window. I'm okay with that.

I'm only a few steps in when I see the first lantern winking through the branches. Then another, and another; at some point, Mason strung up a path. How often has he come here at night? As promised, he's stayed on the phone. I can hear his breathing, the occasional mutter. I listen for more whispers, try to hear a voice like Otto said. But if there are any thoughts besides mine tonight, I can't find them.

There's one rule I'll never break, though: Don't run. It makes you look like prey.

I hold my breath slipping from one lantern to the next, shutting out the weight of the forest, the wind's layers as it breaks through the trees. The trees distort noise, and it could be the song, it could be the wind, it could be earth shifting somewhere. "Leave me *alone*," I say anyway, and I can't tell if I'm imagining the sensation leaving. I get to the creek and clamber up the rope ladder with slippery fingers. There's a groundsheet over the entrance with water sliding off it; I duck under it into the grotto, my hair dripping down my back, then almost gasp at the sudden light.

Mason is sitting under the lantern, unmoving. At first, I think something's happened and I'm too late, but then he stirs and offers me a blanket. There are more tossed around, weighted by books strewn over the floor. The sage and pomegranate candle, the only kind he burns ever since Wren gave him one as a present, flickers in the corner. There are open boxes of cookies and empty soda cans. It looks like he's been practically living here.

"What's going on?" I ask, as I pull the blanket over my shoulders. It's tattered, but the pattern of little black dogs is still visible.

"Cookie?" he asks, ignoring my question.

"No. If you called just because you wanted someone to hear your voice, I'm going to be pissed."

He rolls his eyes, but it's a hollow attempt. He glances at the groundsheet, buffeted inward, translucent with the lamplight. "I thought I heard her."

The plastic ripples and I'm not sure if that's all I'm hearing; I don't trust my senses. Watching Mason is like watching a zoetrope, a blur of color and motion until you focus and see the shuttering panes of black.

I know about shuttering dark. You can find beauty in anything if you stare at it carefully enough, even a long fall. Even the idea of breaking, so everything bad inside you finally makes sense on the surface. One of my classmates did a sculpture with rotting flowers once. They were bright enough to pass for living at a distance, but as you got closer, you started smelling the decay. Started seeing the tips where stalks were going soft, leaves blackening. You could miss the signs of rot until you were so close.

"Hey, are you okay?"

The lantern creaks, pulling us into its cone of light. In here, the unfair world used to become good. No bad grades, no running too slow or talking too loud, no loving the wrong person, no learning that your body changing meant you somehow weren't a little girl anymore. In here, the four of us only had to be ourselves.

But that was before. Now we've built walls in here ourselves and I feel my question hitting one head-on.

"I can't stop thinking about what your mom said," he says instead. "You're right—someone must have told her about the Angel and that it was watching her because she'd done something bad. My money's on the pastor, by the way. Exactly the person you'd go to for help and then be told some shit like that. It would be convenient for everyone that a supernatural force happened to validate their moral code. I doubt half the town even really believes in the Vandersteens' miracle plague purifier. They don't even need the Angel to punish anyone, they can just scare others into thinking it will. So then they get to go, if you'd just followed the rules, you wouldn't have died.

"But sin doesn't kill, shame does, and that shame they make you feel is what draws the Angel in. As long as the Angel is around and kids keep dying though, they'll never consider that they're the ones responsible. The Angel's just a feeder. It almost feels easier to deal with than the people."

"Who's 'they'?" I say, sharper than I mean to. I think he's right about the Angel and shame, but that was a Mason Kane Speech with a capital S. Self-righteous, condemning the whole world— and always forgetting who's sitting in front of him.

Even now he frowns, like he hadn't thought about it. "The Vandersteens. The pastor. Everyone in the church."

"So, me? Zach? Wren? Trish is at church right now. Almost everyone grows up there."

He waves dismissively. "You know I don't mean you guys."

"But if you say everyone, then you should. Because I was everyone. Those people you're lumping all together was everyone who loved me."

To my shock, my voice trips, and before I know it, a speech is pouring out of me too. "I regret leaving almost every day, even when I never want to come back. Now that I'm back, part of me thinks it'd be easier to just beg forgiveness and let the town cuddle me up again. It's really fucking lonely otherwise, and I did that to myself. I hate that to get free, I had to become a stranger to everyone I knew. I wonder every day if I should have tried harder to bring people with me, if I left them behind—or if I just left myself out. That maybe if I'd just had more faith then nothing bad would ever have—" My throat hitches again and I cut myself off abruptly. "So think about the other side. For one second."

"Is that what you think? I can't empathize with people? No, really," he says when I don't reply. "Tell me."

I almost do. It's at the tip of my tongue: *Yes, you used to be so full of ideals and opinions that you couldn't see what was right in front of you. Yes, and maybe that's why Zach ran away, and why*

Wren was alone after he died. But I recognize his tone, asking for self-destruction, and I'm past entertaining that bullshit from me or him. "No. You're just picking a fight."

He smirks, but dead flat, like it's aimed more at himself. "Yeah, well. Leaving town isn't the only alternative. I've been here."

"Are you saying you're not lonely?"

He tips his head to the ceiling. Leans back on his hands, stalling. The rain's echo rolls in the eaves. I've hit the right beat. The light slants in a particular way, and for the first time, I notice the thin scar tucked under his jaw.

"I'm starting to forget what their voices sounded like. I stare at these pictures, at letters and cards with their writing—but sometimes I wake up and realize I've forgotten what 'hi' sounded like. One day I'm going to have nothing left of them. Or at least none of the little things that made what we had real. The best part of my life, the best version of me, just slipping away as I watch. I thought I heard Wren's voice out there, and I almost went after it."

"I'm glad you called instead."

"I tried to find you the day she died, too, that's why I thought you were missing. I went to see her grave after the funeral cleared out. I was going to kill myself."

"Mason," I say, and stop there, but by *Mason* I mean *me too* and I mean *you can't do that* and I mean *but if I want better for you then I have to want better for myself* and I mean *if you deserve to exist just because then I do too* and I mean *oh*. There's suddenly so much blood rushing to my head that I almost miss his next words:

"I saw her grave next to his, and just snapped. I was convinced no one would care. The whole town hated me, and they were gone, and you were gone." He shuts his eyes briefly. "Wren and Zach stopped me. That was the first time I saw them again."

He'd said earlier he first saw them in the cemetery after Wren died, but it had never occurred to me that this was how, this was *why*.

The storm is going to be bad tonight. The groundsheet keeps out the water, but the wind strokes the plastic, pressing it inward in trailing ripples.

It was as though the stone and the waters had fused the children to the earth ...

"She wrote me so many letters after Zach died, telling me she was having nightmares, telling me she really needed me. Letters always used to work when we didn't know how to say things out loud. But I never wrote back. For the first time in my life I couldn't find the words. Then she was dead. And in the last letter she ever wrote, she told her mom she was pregnant."

"But she wasn't."

"No, but *she* was convinced. They read me the letter. She was *convinced*, and she was terrified. She said I ruined her, and she felt sick at the thought of me touching her. And they found those old texts we sent, and they put them all in front of me like they'd never heard of teenagers talking about sex. Like that was proof I killed her. Corrupting her, I guess, was as good as killing her. I think sometimes about whether we could have done better raising a kid than everyone else in town or if we would've just fucked up too. But you know what, I was kind of glad she was already dead when they found those, because if she'd been sitting there with those texts and photos out and the way they were looking at me, I think she would have killed herself anyway."

"*Mason.*"

158

He lifts and drops one shoulder in a shrug that's too casual. I recognize it. It's hiding behind carelessness because having feelings means coming undone.

"You know, I always felt so proud of myself for not falling for the same stupid rules everyone else seemed to—no offense."

"None taken," I mutter.

"But after that I wondered if everything I've ever gotten away with was because of me or because I'm . . . *me*. I keep thinking about shame and whether I just don't feel enough of it. I didn't know how to handle Wren's anxieties; Matthew was fucked up after Zach died, they found meth at his place, did you hear that?"

"No. But Zach had just been cut from the team, too, right? His dad would have gone ballistic."

"It wasn't just the team."

The silence turns liquid in waiting, charged and flowing like the storm outside. I've imagined a hundred possibilities about what happened when they fought: Zach had told Mason he was planning to kill himself, and Mason didn't stop him; Mason snapped at Zach and said something bad enough that Zach went and shot himself; Zach asked for a gun and Mason gave him one; Zach and Mason, Mason and Zach. And then finally:

"He was failing classes."

"Oh."

"He also kissed me."

"Oh."

"I liked it."

"*Oh.*"

"And then he shot himself, and I didn't know what to do with that. It's stupid, isn't it? That's not my brand." His mouth presses and slants upward, some facsimile of a smile. His fever is back, dangerous.

"Did you know?" Mason asks. "Did everyone see this but me? What am I if I loved him and he died before I realized that? What am I if I loved them both at the same time? If everyone I loved is dead, what proof does that leave me?"

"*Mason.* Hey." I grip the sides of his face and his brows crumple, the hard, careless lines of his face giving way. "I like boys and girls too. It's *okay*. But we're more than who we love."

Mason would have been the first person to tell us not to define ourselves by what other people think. But it's easier to argue for something when it isn't personal. Especially when, for the past two years, he's been entirely alone. So now this: Mason Kane, rebel, intellectual, the boy who's better than this town. Undone by a kiss from his best friend.

"It's not just the liking guys. It's that it feels like it should be so easy to ignore. I could have kept dating Wren, married her, and gone my whole life without having to deal with the liking, but it would feel like hiding because I wouldn't be able to stop thinking about how I used to dream sometimes . . . If I accept—this—then I feel like I'm going to have to keep proving myself just so it doesn't feel like I'm taking the easy way out, or like it was just him and I'm just driving myself insane thinking it's more than that." His breath hitches. "If everyone who loved me is dead, what does that make me then? Where else do I have to go?"

"You can go anywhere," I whisper. "The world is so big, and life is so long, and love is so possible."

"Do you believe that?"

The words sound empty in both our mouths, but somehow, something stirs inside me. "I do believe that," I say. I think of sunrises and ice creams, storefronts stuck with flags in June, rooms full of paintings. "I think I do, now. I think I'm losing the memories, too, but—" But I don't think about it the way he does, and I search for why. "But I think I'm making new ones now, and when I do it's not so bad."

His mouth opens and nothing comes out, and that's another first, Mason Kane being wordless. Then he knits his hands behind my neck and touches his forehead to mine, and just breathes.

"There are days"—he swallows—"I feel like all my insides have been carved out, and I could lie still for hours and let time slip away. And most of the time I think too much, but on those days some part of me is relieved because the nothing's more peaceful than thinking. That's messed up, isn't it?" His voice is a murmur. "A couple of times I've come close to praying, just to try it."

I hold him. We hold each other, forehead to forehead, knee to knee, palms to jaw, until our breaths and pulses sync with the pattering of the rain.

"I can feel your heartbeat," he whispers.

It's such a stupid thing to say because of course he can, his lifelines are right up against my jugular, his temple pressed against mine. But no, it's not stupid. Because I got out, but Mason's been here for the past two years, surrounded by ghosts and deaths that never leave him. This simple thing, this core requirement of being alive, is like a miracle.

Maybe it is for me too. The two of us aren't everyone and we never will be *everyone* again, but it's more than something.

I sometimes panic when I meet new people, trying to remember the lies that will make me sound only just damaged enough to be attractive. But there is nothing panicking about this, because we know all there is to know. There's comfort in a familiarity that never needs explanation, never comes with the fear that revealing yourself will change everything. He's heard the excuses and the evasions, seen my attempts at hiding bruises. The ugliest secrets are already in the open. We don't need to be anything except here, just as we are. He is alive. I am alive. Despite it all.

An instinct pulls at me, a panic that isn't mine.

I freeze. It wasn't there and then it is, as though our bullet chamber has clicked around and the barrel is igniting air. The cave's mouth is suddenly gaping. The groundsheet over it too thin.

A gasp flickers in my mind again. Conscious. *Urgent.*

"Something's wrong." I scramble to my feet and rip through the groundsheet, almost tripping onto the ledge. Mason's protests die in the wind as the storm sweeps over me.

Isa!

Trish.

The wind howls louder, soaking me with dread.

"Something's wrong," I repeat, shouting now. Snatching my sopping coat, I launch myself into the rain.

Then, fuck the rules, I can't run fast enough. My stomach is in my throat and the rain tastes sour and the wind looks silver in the corner of my eyes; my senses blend into one another until nothing makes sense. I escape the woods and throw myself into the car; somehow Mason's caught up, wrenching open the passenger door.

I race the wet roads as fast as I dare, wind whistling by outside. I've never been more sure in my entire life that something bad is about to happen. Has happened. Will happen.

Am I too late?

I pull up outside my house in a screech, tumbling up the path, eyes fixed on the house. Two solid walls and then, on one side, curtains whipping into the storm, translucent in the light of the room. I fumble with keys, fumble with the handle, charge in without taking off my shoes.

"Isadora? Take your shoes—" Mom yells as I run past her, but I'm already halfway up the stairs.

Trish's room is empty, curtains swelling over the open frame. My heart seizes for a moment—surely not, surely I would've seen from outside—I run across the room and plunge my head out, look down, fearing the worst. Just grass, black in the night.

Mom has caught up; her head swivels from me to Mason in the doorway.

"Mom, *where's Trish*?"

"Taking a bath! What—"

I shove past her and pound on the bathroom door. "Trish? Trish!"

No response. I whirl around, catch Mason pressing his fingers into his skull, shaking his head with confusion. He doesn't know, either. I take a few steps back and kick. My heel slams; something splinters; I drive my foot in again and the door cracks free, swinging wide open. The tang of metal hits me.

Trish.

Bathtub.

Red water on the tiles.

Bracelets sloughing off her wrists in bright stripes, and above them . . .

I scream.

Like a snap, I feel the song up my spine, bending me toward the blood.

We

A CASKET SITS WITH NO ONE TO MOURN IT

but children.

But that is not the start of this night. No, the night starts when you push into your sister's unlocked room, and tell her you are going to the grave. You would not call Zachary Tai your friend, but you watched him grow up as a younger brother. So you have decided, as you always do, to take everyone's grief into your own hands.

You are strong, Trisha Chang, but there is a point where even mountains break.

The night they give Zachary's body to the ground, however, you can still bear your burden. You manage the feat of taking your sister somewhere she does not want to go—you tell her it is for your sake, and she stands, but you know it must also be for hers. You make her put on a jacket and you steal silently outside to find Wren Carver slipping down the tree that leans toward her window. Your sister is surprised, but while she was hiding away, you were already making plans with all those you thought should care.

So you climb into the cemetery to find Zachary's brother and Mason Kane already there, still as the angels around them. Mason tucks Wren's head into his shoulder as she falls into him, but you notice how little he seems to feel it. You notice everything. We are so alike, in that way. You see, as I do: Alex Tai, not long for this town. Wren Carver, always prepared, breaking down. Mason Kane, always righteous, looking crucified. And your sister, by your side, not running to her friends as she should. They have secrets you cannot reach, and that is our difference.

How will you fix them now? How will you mend these new broken people? You will never be enough. You were not even meant to be. And the presence of another watcher disrupts me, Trisha Chang, distracts needing ears from my voice. I cannot have that. You are difficult to reach, by blood or by temperament or by your attachments, but not impossible. Not with the patience of years, of chipping away night after night when your eyes do not see. You see, to open a rock neatly, you must first score it in lines. Down, and down, and down again. So you did not even notice, when you stepped out from the church of the house of our father, that you were already ready to crack.

Were we not taught, in drastic times, that the firstborns must be taken?

15

MY LUNGS FEEL AS THOUGH THEY CONTRACTED and forgot to expand again. I've been holding Mason's hand so tightly I must have cut off his blood flow, but if I pry my fingers open, I think I might break them. He's tried to say something a few times, but I haven't been able to hear it.

She's alive she's alive she's alive she's *alive*.

Unconscious, in critical condition, but *alive*. We got to her in time. I got to her in time. At some point on the ambulance ride over, I was ready to make a deal—*God, I'm sorry I'm sorry I'm sorry. I'll be good again if she survives.*

When the doctor tells us, yes, she'll be okay; no, we can't see her yet, I finally stop pacing in the waiting room and collapse into the nearest chair. Mom has been sitting all along, face blank. I want to shake her, slap her, anything at all that will shatter that mask and reveal *some* kind of emotion that her oldest daughter could have been dead right now.

If Slater didn't have the history it did, she probably *would* have died. Any other tiny town would have to send someone to the nearest hospital an hour away, but no, not here, not with the Red House, built specially for Slater and its unique wounds. I try not to think of the stories people tell about its strange scarlet walls, not with the image of the bathroom still burned into the back of my eyelids. White ceramic, spill of dark hair, twisting lightning streaks of red on her wrists, a wide, blank smile. I'll never be able to unsee it.

And here Mom is sitting like she's waiting for a flu shot, like *nothing is ever wrong.*

"I'm going to get coffee." Mason rubs his face and finally extricates his other hand from mine. He valiantly tries to shake it out without me seeing. "Do you want anything?"

If I eat, I might throw up.

"Mrs. Chang, do you want anything?"

"Black coffee, please. One sugar." Her voice is clipped but steady. *Normal.*

"Sure." Mason squeezes my shoulder and I feel a surge of gratitude, one that quickly dissipates once he slips out the door. Because now there's nothing standing in between me and Mom. She meets my eyes. A shiver of dust, a keening. Then both of us fire at once.

"This is your fault," I say.

"I told both of you. I told you to keep it out. And you didn't listen."

"*Maybe,*" I interrupt, harsh enough to cut her off, and then louder to block her out, screw the sound carrying, "maybe if you'd been more concerned with the monster *in* the house than the one outside of it, then none of this would have happened in the first place. You were so *worried* about keeping everything inside, making sure no one talked. You pretend not to hear anything, but the Angel *listens.* It knows how to get to us. You know something about it. If you'd told us what we were up against, maybe Trish wouldn't be dying!"

"Don't think the whole town doesn't know what you're doing, poking around with that boy. Pastor Charles came to tell me—"

"Oh, he told you that, did he? Did you tell him about Dad? Do you think the Angel took him, cleansed the evil? Or did the pastor also tell you the Angel was watching you?"

"You want your money?" she snaps. "You want to go back to your school? Then you stop causing all these problems. You know what people ask me when you're gone? They ask me if you're doing drugs, how I can let you run away. They ask me if you're staying with some *man*—"

"Well, I'd be learning from you if I was!"

She slaps me. "Keep talking." Her voice trembles as I reel. "Keep talking! The Angel will hear you too. It will come for you again!"

I stop short, even as she goes white. "*Again?* What do you mean again? *Mom*," I say, as she gestures in frustration, "*what do you mean again?*"

"*Trisha* say," she snaps, driving in the syllables. She's struggling to find words. "She find you on the cliff. She bring you home. She think you just sleepwalk too, but I know you hear the bad song. The next day you don't remember."

No, I don't. What? My brain is grasping now, trying to fit any fragments that make sense around this truth she's suggesting. That despite thinking I'd avoided the Angel by learning to block it out, it had gotten to me after all. And not only had it gotten to me—it failed, because Trish found me, the way I've found her. "When was this?"

She shakes her head. "Trisha fifteen, sixteen."

Which would make me thirteen or fourteen. When I was starting to have feelings for Wren, maybe, but the years are a blur. Nothing stands out, nothing that could have tipped me over. "But I must have woken up. Why don't I remember?"

"*I'm so tired*, you say, and fall asleep. Next day like nothing happened."

Tired. Yeah. That sounds about right. I spent so long just being tired, my whole existence a blur of dreaming and waking without enough to really wake up for. I could see my guard against the song dropping for just a moment because I couldn't be bothered to hold it up any longer, because it was too much effort to pretend the darkness the song called to wasn't me. Don't I dream of edges, sit on rooftops? No, I'm not surprised. But I am more tired than I have been in a long time when I ask, "Why didn't you ever tell me?"

Trish and Mom, Mom and Trish, together in a way I've never been able to join in on, apparently even when it comes to my life. Her mouth opens, but no sound comes. A familiar frustration constricts her expression and I know, I know it's something she can't say in English with all the meaning that's in her head. I can't speak the language she feels in, and without that how are we supposed to really see each other at all? Forget the Angel. One day Mom will die, too, with all these words I couldn't hear even if I tried.

Mason reappears in the doorway with two cups of coffee. He freezes at the obvious trainwreck occurring in front of him, and Mom marches away to find the doctor.

I blink away the pinpricks in my eyes and pull him back out the door. "I need air."

"Your mom's coffee—"

I snatch the cup from him, walking until we're outside. Despite my earlier queasiness, I take a long sip. The warmth smooths out my jagged nerves, and I take another gulp. Slowly I stop feeling like I'm going to explode.

"There really is something—" he starts, but I shake my head. Let me pretend again that there's nothing to say.

Above us the cliffs have folded the sky shut for the night. The shadow turns lit houses into fishbowls; even with everyone's curtains drawn, light from inside seeps around the edges, ringing the frame like an iris. When the wind goes through the crooked gap of the porches and tickles the chimes there, the houses sound like they're whistling after us. Good, normal people don't roam around at night, but good, normal people are welcomed into homes without having to grovel. The things in the dark have gotten to know me over the years. I liked those dark things better than the ones at home.

But now the outside is inside and the inside is outside. The usual numbness that helps me keep going has collapsed. My brain feels like clotted hair in the drain, dripping as I try to pinch it. Tangled voices, images, sensations, all trying to force their way into me at once. Trish always believed me. Trish is almost dead. Trish broke something in herself when she broke the window and let something in. There's so much. So much. But even with my brain on the edge of splitting, it just won't let the thing come through. I can't turn the mess into anything useful because I was told right from the start that I should learn what was real and that no one liked crazy girls who insisted everything was wrong.

But something is so fucking wrong, and I'm not crazy for saying it. I'm not.

. . .

NOTHING'S OPEN this time of night, I'm avoiding Mom, and I can't even think of going home—someone will need to clean up the blood—so we end up in the back of the Red House by the coffee machine. There's a kitchen somewhere in this manor, where they must cook for patients and where Cecily must have once taken her meals, but the only food out in the sitting area is bags of chips and I tear one open listlessly, wincing at the echoing noise.

"Isa," Mason says gently, "I didn't want to say anything until we were sure Trish would be okay, but I have to tell you something."

The sitting room is still decorated how it must have been in Cecily's time, since her taste—and bedside manner—is everywhere in the paintings on the walls. They're all different scenes of old medicine in tarnished frames: a woman in a chair getting blood let from her arm, a group of men in suits holding scalpels cutting open a body part on the operating table, a doctor feeding what looks like a string through a hole in his patient's stomach. More recognizable ones too: Frida Kahlo with her spine ripped out and replaced by a stone column, her skin nailed like Jesus. A window looks out onto a back garden, solid black now.

"Fine," I say finally, tearing my eyes from the frame.

He pulls a folded piece of paper from his pocket. "For a second in your house, right before we found Trish, I heard the song." I try to think if I felt anything, but it's all a blur, like my brain just forgot to hit record between the moment I left the grotto and when I found Trish in the bathroom. "Then you screamed, and it was just gone. But this was in Trish's jacket pocket."

He spreads the paper out, revealing a music composition sheet. Except after a couple lines of regular notes, the black circles unfurl into letters: MAMA MAMA MAMA MAMA CHILD CHILD CHILD

And then the pen starts scribbling sentences all over the bars, almost tearing through the staves.

What else will I lose my body their love? I've always wanted children but what kind of mother would I be now? I let a devil boy ruin me I ruined myself I feel sick thinking of him touching me again he cannot come near me any longer I am waiting for blood I am praying. Mom wishes I would never grow up but I killed the little girl she loves she does not know me anymore she will not love me anymore. There's witches in the water I could be worthy of love again I promise I promise I promise.

"What is this?" But then it becomes familiar from all the notes slipped into my locker, the birthday cards I've lost now. My finger traces the loops of her *y*'s, the dashes in her *i*'s in place of dots, the lines that run into one another. "Wren wrote this."

I think of what Trish said about Wren spending a lot of time in the church in the days leading up to her death. Danny saying that she just spent her time playing the piano. I imagine her hunched over the keys in the chapel, scribbling as the Angel in the stained glass bore down. Trish was at the church earlier tonight. Is that where she got this? The words at the top, MAMA MAMA MAMA MAMA. Mrs. Carver? Or Wren herself? Wren was convinced she was pregnant, even though the autopsy showed otherwise. And something about the sentences is so familiar, even though it doesn't sound like something she'd write at all.

"It's the same words from the letter they found in her room when she went missing," Mason says hoarsely. *"Mama, what else will I lose, my body, their love? I've always wanted children but what kind of mother would I be now? I let him ruin me, I ruined myself. I feel sick thinking of him touching me."* He recites it so clearly, I know the words have looped in his head over and over. "It's longer, even. All this about her mom, and blood. Like she was writing a draft of the letter. Except here she says 'Mom,' not 'you.'"

"Paige was doing the same thing," I realize. "I mean, a more unhinged version. But she was scribbling random words too before she disappeared."

He blinks. "You're right." He sounds almost more shocked he wasn't the one to make the connection. Wren's writing must have distracted him completely.

"Maybe Paige was closer to losing it." It sure sounded like it.

"Or," he says, focus coming over him again, "it's the other way around. Both of them were writing. Paige was in her notes. But Wren was on the piano. The ghosts around here respond to the chimes, a music that's fed back. The vibrations open up a liminal space."

"Is that for real, or are you just being philosophical?"

"Doesn't matter; it works. You've seen Wren when she played. When she was into a song, she'd sit there for hours until she'd learned it, wouldn't even hear you sometimes."

I nod. The music would float across the garden from the piano in her living room, starting and stopping, every note and careful embellishment slowly forming through try after try. When she finally got the song perfect I'd often just pause, listening, an anxious tick waiting for a stumble that never came. When the piece ended, I'd feel a strange sense of loss.

"What if something else slipped in, while she was sitting there with the music?" Mason says. "Maybe it didn't even mean to be heard, but it didn't realize how closely she was listening. What if they were capturing what they were hearing? You and Otto said you sensed feelings. What if this is its voice? What if right before it takes you, there's a moment clear enough for some people to hear it? Paige got words. Wren actually heard it. She just couldn't separate its voice from her thoughts. And you do the same thing with your drawings," he charges on. "I don't know how or why, but you have this connection with it, and sometimes it comes through you instead."

I stare at Wren's paper again, the music that turns into fragments of a voice. My mind traces it and something tugs in my mind, something else that's been scratching at me since Mom's confession. I once had to stare at a Richter painting and share what I saw in the color blurs. The more I looked, the more an image seemed to solidify, but the second I blinked, I was no longer sure if I'd really seen anything. Trying to grab the details of this memory is the same. I feel like I'm just deluding myself.

"The Angel did get through to me, years ago," I say slowly, still reading *I ruined myself I am waiting for blood I am praying*. I stare at Frida Kahlo's broken stone spine, wedged in where her bones should be. "Apparently I was going to jump. My mom said Trish saved me. Maybe it left some part of the Angel in me." Like roots left behind in winter, extending and extending, just waiting for the right time to sprout again. *I could be worthy of love again I promise I promise I promise.* I've sure told myself the exact same thing. For some reason seeing it in Wren's writing is the first time I've ever realized how desperate and young it sounds, how much it makes me just want to hold her.

Where do our thoughts end and the Angel's begin? The slow fusing of thoughts is worse than a spirit just snatching your body. A creeping invasion, twining comfortably between what was already there until it's impossible to actually separate. Then one day you're just made of it and you're lost before you even realize you're losing. Was I ever really blocking it out? Or did I just give up my one way of figuring out how far it had actually spread?

Mason takes my news much more evenly than I did when Mom told me. "Trish saved you from the Angel?" he asks, skipping right over any shock. I didn't realize I was tensing for a reaction until the knot in my chest unwinds. "How?"

"I don't know. Otto said the Angel doesn't like when we're not alone. Maybe she found me just in time."

"Where was this?"

That's a great question. *The cliff,* Mom said, but her language isn't always precise and there are plenty of high drops in this town. "The ledge, maybe. One of the other lookouts. It doesn't matter. Trish saved me from the Angel without realizing that's what she was doing, but Mom's convinced—and I don't remember any of it at all, but now that she's said it, I feel like I'm squinting at something coming through." I can picture a cliff now, sky, Trish running up to me, but I can't tell if it's just my imagination filling in the gaps. "I can't remember so many things. Even the good stuff is out of reach. Then the memories spring up on me without warning."

One of my other school assignments was about memory. It was up to us how we wanted to interpret it—excavation, fluidity, unreliability. Absence. My concept was juxtaposition, the decay of time. I painted a pond, and then, on pieces of drugstore gauze, I painted four kids and a boat with a bedsheet sail, playing pirates. But one stray gust of wind, one careless bump of an elbow, one mistimed sneeze, and gauzes are knocked out of place. Suddenly the kids are floating out of the boat and one is missing entirely. Suddenly they're all gone and there's just one girl on her lone piece of flimsy cloth, laughing at nothing in the middle of the pond like she doesn't realize she's about to drown. From the branches fringing the frame, a pair of moths looked on.

Even if I tried I couldn't get my scattered memories back to their original place. I've never needed to, until that moment with Zach. I've never wanted to, either. But now, this, Trish, the Angel. There's some shred there I need to replace to make the blankness in my memory make sense. And the more I look at Wren's scribbles, the more sense I get that Mason's right. There's almost something speaking there. Something she and Paige were so close to capturing.

"Is that quieter, not remembering?" Mason says. "I remember everything, like I promised I'd hold on to every bit of them and then I just did. But it's like this—" He taps Wren's scrawls. "In my head, all the time. I guess I've kind of resented your peace."

I laugh shortly. "I'm not at peace. I've felt safe. But I also feel like I left some important part of me behind in exchange. And these past few days, I've . . . wondered if I made the right choice."

"Don't feel guilty for saving yourself," he says sharply. "I said I looked for your body, not that I wanted to find it."

Something cracks in my chest and I resort to a watery joke to cover it up. "What, you didn't want to hang out with my ghost? I win, by the way."

"Win what?"

It sounds worse now that I have to say it aloud, but I do it anyway. "Tonight's surprise suicide confessions."

"Jesus." He scrubs his hand over his face, but his mouth twitches.

But something darker occurs to me at the same time. "Mason—your night—could that have been the Angel too?"

He considers this for a long while. "I've thought about it, actually, ever since we realized what the Angel was doing. But I remember everything about that night incredibly clearly. I remember seeing them, just for a moment, and I remember putting the pocketknife down. Honestly, when I realized what your drawing of me meant, I was almost relieved. Like I was finally feeling enough for it to want me."

"Don't—"

"I know it's not rational. But is any of this?" He taps the scribbled sheets. "If we're going to stop the Angel, we have to understand what it is and how it works. Wren and Paige were close to understanding some part of it bleeds over when it gets close, just like what happened when the foreman saw it." He hesitates. "Are you still up for going to the quarry?"

Part of me wants to go sit beside Trish's bed until she wakes up, but how would that help? Now that the terror has faded I'm stripped raw and running on anger. I'm not going to just sit there hoping, when there actually is something I can do about it. Out there around the quarry somewhere is the grave of a man who started stories of an angel. Who saw it the night it first appeared. "Yes. First thing tomorrow."

I suddenly remember we're not the only ones that are supposed to be going. I pull out my phone, intending to text Otto, which is when I see that I've missed several texts from him.

Think I might be onto something trying to find out more tell you tmr

When we're in there walk side by side NOT in single file

If you hear someone who's not each other NO YOU DONT

Those woods might not like my family we'll see I guess

This filing system makes no sense

There was a story about a house in the mountains

His train of thought is once again impossible to predict, but I send him back a quick response just to let him know where we are. I notice I have one more unread message and my heart skips—it's Olivia—but that's too much to deal with for one night. I shut my phone off and notice Mason straining to stay awake, despite the coffee. All those nights might finally be catching up with him.

"Hey," I say. His eyes flutter shut before he jerks upright. "Take a nap."

"I'm fine."

"I'm not asking. I won't do anything stupid, I promise."

"What about you?"

"I don't think I'm sleeping tonight."

He glances warily out at the silent corridors, then types into his phone and sets a timer on the table. "Fifteen minutes." He kicks off his shoes, curls up in the armchair, and buries his head in his arms.

He's out in seconds. Quietly, I pull his phone over. The lock screen flashes obligingly—a different picture of the four of us from Wren's birthday party that I don't even remember taking. Wren has a crown perched on her curls and she's grinning.

I hesitate with the four-digit password. I doubt it's as simple as his birthday, September 27. My thumbs hover over the screen before a date dislodges itself from my memory.

0505.

I'm in. May 5, his and Wren's anniversary, and also her birthday. I glance at him, everything hurting, and turn off his timer.

I can't help but think again about what Mason told me about Zach. Kissing Zach. The sheer terror of realizing you're not who you thought you were seconds before you lose the other person forever. Feeling like he'd betrayed Wren at the same time, weeks before losing her too. *Well*, is all I can really think, to desperately try and siphon off the otherwise crushing sadness, *at least I don't have the most tragic sexual-awakening story anymore.*

I haven't seen Mason asleep since we were kids. Head down, he just looks like a pile of soft things slumped over. Like if you pushed he'd slip right off the chair.

The thing about being bi is that it seems like there's an option for you to just be normal. Like you have an easy way out. A shortcut through a world you would otherwise have to fight a whole lot harder to navigate. But that escape is a slow death in itself, a self-inflicted drowning.

I figured out I was queer like a cliché, falling in love with my best friend who didn't even like me back, but I had perfectly legitimate crushes on boys too. Until something flipped and

Wren crashed through my ribs, I never had to think anything
was abnormal. After she died, I was ready to go right back to
forgetting about it. But then in the city, the tattoo shop had a flag
in the window and my classmates wore pins, and I was given
the words to express myself. And once I had those, it felt almost
natural, really, not to stop that first girl who locked eyes with me
in the summer party from lowering her mouth to mine.

There's something they don't tell you about coming into your
own, though: once you've gotten a taste of love, going back to
the void hurts worse than if you'd never left. I let my skin get
soft out there, and now every blow Slater lands—on me, on my
sister, on this boy who was once my best friend—feels like it
might break me.

And then there's Mason, surrounded by graves and obituaries,
almost like he likes the pain. For a second, I hate him all over
again. He's lying there, pale wisps of hair over his paler face, and
I just want to put my hands around his neck and squeeze.

No. I dig my nails into my palm, warmth rushing to the surface. I'm not violent and I'm not even angry—well, not at Mason,
anyway—I'm terrified. Terrified of seeing him spiral, a victim of
his own worst behaviors. And also of losing him too. In this world
we lose so easily.

I want to drive us all out of here, but I care too much and need
to see it through now. There's Wren and Zach, there's Paige, and
now there's Trish; there's Matthew Accetta, and all the kids that
the Angel's taken and has yet to take. I remember this guy who
came into the tattoo shop to get a big rib piece. He was struggling,
but his friend was unsympathetic—*What are you gonna do? Leave
it half drawn?* It's what this pain feels like now, a piece that needs
to be finished.

I slip through the morning on coffees I stop tasting and drawings I fill napkins with, wandering up to Trish's room several times only to leave when I see Mom's still in there. The doctor is somewhere but I see a couple of the nurses weaving in and out of night rooms when I enter a new corridor, recognizable by their identical off-white uniforms. I sit back down in the middle of Cecily's painted surgeries, and my pen is spiraling, practically moving on its own. It's beyond me to stop now. Eyes in window frames and crooked houses on the water as bones drift by. Water. Why is it always water? When we were old enough to hold our breath, Pastor Charles dipped us in the river and brought us out clean. There's a pond at the bottom of that quarry too, where rain collected in the grave of the mine.

At some point a nurse comes in to refill the coffee machine and says grudgingly, "That's pretty."

I look down in surprise and see I've gone over my hand with flowers, the petals folded over my fingers, bleeding just a little with ink. I say thanks and pick up the coffee cup with my flower hand, looking at the way the petals form rings and realizing that it's the first time I haven't drawn ghosts. But then I notice something else—outside, black is hazing to gray. The sun is coming up. With it we can find our way to the quarry, toward an answer I feel increasingly sure is waiting.

I reach over and tap Mason on the shoulder.

We

YOU DREAM OF A CASKET WITH NO ONE TO
mourn it.

After all these years, I think you would come now. One gunshot, and you are raising your fist to knock on my door. You are
standing in this graveyard as someone who does not know himself. You grip Wren Carver's hand but do not feel her heartbeat,
do not feel yours. See, there too, Isadora Chang standing aside.
Why has she abandoned you now? Why does she never cry? She
does not feel the way you feel. She runs from confrontation. She
will always disappoint you in the end.

They will disappoint. You will disappoint.

I will need time to reach you. But I will, one day, in slips of
sleep and unguarded moments when your stubbornness fades.
For every time you shut your eyes, you dream of a kiss.

See, when you let Zach in and ushered him to your room,
wildness trembled in his eyes. *They kicked me off the team.
Running's all I'm fucking good at. I don't know what to do.*

Your room, an unlived space. You do not like to spend much
time in it. Still, it stores you. It is yours and you were comfortable

in it, enough for your hand to fall so naturally on his shoulder, to make his head turn toward yours.

Why didn't you say something? I thought you were doing better.

I've never been doing better. Some days I'm just less stupid than others. What was I supposed to say? You don't have parents who gave up everything to watch you fail at the easiest fucking things. You've never had to try in your life. I don't understand what you guys go on about, you don't even try, okay, my brain doesn't work like that!

He has always refused to slow down, to reason. Even then you told him as much: *I don't know what you want me to say.*

I don't know. I don't know. I think I need to get out of here.

Let me help you, Zach.

How are you supposed to help me? Tell Burr to let me back on the team? Tell my parents? Leave? Would you—would you leave with me?

You are a great pretender, and here you pretended not to hear. Think of this moment, when he begged you to listen. Of the answers you might have given instead, of how you might not have failed him, of what you would give for a chance to tell him the right one. Instead, you grasped him tighter, fingertips on the back of his neck. This is why they think you are cruel. Was it not your fault, in the end?

You're the most hardworking person I know, Zach. I've got you. No one's going anywhere.

There was a tremor on Zach's mouth that was almost a smile. One feels a collapse before it happens. Shudder the earth, rend the air with a ripple; he pressed his lips to yours and you recoiled in surprise that looked too much like horror. So Zach sprang back, too, crying and saying *sorry*, and he snatched his bag and ran.

Zach, wait!

But you were too late. He was fast and he was gone.

Creak the door in his wake, flutter chimes in the dust, chase the shell of a bullet through bone. You will imagine, in every dream, the exact shade of red, whether the river was as wet as his lips. You will wake with loathing.

For now, however, it is still your last peaceful evening, and I am with you once more. Your hands move across paper so fiercely—a dangerous power, giving shape to thoughts. Unlike your friends, however, you are self-centered. You presume, and you postulate. You are not open enough to hear me, just yet. See, even now you write: *Shame keeps everyone wired at the seams until they suffocate. Wren's ashamed of the things that give her pleasure. Isa's ashamed of the things that hurt her.*

What would we be, Mason Kane, if the earth had crushed us together instead? What tongues would we share, what hands, what voice? *Zach is ashamed of the things he can't do and the people he can't let himself love. I want to tell them how obvious it is that it's tearing them all apart from the inside. But it's not their fault. We learn shame and inherit it. There's nothing shameful about pleasure or pain or failure—*

You have never given it air in your consciousness, but I hear, too, what lips whisper in dreams. Stray your hand to those lips as though touching a ghost. Flicker something buried on your face.

You have written awkward sonnets in the shape of Wren Carver, but beneath that love pools a quieter longing. *A never-ending ocean*, you wrote once of that dream, *and its changing currents*: at once women, slick shapes glittering as they bobbed in

the tides; at once . . . squarer bodies, gold in the light off the
waves. Indiscriminate faces. Indiscriminate mouths.

Sometimes, they look like Zach.

And now, another night, another dream. What do you see in
the water on the tiles, wet under your soles? Do you see the lover
in the pond or the lover by the river? Do you remember betraying
them both? Does the smell of blood dredge up sorrow? Does the
sound of Isadora screaming feel like justice? Your original flaw,
this opening yourself up to love, this unknowable thing. Your
mother was never present to love you, but nonetheless you try,
try, try. And oh, I feel you both now, so close again. You reopen
your old wounds of your own accord, for me, for me, finally,
patiently, to me—

16

"I STILL CAN'T BELIEVE YOU TURNED OFF MY alarm," Mason grumbles as we get into his car.

"You no longer look close to death. You're welcome." I check my phone for the fifth time. Otto hasn't shown up, and he's not responding to my messages. I tell him to meet us at the spot we found on the map instead, then text Mom to make sure she stays with Trish.

In some places the town runs right up against the forest around the quarry, but the stretch toward the descent point we mapped, a short drive from the Red House, is sparse. Broken rock plinths woven with creepers, a bin that hasn't been filled or emptied in months, the lingering smell of old weed. I lower the window; after the Red House's claustrophobia, the cold smell of the forest calms me.

Still, cars always feel like a trap. I'm already bracing for the question when Mason asks, "Why did you start avoiding us? It was like everything was fine one day, and then overnight you were gone. I've never figured out what we did. You didn't even tell us you were thinking of leaving town."

"My dad wouldn't have let me. I didn't know I was leaving until I left."

"So it wasn't about us?"

"It's stupid now."

"So's a lot of things."

I drum on the window. "I was jealous." Jesus, that's embarrassing to say when we have such bigger problems. But isn't that the point, that we were—are—kids with stupid problems that feel like our whole world, and it doesn't mean we deserve any less? "I wanted to rip out my guts around you guys."

He blinks rapidly. "Jealous of—"

"You," I say immediately, before this gets weird. "And you made it worse because you were, like, entranced by her, and I didn't think I could ever show myself to someone like that."

Mason considers this quietly. "Do you have friends in school?"

I still haven't responded to Olivia. "My roommate, I guess." I hope. "And my bosses at the shop are way nicer than they need to be. People are friend*ly* . . . I don't think it makes us friends. But I feel like I don't know what a friend actually is, the way other people seem to so easily. Like there's this gulf I can never fully cross. I'm just . . . mysterious; that's my thing."

"Aren't we friends?"

"*I mean*—now, after everything that happened. With someone I haven't known for so long it's basically a sunk cost fallacy, and who I'm not basically trauma bonded to."

"So you *do* think we're bonding."

"As if you've talked to anyone in the last two years who isn't dead or my sister."

Surprisingly he laughs. "I'm sorry you felt that way about me and Wren. I'm sorry to Zach, too, I guess. Honestly, I don't even know how that happened. Just felt like one day I was still pining and the next we were hanging out every day after that summer fair."

This stops me. "Mason Gabriel Kane, don't tell me you and your gigantic brain still think you and Wren ended up at the fair alone by *accident*."

"We . . . didn't?"

"No, idiot, she made me meet Zach somewhere else and told you we'd bounced. Don't stare at me like that. What was I supposed to do, say no? She had you wrapped around her finger. I didn't stand a chance."

He exhales in another laugh. We pull up in a clearing as far as the car will go and get out, cold earth scrunching beneath our soles. Mason looks back at where the Red House is still just visible. "Birnam Wood come to Dunsinane," he mutters, which I assume is another reference, but before I can respond, my muscles lock. The particular smell of the forest touches my mouth, something about the way the evergreens part. I've been here before.

No more running, Isadora. Do you not tire of yourself?

I stumble against the car.

Mason's voice rings in my ears, but my muscles feel like they're being compressed beneath a horrible weight. Ice splices my spine, spiraling through my nervous system. A voice, the song, but filtered through murky layers. A memory fighting to return. A night I let my guard down, got too tired of blocking out the song. Maybe even welcomed the feelings it pulled out. *Yes*, I thought, looking at the dark, *that's me.*

And then my feet are walking. My thoughts push in and out with the stronger voice trying to intertwine with them. *Just let me show you*, I think—whose voice was that? "Get away from me," I murmured. Firmer, then, a grip clamping shut around me and pushing me along. "Get away from me!"

Isa, get the hell away from there!

Trish? Suddenly all the voices vanish. Trish is not here. We're surrounded by trees. In front of me Mason spreads his hands, eyes wide. "I'm not touching you."

A scratch has opened his skin from cheek to jaw. I know without looking that I'll find blood under my nail. I don't even remember fighting him; there was a voice in my head, trying to take me over, and I . . . It slips away. "You're bleeding."

He swipes it off with his thumb, but more beads well up, like hatching ladybugs. "I'm fine. What was that?"

"It was here." The actual voices are still a swirl of confusion, but that understanding cuts through cleanly. "The edge Trish found me on. It was the quarry. I've been here. I think I heard its voice in the song like Otto said. It was telling me about myself, trying to lead me to . . ." I look around. I can just about make out the clearing we parked in, but otherwise the trees are the same in every direction. "Let's not get sidetracked."

"If you're sure," Mason says doubtfully. "I think we should keep heading east. It doesn't seem like Otto's showing up." He pauses, and I know we both have the same beat of worry, but Otto knows when the Angel's watching him, and I can't make myself turn around. I'm being drawn deeper into the forest by a muscle memory.

We push into the trees. I don't mention that I still feel it, a force pressing through my chest like it wants to split me. Guilt, yes, shame, echoes of the song from that night stirring up my emotions, but also something else I heard in its voice that's coming through in shreds.

No more running. It will be so peaceful.

The ground crunches under my boots. Shriveled lichen and twining creepers cling to bleached needle trees. The forest feels flayed and brittle, like too quick a breath would make it all fall to pieces. It's been sixty years or so since the quarry closed. The remaining buildings are cloaked around us somewhere, scarring the undergrowth.

Mason checks the picture of the old map from the library, trying to match the landscape to the drawing while I tap at my phone compass and hope it still works. In theory it should just be a straight path to the quarry, but in the middle of the trees, you can get lost with one step. As we walk, however, I'm more and more sure that I've taken this exact path before. The certainty ripples from heel to heart and back to heel again, my feet finding impressions in the ground they remember making in the past.

The whine in my head grows louder. Guilt drags itself from my chest—but compared to what I've confronted over the past few days, it feels oddly small. Young. Still a memory, from before the deaths. A voice in my head that both is and isn't my own: *No more running, Isadora. Do you not tire of yourself? Do you not tire of all your own lies? You are such a hurt child. You do not belong in this house, or this town. Why should they care for you when you are unable to care for them? You are broken. You have rejected love for so long you are almost incapable of it. But only almost. Run to me, Isadora. I have love for you. It will be so calm, so peaceful. Just let me show you. You, you, you.*

I'm so close. I take off running, chasing the end of the memory even as the path welcomes me back. The tree line breaks, and suddenly all that's between me and a crater in the world is a bare strip of earth. I cross it in five steps, drop down, and then I'm curled on my knees staring down over the edge of the quarry. I'm here now, scrunching my fists against the cold gravel. Overlaid like a gauze is me here years ago, with a voice saying, *The fall will be so freeing.*

The plummeting depths swallow me, both present and past, but they're starting to separate out like a sieve. In one layer I'm conscious of sharp terror, seeing myself move without meaning to. In the other, I think about tipping over and just free-falling through all that empty space. Letting go of any pretense at control entirely. The idea is soft, breathtaking. Liberating. And not mine.

"Isa. Isa." Trish appears right in front of me, grabbing my face, staring into my eyes. Doesn't ask, just says, "Get the hell away from there."

The image of her dissolves as Mason's footsteps crash beside me; he yanks me back from the edge even as I grip his wrists, stunned by the sudden onslaught of memory. "Isa, you need to talk to me right now."

"I remember. *I remember.* I could hear what the Angel was saying to me. And I remember what it was saying. It reminds you of everything you hate about yourself." I'm working backward now, sorting through. Once I've peeled the Angel's voice from my own, I can make out the way its influence twists and turns, the way its words contain both my secrets and a promise to show me a better place. "It tells you it's the only one that's listening to you, that it's the only one that loves you. That it's the only way out. It says, take my hand and I'll show you. Nothing else had ever loved me that much."

"It thinks it's a savior," Mason says slowly.

My fingers itch. "It thinks it's killing for our own good."

Just beside us, a large step away, the earth yawns. Gray water pools at the base of its throat from decades of disuse. The sides are ridged with worn paths, pockmarked with tunnels. Faintly, I think I hear a song ringing around the steep walls up to us. Not the Angel's song, just a hum like lilting dust or distant wings. There are old songs here, Otto said. But somehow, in this pit, in a storm that trapped five kids, they birthed a new one. A dark one.

There's a piece we're missing, I think. Something about why the mine collapse was the Angel's first act of twisted grace.

"Hawthorne Redford," I say out loud, and don't know if I imagine the air stirring, "you better have some goddamn answers."

17

THE QUARRY ENGULFS US, CUT WALLS LOOM-
ing like a fortress, the water mirroring the gray sky. These walls
have been here for a century, being cut ever down and outward.

The path is strangely well-preserved, only partly eroded at the
edges and still wide enough to walk safely down. We decide to try
to get as close to the mine collapse as possible to try to summon
Thorn, but the original floor of the quarry is now flooded, so we
settle on a low ridge on the other side that still has a pile of rock
in one corner and is scuffed by equipment marks.

"I've been thinking," Mason says, as we pick the spot. "Maybe
surviving the Angel left you with some piece of it, and that's why
your senses are so dialed-up."

"I was sensing it before that, though." I walk a circle, then sit
awkwardly, deciding my best course of action is to sketch on the
ground. "I can't do this with an audience."

He sighs and turns away.

"I can still feel you judging me."

He throws up his hands, still facing the sky. "What do you
want me to do?"

It's a striking image, his slender frame against the stark vastness of the cliffs and the flooded pool, hands almost worshipful, but that's not what I need to capture. "Take a walk."

He stalks off, probably rolling his eyes. I sweep my hand over the grainy dirt, smoothing my makeshift canvas. I have no idea where to start. The dowsing, as Mason wants to call it, has always happened when I'm not trying. Is that just how it works? Or would my subconscious work with me if I actually let it?

I drag my fingernail through the ground. I can already feel my reluctance building into a wall the longer I hesitate. Every time I've let this sensation come out of me it's just made me feel worse and worse—the scratching on my skin, the portraits, Zach's death, Trish in the bathroom, the suffocating voice of the Angel, ghosts upon bodies upon wounds. I miss who I was two weeks ago, when all I had to feel bad about was messing up a date.

Except that's not true either, is it? Why did I mess up that date? Because her laugh was a shade too much like Wren's, because the sound of it alone snapped a chain on a monster that took over my body? People doing well don't give other people first-degree burns and run away to hyperventilate in a coffee shop's single bathroom because of a *laugh*. And as much as I'd like to think otherwise, now that I've gotten those memories back—now that those instincts might have saved Trish's life, even if I can't close my eyes without seeing her bleeding out—I can't imagine losing them again. I'd rather see exactly what's fucking me up than go around convinced I was just born broken.

Which means Hawthorne Redford needs to show his goddamn face, so he can tell me about this demented Jesus-lite that popped out from the mountains to kill my friends—and tell me how to stop it.

"Hawthorne Redford," I mutter. "Hey, old man. I know you're out there. Are you listening to me?"

Just like free drawing, I think, sketching the vaguest outline of a man's head. Fill in the basics that could belong to anyone— brow ridges, ears, shadow of the mouth. Just a quick, fifteen-minute warm-up. Let your creativity flow. I was always terrible at free drawing. Even now I start feeling my anxiety tick up as I go in with more details—close-set, heavy eyes; crooked nose; narrow jaw. There's no way I'm not just making this shit up. I should start over.

No. I slap that urge away and keep going. I maybe hear something in the air, a noise once gestated in the earth released by the Vandersteens' hunger for stone, piped through the tunnels like the holes of an ancient flute. It's not quite the Angel's song. It drifts past and I get a touch of almost curiosity, a deep, comfortable hum.

A man is forming himself under my fingers. Not someone I've ever seen. A beard, I think, and don't know why I think that, but I use the tip of my nail to work in fine hairs across his chin, hairs that would trap mist in a storm.

I don't realize Mason's been watching me until he touches my shoulder, says, "Hawthorne Redford," and rings his chime in my ear.

The ghost unfolds from the ground so suddenly I almost jerk away. Mason's grip tightens before we can lose contact, and he pulls me to my feet so we're standing face-to-face with the former foreman.

"Finally," Mason mutters, as I stare at the translucent, ebbing figure of the man I was just drawing in the dirt. "A *normal* ghost."

· · ·

THORN IS DRESSED in work clothes. He looks a rough thir-
ties, younger than I expected considering he died when he was
over ninety. But maybe this is the version of him we need.

I can tell now why Mason immediately clocked something
wrong with the Angel's ghosts. There's no struggle to keep Thorn
here, no sense that he's constantly being pulled away. In fact, he
looks almost annoyed. "Who are you?"

Hearing his voice startles me again. It's unexpectedly normal,
something I'd hear in the street and forget in the next second.

"My name is Mason and this is Isadora," Mason says, unfazed.
"We want to ask you about the Angel."

Hawthorne pauses. Then, to my surprise, he starts laughing.
"And what do you know about it?"

"We know you saw it that night the mine collapsed. Whatever you saw, you couldn't forget. We read your logs. Did the
Vandersteens fire you when you tried to shut the mine down?"

The man's amused expression collapses so quickly my adrena-
line jumps, fight or flight kicking in. "Did they?" he says, his face
leathering all of a sudden, gaining fifty years that disappear again
the next time I blink. "Did they fire me? Did they lock me up? Did
they bury me?"

"Yes," Mason says unexpectedly, with an even, strong voice
that sounds like a spell. "Yes, yes, yes."

Hawthorne's eyes have a bright fever to them. Whatever con-
versational trick Mason's spinning, or power he's injecting into
his voice, it's clearly gotten the ghost on board. "They did," he
says. "I tried to warn them. I told them to fill it all back up. Fill in
this gash they cut from the mountain, let the things they dug up

198

lie back underground. It'll keep taking the kids, I told them. Take and take and take. I looked at it and knew it had purpose. It wouldn't stop till it was done. But when's it done? When's it ever done?"

"You *saw* the Angel?" Thorn's gaze snaps to me. Looks at me for a while with a leer he didn't have before.

"Just for a lightning flash. In the storm there was a crack so loud it woke me up. I was in the foreman's hut, see, I could see everything. That flash of light filled the whole pit, and the fallen tunnel was broken back open, and that thing was picking itself out from the rocks. All that sobbing turned into singing. Then it was gone like the wind blew it to pieces."

"Picking out from the rocks?" Mason asks. "Coming out of the tunnel, where the kids were?"

"Crawling like a babe. And after that the kids were losing their minds, jumping off the edges, sticking their heads in the river . . . starting with their friends, right, and I said that, I said it would take the ones it knew and they laughed at me. Locked me up. Buried me. Only that what's-her-name wants to talk."

Sarai, I think. Then: *Wants?* But Mason's got hold of another thread. "What do you mean the ones it knew? The Angel knew those kids to start with?"

"Why wouldn't it? They were friends, weren't they? The families too. Brothers, sisters, cousins. Lots of deadly things you can blame on these forests if a child's not careful, and the Vandersteens didn't care, the babes were easy enough to replace. Said it was my fault if anything for not managing the lot. Locked me up, buried me . . ."

"What do you mean the families?" Mason demands. "Of the kids it killed?"

"Now where did I say that? I said taken, taken, pulled into itself—"

"Are you saying the Angel didn't cause the deaths of those kids in the tunnel?"

Hawthorne fixes him with a hundred-yard stare. "Those boys were the Angel. I told you. I sent 'em in there. And the mountain swallowed them. And an angel crawled out. We had to hack the bodies apart to carry 'em out. Buried them on the far lot, no names or anything. Pastor and the Vandersteens all said the corpses were an abomination, but they didn't see what I did."

"What makes you so sure?" Mason presses, even as my tongue goes sour. "You recognized them? Why do you call it an angel, then?"

"So many faces," Hawthorne whispers. "So many eyes. Their eyes. All lit up in lightning, black dusted . . . It knew what we'd done to it. I was sorry. I'd pay it back, I said. We'd pay it whatever it asked. But the Vandersteens wouldn't listen. Locked me up—"

"What were their names?"

"Buried—"

"What were their names?"

Hawthorne's eyes snap to me again. Am I imagining it, or are they actually bright now, the black of his pupils starting to spread specks across his whites like soil scattered on water? "Stanley McLean," he moans, like in prayer. "Stan, Gil—"

A vacuum descends over my ears. His syllables turn soundless, mouth opening and closing.

"We need to get out," I exclaim, but I can't hear my own voice and I don't think Mason can either. His knuckles are buried in the drawing, turning white, the chime squeezed between them. His other hand has a death grip on me. "Mason!"

Child.

A ribbon slides over me, light and cold, and I realize it's wind, merely silent. I try to block it out, as I've done for years and years, but I'm still too open with bringing Hawthorne here, and I hear its voice, gliding past my ear:

You do not know what you do not understand.

Its lilt has layers. Parts upon parts upon parts, spread over each other. An unbreakable harmony, sewn into a single chastising voice, cupping the side of my face. Part of me wants to sink into it and beg for forgiveness. But the conscious part of me gasps, and the wind dies as my senses return in a flood. My skin feels stripped raw.

The ghost is still frozen before us, on his knees now, mouthing incomprehensible things over and over. Tears are streaming down his face. Mason is still transfixed. He's not hearing me.

Then, behind Hawthorne, arms burst from nothingness. I cry out as they wrap their hands around his body, dragging him backward as he ages rapidly.

Mason jerks alert. We watch in horror as other spirits— barefooted children with smudged faces—pull him into them until the ghosts begin to blur together. One of them encircles his waist and buries its head in his shoulder, indistinguishable mouth tilted up to whisper in his ear. As they merge, webs begin to unfurl over them. No, not webs—roots, like the irises, racing over their heads and torsos and unfurling more and more feelers as the entire mass of them fades away, swallowed back into where they came from.

The air pops. Mason doubles over, gasping, sweat slicking his forehead. It takes me a moment to remember how to breathe. I can't shake the sight of their blurry faces—*eroded*, Mason said. I can't unhear the Angel's voice, the way it sounded almost *disappointed*.

"Did you hear that?" I start, but he's not listening. He stares over into the water.

"There's something moving down there."

I look down. At first, I don't see anything, just a flat murky surface that time has filled. But then I lean forward into his line of sight, I see the ripples in the water, radiating out from under us. He's right. Something's moving under the surface. We must be standing right on top of one of the submerged tunnels. I grab his wrist, about to pull him back from the edge, when a pale shape breaks the water and a slim rib cage floats out from the rock.

I stumble backward, hitting the ground. It almost vanishes from sight, but one second passes, then two, and it floats far enough that I can see it even from here, buoyed across the water like a jagged white ship. Bones don't float. Do they? No, I'm sure they don't. But then Mason falls to his knees, and I see a second long white shape float out, almost too evenly, like a hand is pushing it across the surface.

Missing presumed dead, I think, and then feel like throwing up. There's no way to prove I'm right. But I know, like I knew about Trish and Zach and Hawthorne and all the people I pulled out into my drawings, that I am. I don't know for sure whether the Angel picks the death or just pushes someone toward it, but it's not all exactly the same. Some die with guns, some with ropes, some just by water.

Others, like me, must have come here. Stepped off the edge and drowned, or broken right on the surface.

Then Mason says, "Oh, fuck."

He has his sleeve pressed to his nose, and dread settles in a pit in my stomach as the smell, garbage-sweet and meat-sour, comes to me a second later. I can't move, even as his shoulders heave. Even as shoes drift out into view.

Shoes. Not bones, which I'd almost gotten used to, which I could file away as some hallucination because something like that just wasn't possible. Shoes, purple Converse, one set of custom yellow laces untied and drifting on the current. Purple Converse followed by the purple-black flesh of two legs.

I haven't eaten in hours but acid comes up anyway, burning through my lips and sharpening the air as I press my elbows to the ground, unwilling to look back and yet unable to stop myself from looking over my arms, to where Mason is still kneeling and staring at the body, which has stopped moving.

Then he leans forward and reaches for it.

"*Mason!*"

This part I really can't see, this part I have to leave to him and all his nights prepping bodies for burials. This part I shut my eyes and press my face into my curled fists willing my breaths to still, until there's the sound of a wet thud on the ground a short way from me.

For a moment there's only silence and our heavy breathing. I know what I'll see when I open my eyes. I know, and I don't want to see it. I want to go forever just with my knuckles in my lids, the world black and starry.

But eventually I open them and find Mason sitting there entirely expressionless with a dead Paige Vandersteen lying in front of him.

The first thing I notice is how pale her hair still is, almost silvery strands wrapped around her shoulders and throat like a tangled glowing moss. The second thing I notice is that under the hair, her neck is broken, just like how I drew it.

The third is that her bloated lips are curved gently, as though she simply fell into a peaceful sleep. Like she was saved.

A laugh bursts from my chest.

Mason's head snaps around. I press my hand to my mouth as another spikes up my throat. I taste the remnants of vomit, and then laugh until I collapse into the ground like I was supposed to all those years ago, except why would someone save me and not all these other kids just left here behind? Why not Wren? Why not Zach?

It's unfair, it's so fucking unfair. I hate it. I miss them. I miss them. I miss them.

"I know," Mason says, and I realize I'm speaking aloud again as he pulls me into him. Only then do I start gasping into his shoulder. I think he might be crying too. *Isa*, a voice pleads urgently. Then another, *Isa*, and a third, *Isa*. They sound a bit like Wren and a bit like Zach and a bit like Paige and a bit like Mason. I feel delirious and detached, sobs and garbled words spasming their way out of my mouth with no barrier. I think I'm just fully broken, I don't know who I was kidding, I'm so angry and tired and the loneliness of all these abandoned bodies are ripping me open, spilling out of me. It could've been me. *Isa. Isa.* I hear them, is that it? Because I should be part of them? Why aren't I? Why? *Why?* Because I fought for it? Did they not fight hard enough? Isn't that what we say to convince ourselves it won't be us?

But then one clear voice cuts through the screaming in my head. Mason is speaking out loud. "Isa. Isa."

His voice and the grip on my shoulders are hardening rapidly, dragging me back together. I swallow with a shuddering breath and follow his gaze up to the police chief standing at the edge of the quarry, looking down at us and the body lying there.

We

I WATCH UNTIL I AM NEEDED, WHISPER UNTIL you are ready to take my hand. I have learned not to jeopardize my mission by entering the sight of the closed-minded who would try to stop me. I am patient. I can take my time, give first to those who truly need me.

I am the only one who knows; I am the only one who cares. I am the only one who sees right through each of your walls, who cares to break them to bring us together. How fissures spread, between children trapped in the same place. A single fracture opens another and another. Call this cataclasis; call this catechism; call this comminution; call this communion.

Can I tell you a secret, Isadora Chang? We were abandoned too. The darkness swallowed us. We, too, heard our names being cried. At first, only from the outside. Faint shouts from beyond the stone. But then we heard the song from within the earth, and we heard it from each other. Our names from each other's mouths. Our names each other's mouths. Our names our mouths. Our other mouths. We were one body and one of another, bloody and sharing air. As children grow in their mothers so we grew into each other. The sound of shared heartbeats is the rhythm of the earth. To be buried is to be born again.

Do you not miss being swaddled? Do you remember how much you long for love, and how much of it I have to offer? I have followed you all your days and touched all your nights, even when you would not take me in, and you will remember you are grateful when you are safe in my keeping forever.

You see, I was lost, but in the dark, I was found by purpose, and even as our mamas wept, I was reborn. And didn't mama speak of lost sheep that need finding? So I will gather them all. I am patient. I am kind. To lose you once, I know, is to have walls put in your heart, separating you from me. But now your sister is no longer in our way.

Do you understand now what she took from us? You could have avoided all this pain. We could have had so much time. Will you listen to me now, Isadora?

18

SITTING ALONE IN THIS INTERROGATION
room, coming down from the whiplash of the past twelve or so
hours, the tide that overwhelmed me has receded once again to a
hollow knot in my chest and stomach. It's indistinct enough to
ignore if I want to. For the first time, though, I don't feel relieved.
I can think much more clearly, start putting together my cover
story. But it also feels like I just lost something after coming close
to it. I was close to grasping onto . . . what? Everything after finding Paige's body is a blur.

After minutes, hours, Officer Tai walks into the room.

Slater only has four policemen, so there was about a twenty-
five percent chance, but I still flinch inside when he sits down
across from me. After hours of being locked in with my own
thoughts, I've managed to pull myself together again, stop the
tears, stop the spiraling, but it's taken everything in me not to
start embossing my skin with my nails again. No one's told me
what's going on. I don't know where Mason is, what they're doing
with the quarry. Are they draining it? Or is finding Paige enough?

Officer Tai was the one who found Zach's body. He was doing
his early rounds and went down the river road, expecting to see

nothing but some stray trash. Instead, he found his son lying face down in the water with Officer Tai's own revolver inches from his flung-out palm.

He looks even more haggard than he did at Dad's funeral; there are rumors he's developed an alcohol problem. "We'll bring in your mom soon, but you want to tell me what you were doing down there, Isadora?"

We were trying to investigate the evil spirit that we believe made your son steal your gun and shoot himself. "We were exploring. We didn't know any of that was down there."

He leans forward. "You just happened to be there? With Mason?"

"What does Mason have to do with it?"

Officer Tai's jaw sets. "I'm sure you've heard, but Mason was one of the last people to see Paige before she disappeared. So it's suspicious that he happens to be the one to find her body, all the way down there."

"How did you even find us?"

Now he looks even unhappier. "Otto Vandersteen."

Shit. I forgot. At least he's safe, but he wouldn't have snitched on us, at least not by himself. From the blank snarl of my emotions, worry manages to identify itself.

"I don't know how you managed to get into so much trouble coming back for a few days," Officer Tai continues. "From what I heard you seemed to be doing well in school. But this? Did Mason put you up to this? The Vandersteens are not happy. Otto is a troubled—boy; he doesn't need more people getting in his head. Least of all Mason Kane. This isn't the city, Isadora."

"I know that." Jesus, do I know that. "Otto's not *confused*. He was just looking for his sister. We didn't do anything."

"His parents found him hysterical—"

"Is that the problem? That he's upset his sister is *dead*? Would that be a problem if he was still a girl?"

Officer Tai's expression is stony. "I don't know what you're talking about."

A clear anger manages to thread through me. "He cared what you thought so much. And he was *never* enough for you." I'm not talking about Otto anymore and Officer Tai knows it. The tears are coming back, pricking the corners of my eyes. I could shut up and blink them away, but the wet sensation of them on my lashes suddenly feels like I'm closer to whatever it was I almost had in the quarry. "You told him you wouldn't know how to show your face in public if he kept failing. You said he was stupid. You wouldn't speak to him if he lost a race. And you taught him to shoot, by the way."

Part of me instantly regrets that one. He used to take his sons out camping, a boys' trip type thing where they'd toughen up, climb rocks, and shoot stuff. No one could have anticipated what Zach would do, but Officer Tai deserves it at least a bit. Zach and I shared a raw, pleading anger. He always felt guilty about letting it out too. But we deserve to be angry. I deserve to be angry. And now that they're dead, I'm angry that my friends died because they were made to feel like they didn't have anywhere else to go.

I wait for Officer Tai to shout, but he just stands, expression hard. "You're not as grown up as you think, Isadora."

"So can I go?"

He opens the door, stands in the doorway. "The Vandersteens want to talk to you."

. . . .

MASON IS ALREADY sitting opposite them in the sitting room. Otto's mother wears her dark hair in an updo; she has an elegant, heart-shaped face and a mouth for society. They say Emma was a disgraced socialite in some city, come to hide in the old money of the Purple House.

Her husband, on the other hand, is Vandersteen blood through and through: a slate-cut, stiff-shouldered figure of hewn cheeks and hair like watery sun. The current head of workshop and de facto second principal of the school, since he funds half of it. He's got an eye for measurements—in some of the demonstrations he'd run he would chisel a piece of slate into the exact right shape with one look. That exacting gaze, a shade more desaturated than Otto's, whittles me down now, even as he holds and strokes his wife's hand.

"We were just saying to Mason," he says to me, "we'd like to thank you for finding Paige and bringing her home to us. These past few days have been difficult."

"Where *is* Otto?" Mason interrupts. My nerves light up, already anticipating this going badly. The Vandersteens' marbled silver gazes slide into one another and then back onto us again.

"Paige's sibling is at home. She's very sensitive about these matters," Mrs. Vandersteen says.

I grit my teeth, already itching to get away, but Mason's voice evens into something dangerous. "Would you be conducting an investigation if he'd died instead, Mrs. Vandersteen?"

"You'd be an expert in investigating dead girls, wouldn't you?" she replies. Mason stiffens, and her mouth ghosts upward at the corners. She leans a little into her husband, as if for comfort, and her chestnut hair spills into his brown suit. He's still stroking her hand.

"How's your sister?" she asks me, in a knowing way I don't like. "It was terrible to hear about."

Her tone makes my teeth grind, but I can't snap at her like I did at Zach's dad. "Unconscious, I think. But they said she'll be fine."

"That's good to hear. We'll have to check in with the doctor. We always found her such a blessing to have around; I couldn't believe when I heard."

I almost don't catch the past tense of *found*, slipped in there like poison. "It was an accident."

"No one cuts their wrists by accident, Isadora." I flinch. He says it like he's explaining to a kid. "We're concerned for her, and especially since she was tutoring our daughter, we're concerned what kind of influence she was exerting."

I'm so stunned by what I think she's implying that Mason has to say it for me. "Are you blaming Trish for Paige's death?" Right. So I'm not imagining it.

"No one's blaming anyone," Mr. Vandersteen says, in a voice layered thick with blame. "We're only concerned. The twins have been having all these attitudes for years now—"

"You are *not* pinning this on Trish!" I regret the outburst once it escapes me. Danger thrums in my ears, rises in a whine as the Vandersteens simply look at me with identical flat eyes and hands intertwined, Mrs. Vandersteen leaning into his shoulder. I feel crazy. I'm *not*, but they're just looking at me like they have no idea why I'm reacting like this, like a child who can't take things rationally; like I'm the one ruining this calm civilized conversation. Otto's not the only one hysterical today.

"You were the most promising student in your sculpture class, you know," Mr. Vandersteen says. "I remember being impressed. It's a shame you decided to leave."

That implication is clear, too: *You won't be welcome back.* Once his approval might have been all I wanted—his workshop was where I felt safest, where I felt like I could actually do something. He was an artist and a good teacher, on the few times he took over the class. Even now sometimes I wish Slater would be a place that let me love it unconditionally. But their prestige and protection means nothing when they'll cut you off the moment they deem you unfit. At some point you have to stop trying to become what they want before you lose yourself entirely. Holding on to hope is just a slow death. Worse: hope is the reason you let them get away with so much.

But I can't help feeling that maybe I picked the wrong battle to finally fight. As they so helpfully reminded me, they feed my family. I don't know where Trish and Mom would go if we've all pissed the Vandersteens off.

Unfortunately, Mason can't read my thoughts, and he's allergic to shutting the fuck up. "This seems to run in your family, though. Wasn't there another twin who jumped off something?"

"*Mason*," I hiss. Emma smiles thinly. It's the disinterest that gets me, the threat delivered with the complete lack of concern. They're so comfortable with their power, how easily they can just chip unsavory things away.

"You might think yourself grown-up, Mason Kane, but all you are is playing pretend. You're clearly intelligent. It's a shame that you chose to use those gifts to corrupt everyone around you."

"I'd suggest you get your story straight. Was I the corruption here or was it Trish? It's starting to get unclear."

I kick him in the ankle, but the damage is done. Pierce and Emma exchange another look and stand. Suddenly they're looming over us, and I hate how small I feel.

The Angel took those kids' lives, but it was living people that created the shame that drove the kids to the Angel in the first place. And it was living people that created the Angel—the foreman's mission and the Vandersteens' mine killed it first, even, crushed it to pieces that were rearranged back together with whatever force of space and age is in those mountains. Whatever sympathy I might have had for the Angel was permanently buried at the sight of Paige's body, but I can understand, at the least, how the right pressure can squeeze darkness into you. I was suffocating from the moment I was born. I would have died for a breath of fresh air.

The original monster here has always been human. We can outlive that, but we need to be allowed the chance to. The Angel doesn't get to decide when we give up.

"We'll have to talk to your mothers," Mr. Vandersteen says. "Don't come near our family again."

Mason shakes his head and walks right out. Mr. Vandersteen raises his eyebrows at me. Once upon a time, I felt safer around him than I did Dad. He never tried anything and I don't think he ever would, even if he is a shitty man otherwise, but in hindsight I see so easily how abandoned kids end up being prey to even more dangerous things. The right words, private lessons, enough praise, and I might have followed him anywhere too.

I stand and follow Mason out.

THE CHIEF MUST be superstitious; chimes dangle outside the station and tinkle lightly. Their light metallic ringing reminds me of the melodic voice: *You do not know what you do not understand.*

If I let the anger and shock take over me right now, I just wouldn't move at all. Instead, by some silent agreement, we turn over what we know about the Angel, the quarry, the plague. There's something that feels important about the plague night still; like the original storm that created the Angel, the plague house stands out from the pattern of its usual methods. It makes sense the Angel was drawn to their suffering, would want to save them from it, but the plague kids were too many at once, too quick. What let the Angel have that kind of control, when it never seemed to before?

And why has it never used that kind of power again?

We keep going around the names of the original boys that became the Angel. Mason was determined to get them back when we were talking to Hawthorne. The Angel clearly doesn't want us to, judging by the way it destroyed our connection with Hawthorne just as he was about to give them away. But names have power in dealing with spirits, grabs the core of them and lets you hold on. The Angel's talked at us long enough. Knowing who it is might let us do something more back.

Hawthorne did manage to give us one name: Stanley McLean. Burial records from that long ago are scattered, and the grave is unmarked, but we know the general location, and we have me. It's a start. Even with just one name out of six, we might be able to summon the Angel, instead of waiting for it to hijack our séances. Except what are we supposed to do against a voice on the wind?

As we talk about Hawthorne, though, something else occurs to me. "He mentioned Sarai."

"Yeah, that she talked to him all the time. Cecily said that."

"No—" The details are hazy, but I'm sure of it. "Hawthorne said she *talks* to him."

Mason pauses. "I don't think ghosts talk to each other."

My phone vibrates in my pocket, making me jump. I'm afraid for a moment it's Mom, or even the police, but it's Otto. I fumble with my phone and put it on speaker. "Hello?"

"Sarai's alive."

His bluntness catches me off guard, as does the answer to the thread we were following dropped right in our lap. But he's steamrolling ahead. "My parents found me going through their stuff last night and I'm on house arrest. Sorry. I just stole a phone back—Sarai's alive and she's still in Slater. That passage about the witches in the woods being bribed to keep away from town— someone told me that same story once, about a house deep in the mountains. I dug through my parents' office, and there's payments for supplies every month started by my grandparents. I didn't even know this property existed. It's up one of the mountain roads. I just sent you the address."

"Hang on." I'm struggling to keep up. Do we talk about Paige? The quarry? His parents' threats? But he hasn't brought it up, so I latch on to the thing he's telling us. The thing Hawthorne actually gave away, if I'd been sharp enough to realize it. The thing we might have already known, going in, if Otto had been a little clearer about his theory in his texts, or if his parents hadn't caught him. "Sarai survived the plague house. She knows what happened that night."

One of our questions answered, at least. We were going to go to the cemetery, but Mason nods. "She has to know something

about the Angel that we're missing. We've said the Angel struggles when someone's not alone. That plague house had dozens of
kids in it. Sarai was the whole reason we went to the plague house
in the first place, and the reason Theodore and Cecily named the
town's savior the Angel."

I glance at the route Otto's texted me. "I don't even recognize
this road."

"It's deep. Might not be on GPS, but the town maps will have it."

Mason covers the speaker with his hand. "My car's still back
at the quarry."

"It's not that far." Still, I can't help but glance over my shoulder as we head in that direction, almost expecting to see our
mothers or the police coming after us.

We've been walking for a few seconds before I realize there's
silence on the phone. "Otto?"

A scuffling comes from the other end. "Otto," Mason demands,
"are you there?"

"I'm here," he says faintly. "I dreamt that she was under the
earth. Right outside. Like she's right there. I could just . . . dig her
back up."

I've had that dream before. I wrap my coat as a wind picks up,
but I don't hear anything in it. "It's not real, okay?" I hesitate, not
wanting to divert, but I can't let him be in danger either. "Do you
want us to come to you?"

"No. I'm not worth the time." His voice drops off again before
returning, soft: "It doesn't like that I know about it. It doesn't
like the walls of this house . . . but I feel it every time I go to the
window. A shadow passing back and forth, trying to catch me
unaware. It wants to land where I don't see it. Grow through my
cracks. But I keep . . . shining a light on it. I see it. I feel it every

time it tries to come close. I think that's our power, you know? We know it's there. So it can't hurt us, not the same way. And that makes it mad."

"Listen to us," Mason says, as we cut through the park. "Stay on the line. It doesn't like when you're not alone, and it can't get to you if you know how to hear it. Just focus on our voices, okay?"

"That's what your mother used to say. When we were kids, they tried to ask her to fix me. It didn't work."

"Just keep him talking," I whisper.

Mason gestures wildly. "Hey, tell me about . . . different kinds of slate."

A pause. Mason winces. Then, unevenly: "What do you want to know?"

I, personally, have less than zero interest in hearing about rocks, but if there's one thing Mason can do, it's talk for a long time about pointless things. "Whatever you know."

"Um—it starts with . . . ash or clay—genesis—diagenesis—"

The sun today is entirely shrouded behind filmy clouds, casting the whole town in the mountains' overlapping shadows. Mason keeps Otto talking as the houses thin out toward the quarry, and he gestures at his car in the clearing. He passes me the keys; I fumble with them and get it in on the second try as he tries to find the address on his phone, realizes it's not marked on GPS, and scrambles for the paper map in his glove compartment instead.

Mason's still talking to Otto. I'm already driving, heading toward the valley roads with the map propped on the dash, when Otto says, "It's gone." A pause. A long, unsteady breath. "She's gone."

"I'm sorry," I tell him. It's a completely useless phrase and I never wanted to hear it myself, but I don't know what else to say. I am sorry, that his sister is dead and that the hard part is really only just starting. That this will be with him for months, years, the rest of his life.

"I'll see if they let me visit Trish." The signal's getting worse; he's barely coming through. Then, abruptly: "I lied," he says. "I mean, kind of. I do want to get out of town, for a bit. To the beach and everything. But I'm going to end up coming back here. I can't leave the mountains. We know each other too well."

I exchange a look with Mason. "Otto—are you going to be okay?"

"Don't worry. The Purple House knows its children too."

The line clicks off. "He'll be fine," I say, not sure who I'm reassuring.

The road is steep and bumpy, curving into the valley of the peaks that surround Slater. Vast rock, vast shadow, vast forest. I've never driven up here before, never had a reason to. These are the trails with no names. It's even more remote than the rest of Slater. Any number of things could be hidden away here.

I like driving, although I'm a little rusty because I haven't had a chance to since I left. It's the more grown-up version of being able to just wander. By some agreement, we don't talk after that, just let the valleys fold us in until the house appears.

Finally, I pull up at the fence where the Vandersteens have kept their biggest secret.

19

SARAI'S HOUSE IS LOW, DEEPER RATHER THAN
wide, nestled on an incline and walled in by forest. Neglect flakes
off it. Too many wind chimes hang from the porch, making the
beams look like they've sprouted silver teeth, and between them
are strange brown objects wrapped in cloth.

Mason gets out of the car and pauses. "Some people make
questionable choices in real estate."

Despite the jokes, I feel a deep unease as we walk up to the
door. The yard is covered in mounds, like someone's been digging
all over the place. Closer to the patio, the brown objects I couldn't
identify become clearer: they're ginseng roots, dressed in clothes
to look like dolls, so old and petrified they're probably worth
nothing. The clothes are handsewn, decorated with lace and buttons. Whoever the roots are supposed to represent, they just turn
slowly between the chimes.

I don't think we should be here. And yet I'm tugging the cord
for the ancient doorbell, and waiting to see who responds to its
ringing.

The door opens to an old white woman with long braided hair and a puckered face, like it was crumpled once and never smoothed back out.

"Sarai?" Mason says, and she looks right past me at him. The moment she does, something in her gray eyes lights up. I don't like it. She's looking at him like she knows something, and I can't think what it would be—only that Mason is in my portraits of now-dead people, and I feel like we've finally arrived at the moment his comes true.

"Oh," Sarai says, smiling. Her voice is rough like smoke. "I don't get many visitors up here. Come in."

"You don't want to know who we are?"

"I know who you are," she says, and turns back into the house, waiting for us to follow. Mason and I exchange looks. We don't have much choice if we want to learn what really happened at the plague house.

"Ladies first," Mason says.

"What a gentleman." I step inside.

THE HALLWAY IS COATED with angels. Every inch of the walls is a different painting, a different case of a figurine carved from wood. If I had doubts before that Sarai was the right person, they're entirely gone now, replaced by the sheer realization that we have possibly fucked up, and Sarai is definitely about to kill us, put us in lace, and hang us from her patio.

"You believe in the Angel," Mason remarks, but even he can't manage to sound totally casual.

"And what angel is that?" Sarai waves us into the living room, once more crowded with angels and scraps of cloth, smelling like earth. She steps into the kitchen, but calls, "Gabriel? Michael? Uriel? Strange, isn't it, how we don't have a name for our savior?"

"It's not a real angel. Hawthorne just told you that because he didn't know what else to call it."

"Oh, you've talked to *Thorn*?" Sarai stands in the kitchen doorway, pot in hand, a smile creeping over her. "Smart children, aren't you? How did you find his grave?"

"How did you?" Mason deflects.

"I was there when they buried him. I wasn't going to forget just because there's a forest there. We talk about all sorts of things. How we'd kill all the Vandersteens dead if we could. One of those kids just offed herself, didn't she? One more to go. Tea?" I can't decide if saying yes or no feels more dangerous, so I just take the cup when she pours it and sits us around a square table. "Sugar's in that tin."

I pause, then cautiously pry open the rusting tin. I almost drop it: nestled on top of the sugar is a mound of pink squirming rats, hairless, eyes not even open. "Uh . . ."

"Oh, did the rats get in there again? I meant to throw them into the salt," she says, grabbing the tin away from me, "dries them out, you know. Sucks all the water from their bodies."

I can't think of a single response that isn't *get out, get out now.* "You have rats too?"

"They like the survivors, especially if you don't go out and about too much. They can sniff you right out." She flashes her remaining teeth at me like she can smell my truths too. Like she's looked into our house, pried inside our walls. I don't like how easily she's admitted to her experience with the Angel. After all the secrets and evasions, she's just telling us freely? But she's still looking at Mason in that sly bright-eyed way that makes my skin prickle. Something's still hiding here, and I don't know what it is.

Mason smoothly takes over. "So, you were in the plague house. You're Ida Vandersteen's daughter," he says, as I realize it's the first time I've ever been given the word *survivor*. It sits with me like Mom does, uncomfortable and too intimate at once.

"*Aren't* I," Sarai says, then hums. "I dream of that ridge, you know. Locked up on that shore to die, knowing it was because, just a few feet away, my mother spread her legs for some pirate and then dumped me on a witch doctor who couldn't wait to get rid of me."

Mason waves this away, though I can't help but feel sorry for her. I wonder if she knows the town still sings songs about Ida's affair, if Ida herself ever thought about the daughter she'd left behind. How long has Sarai been hiding here? How has she been surviving up here anyway? "But you heard the Angel that night," Mason says. "You survived."

Sarai laughs. "I didn't just hear it. It *came* to us. Real as anything."

I jerk forward. "You mean you saw it?" Like Hawthorne did. Something that let it manifest. "Just for a flash?"

"A flash? It looked at me. It sang right to me. It was the sweetest sound I'd ever heard. Who would have sung to me like that? Not my mother. Not *Cecily*. I wanted to go to it, everyone else were cowards. But I wasn't, I knew it would save me and love me. I've waited every day for it to come back for me, but I've never seen it again. Suppose there's not enough of us, just me. It won't come back just for me."

Suddenly I realize something that's been nagging me this whole time. "You don't have their eyes."

When she looks at me straight on, it's perfectly clear. She has gray irises, like stone, but without silver marbling. They look strangely familiar, but they're not the same as Otto's or Mr. Vandersteen's, or what must have been Ida's and Cecily's. "The Vandersteen eyes," I clarify. I couldn't have imagined it all. "Or is that just a story?"

"Not a story at all." She sounds darkly satisfied. "Have you ever seen a Vandersteen baby, girl? Or a husband or wife before they marry in?"

I try to think if I've ever seen pictures of pre-Slater Emma Vandersteen. I've never thought about why she has their eyes, too, if she wasn't born with their blood. "No."

"The babies' eyes look just like mine. Everyone else's start with other color. It's the house that does it to them. Breathe in all that dust from all those years and it changes them from the inside, makes you one of them."

Then that sly, knowing smile again; there's something she's not telling us. My instinct to leave spikes so strongly I can't ignore it anymore. "Wait," Mason says. "How did you talk to Thorn? Do you talk to ghosts?" I touch his elbow to nudge him, but as I do there's motion in the doorway at the end of the kitchen opposite me, and when I glance up my heart stops.

Another Mason is standing in the doorway, covered in moths, like I drew him days ago. He turns and it's like watching an eclipse: the other half of his face is a ruined mask of necrotic flesh spreading up to his ear. His eyes, one sharp and one sunken, feathered by wings, lock on to us and widen. "Mason?" I whisper, not knowing to who.

Beside me at the table, he cocks his head. "And how did you escape the Angel to begin with?"

In the doorway, he flexes his hands and starts to run toward us. "Mason!"

Both Mason and Sarai whip around. Sarai starts laughing, just as the ghost leaps onto Mason and closes his hands around his throat.

I LOSE CONTACT as Mason's knocked backward off his chair. I touched him, that's how I saw the ghost, but now he flails desperately under an invisible thrashing force. Sarai's still smirking. I can't do anything against something I can't see and my mind is still trying to catch up to why there's two of them, why I drew one and not the other.

Mason chokes, grappling at his throat. This finally jolts me, but my hands hit nothing. Whatever's letting him touch the ghost must be something just for the Kanes.

As a suspicion rolls in, there's the sound of tires outside, the door slamming open, footsteps running in. Then Sharlene Kane appears with two metal objects in her hands, which she strikes together in a shrill metallic screech that rips into the air.

Mason gasps and rolls onto his side, evidently freed. I grab his wrist, half to check if he's okay and half to see the ghost, which is staggering away from him, a swarm of moths bursting from his shoulders in a panicked spiral. With the ghost's one good, widened eye, Mason right next to me, Sharlene striding over to us, and Sarai at the table now looking sour, I match the final pieces.

Sharlene appearing in town out of nowhere. Sarai seemingly rec-
ognizing Mason straight away. Her eyes, not quite Vandersteen
and yet somehow familiar. Familiar because they're the Kanes'.
Because the ghost is Mason's grandfather, who has the only blue
eyes in the room, which makes Sarai . . .

Mason pushes himself up, staring at the old woman. Time
slows for a second. I think I'm about to be left behind again.
Everything forms around him, still; some kinds of people just get
the story, the history, the family, and others don't.

But when Mason speaks he just sounds bitter. "Are you my
grandmother?"

20

SHARLENE SITS US BACK DOWN. SHE DOESN'T
look much like a Vandersteen or her son: curvy, brunette, smiley, more like a flower shop owner than someone who spends time rooting out ghosts. She's insisted on us calling her Sharlene since we were kids, which always made me incredibly uncomfortable, but that's been her approach to parenting—not doing any of the traditional stuff. I used to think that made her the coolest mom, but eventually I realized it was just another kind of abandonment.

Good parent or not, though, she *is* a practiced medium, and she is Sarai's daughter. So she tells us a few things, as the ghost of Enoch Kane hovers resentfully in the corner.

One: Ghosts are often trapped in the form they're most defined by.

Two: While the chimes call them, dissonance destabilizes them.

Three: "Your grandparents were the only survivors of the plague house. The Vandersteens were afraid they would tell people what had happened, so they gave them and Enoch's family a place to stay, promised to provide them with everything as long as they didn't come back. Eventually he and Sarai had me. I was born here and grew up here. I knew the main town existed, but I was told I couldn't go down there, and that I didn't need to. We grew vegetables and every now and then a car would come to deliver meat and flour and other things, and leave.

"But then I realized I could see ghosts. It's passed down. The children that escape it have its mark, some little bit of power passing through them and their children after that. I could pass off the figures in the trees, but one day I saw my grandfather standing where we'd buried him. My mother wanted to use my abilities to call the Angel back. But I couldn't call what I didn't know, no matter how many angel figures we made. My father had seen the Angel, but when he found out what we were doing, he tried to drown me in the bathtub."

She says this matter-of-factly, but over her shoulder, Enoch seems to have wandered far too close. Of course Sarai was smiling. Of course he'd attacked Mason. The irony of a grandson who'd inherited the same powers he'd tried to eliminate. *Tried* being the key word—

"What stopped him?" Mason asks, also eying his grandfather.

"I shot him with a double barrel." Sarai grins. I startle. She hasn't spoken in a while. "I didn't love that man, just needed him, right? Just needed the baby. The only other useful thing he wouldn't give up anyway, and Sharlene could still reach him if he was dead. Except my bitch daughter left."

Sharlene ignores this. "I risked going into town. Found the Purple House just like they told me about. When I told the Vandersteens what had happened, and what I could do, they made me a new deal. The Vandersteens have ghosts in their family too, more than anybody in town, and they're very interested nowadays in cutting all that out. I still couldn't talk to other townspeople, but I'd do their jobs quiet, keep an eye on my mother, and I'd get to stay."

"So they've known who you are, this whole time?" Mason says.

"I don't think Pierce and Emma do," Sharlene replies. "Pierce's parents made me the deal. All Pierce seems to know is that the terms must be kept—not why. If he had, he might have gotten in the way of sending you to school. Or me having you at all."

"But you didn't tell me shit either. You've known about the Angel this whole time. For two years you watched me try to reach Wren and Zach, and you said *nothing*."

Sharlene looks stricken. "Wren and—oh." She covers her mouth. "*Oh*. I never made the connection, Mason, I swear—"

"But you know how we can stop it?" I interrupt. "You know how to stop spirits."

"You're damn well not going to stop it," Sarai snaps. "You find it, you tell it to take me back!"

"I don't think the Angel is like other ghosts," Sharlene says helplessly. "Even if I did know, I'd have to summon it first, and I could never manage that."

"We've got that covered," Mason says. "We just need a way to defeat it. To actually stop the Angel instead of just hoping we're resilient enough to keep surviving." He turns to Sarai. "*What happened that night?*"

"*Angels we have heard on high,*" she sings in her woodsmoke scratch, ignoring him entirely. "*And the mountains in reply, echoing their joy, their joy, their joy—*"

"She didn't see it," Sharlene says quietly. "I've heard her scream at him. He knocked her out. That's what saved her."

"Him, as in . . . Enoch?" We all turn to the ghost in the corner, and of course, that's when he vanishes.

MASON RESPONDS QUICKER than Sharlene, whipping out his necklace so the chimes ring and shouting, "Enoch Kane!" Sharlene looks taken aback by this, but she recovers quickly and is already moving when the ghost shudders back into view, turning toward the chime in the trance. The reverberations hang in the air. He seems paralyzed by them. Sharlene gives it a second ring with her own set of chimes from her pocket, then rapidly places a handful of stones in a circle around him.

"He won't talk to you," Sarai sneers. "Son of a bitch."

"Not to us," Mason agrees. "But Isa's abilities work a little differently."

Sharlene turns to me, surprised again. "You too?" Pity flickers across her face, realizing what this means.

I try to ignore it. "Kind of. But I don't know how to do what you're asking. I can barely control it."

"She's like a prism," Mason clarifies. "They're linked, and whatever power the Angel is comes through her in a way we can access. She can find things without an anchor."

"Interesting," Sharlene says. "That could work."

"*What* could work?"

Sharlene sighs. "Think of the supernatural as . . . infinite sound waves, and you're a radio. If you're tuned into the right frequency, you could hear just about anything. The difficult part is identifying that frequency. Mason and I have a particular one. You seem to be tuned into the Angel itself, and its song."

THE DARK WE KNOW

"And where it's crossed with people," Mason adds.

"Once a person dies, they and all they are become part of those waves. With an anchor, I can pull those scattered pieces together again, but I can't see exactly what I pulled out. But if Mason's right about the way your abilities work, you could draw a single piece through you. If you were honed to the right part of them, the one that's linked to the Angel . . ."

"I could pull it out," I finish.

Sharlene nods. "Theoretically."

Mason shrugs. "All of science is conjecture. Isa?"

After everything that's already happened it should be an easy yes. I know what they want, and I'm even starting to understand it myself. Otto can sense the song, too, make out its emotions, but I'm the only one—the only one still alive—who actually hears its voice. And not just its voice, but the voices within it. When I was crying in the quarry, I could swear now they were reaching for me too, breaking away from the Angel somehow.

My whole life I've needed to keep myself exactly within the lines, because it was risking too much to spill out of them. But I've lost Zach and Wren; we've lost Paige and all the others and now I might lose Trish, and this is the closest we've ever been to understanding how to stop the Angel. Enoch was there that night. He saw the Angel and he survived it.

I'm supposed to be braver now.

I nod at Mason, remember out of nowhere being on the same tag team once and chasing Wren and Zach in the woods. We lost that day, because they were better at catching us than we were at going after them. But this time the game's changed. This time we win.

Before I can regret it, I say, "I'm going to need a pencil."

. . .

"YOU MIGHT NOT actually need the drawing," Sharlene remarks as she hands over the pencil and paper. "It's a focusing tool, like the chimes, but theoretically you should also be able to do without it."

"It's the only way I know how." My throat feels dry. "So—can we please—"

I try not to notice Sarai sitting there watching us hungrily. She's a little too excited that I might somehow bring us closer to the Angel. I still don't know how I'm going to do this, but Sharlene assures me it's instinctive. I need to reach through Enoch, find the resonance of the Angel within him, and form it into something we can use. Could be a memory, a feeling, an image. "All the same to them," Sharlene says. "Don't try to define it."

So I sit down in front of the bound ghost, take a deep breath, and draw. Basic outline first, the rough slope of the jaw, the shape of his nose. So similar to Mason's, but the differences are much more obvious now that I'm paying attention. As the sketch blooms, he starts to hiss. "I escaped! Leave me—ghosts—you don't see a thing. The Angel can't touch me. *I beat it.*"

"Ignore him," Mason murmurs. "Unpack the sensations, find the strange one. It's there, it's always been there, tucked away. Sort it out from the rest."

I breathe slowly as his voice lulls me into a different space, reminds me of listening to stories as a kid. Slipping into fantasy worlds, other people's lives. He shifts again, and then ever so gently, a chime rings again.

It's a dark, choral vibration in the soft bones of my ear. I hear valleys and deep deep earth. *Portrait,* a professor's voice says, portra *here in Latin, meaning to drag out, to reveal, to expose.* The chime rings again. Enoch Kane is an observable thing, I think. A portrait is a relationship, a reflection of the artist and its object of representation. A portrait is a communication in every line. Back, and forth, and back, and forth. This time, I'm more conscious of the slipping. Of the way the resonance twines in me, draws something out not just from me, but through me. I feel my hand shift without thinking about it. I bury the impulse to freak out, shut my eyes, and let it pull me in.

I hear a splash of water, see dark walls. The plague house? I'm hopping across the threshold, the smell of river water molding into the damp—no, that's not right, that's not where it's going. Follow it: splash of water, dark walls, shouting—isn't this the flood? Doesn't it have to be the flood? But the walls are solid, not broken down, and there is the kitchen tap, soapy dishes, shouting—no, that's not . . . why am I here? Dad is shouting. A boy is shouting. I can't tell what's me and what's Enoch. Water going everywhere, a female voice crying out and then going silent. Where am I in all of this? Hiding upstairs. Running away. The current starts to slip. No, I need to follow it. Let it pull me in.

I beat it, Enoch said. That stands out. *I beat it.* I imagine my hands closing. Not into fists. Around something thin and hard.

A poker. Warped, antique, wet with pouring—*rain. I'm crawling through mud, crying, with it gripped in front of me. Wind beats at me, and there's a song, but it's so muffled I can push through it. I can barely hear anything at all. The plague, I think, it's taken my hearing. It didn't take the other girl's; that's why I hit her, pushed her down under blankets before she could run out into the flood like all the others.*

The others. I can still see some of their bodies. They jumped straight into the water laughing. I screamed at them to stop—until I saw what was outside. What they were all running toward.

What I'm crawling toward now, with the first weapon I could find in my hand. If I can kill it, maybe the others will all be okay. I don't know how. My body is burning. I don't know why they all ran to it or why I didn't. Because I'm special. Because I'm supposed to save them.

The thing standing in front of the sick house is made of stone and seeds. It plays a gray pipe that I can barely hear through my ruined ears. I grip the poker. The thing is focused on the house; it didn't see me sneak out the back. It's standing in the water and all the other kids are drifting toward it like a whirlpool. You have to do it now, Enoch, you have to do it now.

I jump up from the mud and swing at its head. Stupid, *I think at the last second,* can't hurt a demon like that, *but the poker crashes right into its head and knocks a chunk off. The pieces of its jaw scatter like gravel. It whirls toward me. It's covered with eyes and faces, and one of them belongs to the boy that had the bed beside me.*

I run and run and run. I—

As Enoch escapes up the Ridge tunnel, stumbling back into Slater proper and collapsing in the grass, I'm jerked sharply back to myself and to silence. The Angel's faces are seared into my mind, gliding in and out the corner of my vision in frozen masks. So many faces. So many eyes. Just like Hawthorne said. All belong to the kids it's collected.

Sarai was right. Somehow I understood that the anguish of the plague house kids was enough to pull the Angel into the physical world for the first time since the mine collapse, let it exert an amount of power it didn't even know it had. In doing so, it made mistakes. Enoch saw the Angel—and he *hurt* it. Once it's in that form, it can be physically hurt, just like anything else. All we have to do is summon it.

But I realize, then, that I don't know where I am. The pus-tinged storm and the plague house have vanished, and I'm surrounded by a wet, quiet darkness.

White light flickers from an invisible source, enough to illuminate a tunnel with strange contours on the stone walls. A second later I recognize noses, chins, foreheads, hands. I've studied enough features for reference to be able to see their shapes anywhere. Except here, all their faces have been sanded into blank sheets. This isn't Enoch's memory. What the hell is this? What layer of waves have I fallen into?

You should not be here.

That sliding harmony fills the entire tunnel. The tone shakes me more than anything. Where earlier, it was disappointed, like I was just a stupid child who'd gone somewhere I wasn't supposed to, now its voice is suppressed anger. *I have been patient. I have been forbearing, as you are ungrateful for my love again and again. You are both beyond me now.*

Cold presses me in. I have nowhere to go. I've fallen too deep. It would be so easy to just sink into it, but images flicker through my mind unsolicited. Broken necks. Bloated bodies. Shattered brains. Blood on the floor. Night after night after night. "That is *not* love!"

You see, child, you do not know what you want. Do not accept me, then. But you will not get in my way.

Fuck this. Maybe it got screwed over too. Maybe I even understand its twisted mind, because no one deserves to die like those
quarry boys did. But that doesn't mean any of this is okay. My
brain is screwed up, too, but I'm not going around murdering
people and telling them that's love. I'm sick of being conde-
scended to by an ancient evil with a savior complex made out of
five fucked-up kids smashed together. I'm sick of being told we
should be grateful for violence.

"We won't get in your way," I say. "We're going to destroy you."

A long silence falls. The tunnel seems to tighten, and my
breath shallows. Around me, the air shifts. A new tapping sound,
one I can't place, and I think maybe it's coming from inside me,
something breaking out or something breaking in, and if it lands
in the right spot, it will cleave me straight through. "I don't need
you anymore!" I don't know where my words come from, but it
feels like the most honest thing I've ever said—that once I would
have gone with the Angel because I felt like I didn't have anywhere else to go and its voice was the kindest thing I heard, but
I don't feel like that anymore. Sometimes, maybe, sometimes I
still hear the song in my dreams, and it sounds like home. But
I've gotten out. Despite my life falling apart in the city, I can fix
it. I don't know exactly where I want to go, but I *can* see the
roads out. Which means the Angel has no power over me. It
never has.

The realization grips me. "I don't have to listen to you
anymore."

A pause. Then an awful, sliding shaft of air, humming against
my jaw. *But you will. And you will regret*, it says, its voice coming

from everywhere. My vision flickers; one of the carvings with a clearer face still seems to bend toward the light, and it almost looks like Wren.

Remember, this is me being kind.

A metallic screech slices through the tunnel. When my vision clears, I'm back in Sarai's house. Sharlene drops her metal tines as she and Mason pull me upright. I don't even remember falling, but my palms are wet, and I realize my nails have scratched diamond eyes so deep they broke skin.

"I'm going to assume that worked," Mason says, as Sharlene scrambles for paper towels.

"We can hurt it. I saw it. I think I pissed it off." My head is pounding, still hearing a lilting layered voice, still seeing its faces. I press the tissues to the cuts, not even really feeling them.

"You *spoke* to it?"

"I reached it somewhere in between." But it's somewhere. Those statues, my drawings—what if I wasn't just drawing omens, but a shard of the Angel's fixation, carried across our connection somehow? I can reach into it, somehow, and that *scares* it. That was the emotion there. Not just mine. The Angel didn't like me either. This whole time the Angel has thought itself a savior; the last time I met it, at least, it pretended to be kind, whispered in my mind over seasons. But Wren's death was different. Sudden, and struggling for control. *Paige's* death was different. And both of them had been close to finding out something about it that would make it vulnerable. Just like I am now. *You will listen*, it said, like it was sure.

I've survived its twisted kindness before. But anger? Revenge? Self-defense? There's no telling what it could do.

"Isa." Mason's tap alerts me to my vibrating phone. I can't deal with a call right now, but when I look at it, it's Mom.

"Isadora? Are you there? Hello?"

Her voice is garbled. The connection is flickering in and out. I grip the phone tighter, trying to hear past the danger blooming in me. "Mom? Mom! What is it?"

"I go to get food, and when I come back, she's—"

"Mom?" She's cut off again, but she's talking about Trish. "She's what?"

"—is—saw her—"

"*Mom!* I can't hear you! What happened to Trish?"

"She's gone!" The line pops into full volume suddenly. "She's not in the hospital. No one can find her."

I'm already moving, fumbling for car keys as Mason yells, "Wait!" He runs after me as I dash out of the house, throwing myself back into the driver's seat and missing the ignition once, twice, before the car starts up. "What's going on?" he demands. Mom's voice is still crackling. I throw him my phone, pull sharply away from Sarai's gate. I feel it now, the spark of Trish on my senses. She's there. She's missing. She's there, yanking me toward her. I floor it as fast as I dare down the valley road, needing to not be too late again.

21

THE VALLEY ROAD BLURS PAST IN A SEA OF trees, cliffs, and a paint-water sky. I'm going as fast as I dare, but the road is cold and at certain bends the valley dips away into a drop. I don't drive in the city; I'm out of practice. I'm not going to do the Angel's job for it. And yet with every call Mason tries to make to Mom or Trish that gets dropped, I let myself go just a little bit faster. Trish is yanking at me. I'm getting closer. I don't even recognize this road, but it's taking me to her.

Mason drums his fingers on the car door handle. "What I don't understand is why it wouldn't just appear every time if it's so much faster. Why spend the time getting in our heads?" Another call. Another flatline beep.

"Because that makes it visible. And vulnerable. It doesn't like that I can get to it more easily than it can get to me. Shitty people who know they're being shitty don't like the people who can see it." I jerk the wheel a little too hard on a turn and wince as something scrapes against rock. Hope Mason's not too attached to his paint job.

"You said you saw Wren in that place with the carvings of all the kids."

"I don't know what I saw, Mason. Maybe. It kind of looked like her, but I was kind of focused on something else at the time."

"What if they really are somewhere we can reach?" His voice picks up in urgency. Another call. This one actually rings a couple times before the signal is swallowed by the peaks. My chest tightens. We're almost back in town. She's close. "What if they can be freed? What if we can still get them back?"

I glance at him. I can see the montage in his eyes: Wren and Zach, back with us, a little taller, a little older; the four of us getting pink milkshakes and sharing fries; piling into this car and sailing away, Zach on the music beside me and Mason yelling directions from the back seat and Wren laughing next to him with her bag of Sour Patch Kids; us, roommates in some overpriced apartment, sharing dishes and a broken light switch and pizzas on movie nights. The sheer force of his yearning punches the breath out of me.

I shove him with one hand, blinking back tears as I refocus on the road. "Don't do that."

He sounds genuinely confused. "Do what?"

"They're gone. *They're gone.* Whatever you believe about their spirits, their bodies have been decomposing in the ground for two years, and they weren't exactly in the best state when they got put in. They're gone!"

"But what if—"

"No! You can't will your way out of this one, Mason! Death is the one thing that is not going to listen to you." I whirl on him as we go round another bend, and in that second Mason shouts, "Isa!"

I look back and see Trish in the middle of the road.

My foot reacts faster than my brain, slamming into the brakes. Trish is smiling in her hospital gown as the car screeches and jerks, but then the wheels slip on a slick patch of road and we're spinning. My ears ricochet with shouts and shrieking tires. Trees and road whirl and blur and there, still smiling, Trish rapidly being swallowed from sight as we rush down on her.

Desperately I wrench the wheel and miraculously the car pulls itself together.

"Isa!"

"Shut up!" I drive my heel into the brake again, a second before we ram headfirst into a tree.

Screaming shock wave. Crunching metal. Then a sharp slam against my chest that knocks the wind out of me, and a shattering wail as my elbow lands on the horn. I jerk back, gasping, and the sound cuts out. Billowing smoke from the crumpled hood rapidly engulfs the windshield.

Outside, Trish pitches sideways.

I fumble with the door. It takes three tries pushing it violently before it opens, and then I hurl myself out onto the road. "Trish. *Trish!*" I grab at her arms, but I can't get a grip on her.

Mason helps me drag Trish off to the side. I pull her into my lap and wrap myself around her. "What the fuck. What the fuck. *What the fuck.*"

"She was just standing there; it could have been anyone driving by."

"No! The Angel knew. It knew we were coming. It was just here. I knew it was still latched on to Trish. It *sent her here.*" Pain throbs in my chest from my impacted seat belt, but I clutch her tighter into my ribs anyway. "Trish. *Trish.*"

Miraculously, her eyes crack open. "Isa?" she mumbles. She catches my arms as I gasp at her. "I heard it. I was in the church. I just remembered seeing Wren there on the piano for hours after Zach died—then I found this music sheet, and—"

"Calm down," Mason says rapidly, shrugging off his coat to drape over her as she shivers. "I'll call the tow truck and your mom."

"I heard it," she tells me again. "The voice."

"*The* voice? You've heard it before?"

"I didn't think I had until I saw Wren's sheet. I read it and it was like I could suddenly hear that same voice every single time."

"Every single time what?"

"Every time I fell asleep. Every time you were too far away. Every time I saw Mom cry. Every time I saw you want to." Her eyes shut briefly, then open again, hard and cold. "Maybe that's just all the time."

I've never seen Mom cry. I wonder how much Trish knows about our house that I don't. Whether I want to know, or ever can know. "How do you know it was the same voice?"

"I don't know," she says. "It sounded like Dad."

THE TOWMAN doesn't ask questions when we load into his truck, leaving behind my crumpled car, but I expect word will get around by tomorrow. I help Trish into the back while Mason sits up front, gazing out at the road. Trish leans into my shoulder.

"I know the Angel led me to hurt myself," she says after a while, "but I'd be lying if I said it's never crossed my mind before. The Angel didn't put the idea into my head. It took a seed that was already there, and it took away that fear. I remember feeling only calm. Happy, even. Happier than I was for a long time. I heard someone calling my name, and it sounded so beautiful, like it *knew* me. So I followed it. And there was . . . I was surrounded by earth. It's like a nightmare in pieces now."

"I know the feeling."

She pauses, trying to figure out what I know.

"Mom told me you found me at the quarry. And then I remembered it." She gnaws at her lip. I squeeze her hand. "You pulled me out of it. The Angel targets people who are alone. It has to convince you it's the only one who understands. I think having people around you, someone who really knows you, stops its power."

Even as I speak, I see Zach all over again. How I didn't try harder to break through to him, how quickly I ran away and left him alone. I didn't know exactly what he was hiding, but maybe it's not the knowing but the caring. Maybe it's *wanting* to know. It's too late either way. Still, instead of hopelessness, the feeling that rises to meet that thought is furious determination. It's simmering steadily now, radiating outward. Like submerging from a dive and realizing I don't have to survive on held breaths. I've spent enough time feeling sorry for myself. I've paid in all that frozen time. There's something out there that hasn't paid at all for what it's done. But it will. I will make sure it does.

"Hey," Trish says, frowning at me. "You okay?"

"Yeah." Damn. I cry so easily these days. I swipe my hand over my eyes. "I just—I'm glad I found you again." I pause, and it feels like I can make a joke. "And that I didn't run you over."

"Yeah, *about that*," Trish starts, making me sob-laugh pathetically. She wraps an arm around me and runs her fingers through my hair again. "Don't worry about it. And hey." She shakes the bandages on her wrist. "Now I have a better reason to wear those bracelets."

"Oh my God, you can't say that."

She laughs again, and it's the best sound I've ever heard, and I can't help but laugh too. "I would have done it if she hadn't," she murmurs. Before I can ask what she means, she shuts her eyes and is asleep.

We

FOR YOU, ANYTHING LESS THAN PERFECT IS failure. To be seen trying is to be flayed open, wet heart bared to the elements; to falter is to fall.

So the question: How do you correctly grieve? You are not meant to feel sorrow for the way Zachary Tai died. Yet it overwhelms you, and you do not know where to direct it. Your elders would condemn it. The boy you love sits by the grave and will not speak. The girl next door is never home. Your brother is too young to be burdened.

So you enter the church and seek hymns instead, seek the solace of your instrument. Grief twists out of you, calls me to you. You have kept yourself molded for so long, and now you finally seep past your limits.

Yet it is hardly the first time you have called to me. You see, they are right about what you feared: Wren Carver has been undone by love.

YOU WERE FRIENDS your whole lives, but you are precise clockwork in the shape of a girl, and you did not stop until you found yourself loved. They would call you a schemer if they knew. But see: he made a rebel of a careful girl and you made a lover from a cynic. After so long trying to be the princess your family and best friend called you, you felt as though you finally found your fairy tale. Wasn't this the kind of tale they write about: two friends growing up together and falling in love? It took you some time to believe that you, too, deserve fairy tales simply handed to you, instead of needing to always work to be worthy of them. Your classmates talked, and you worried that they would find out, but he made you feel not just like a new beginning but the happy ever after to come.

You learned to climb out your window, to steal kisses at night. You learned the names of stars that suddenly seem easier to touch and made plans you could not yet afford: that school, that city, that beach. You thought that if you studied love, it would not punish you, but you were unmoored by the speed at which you lost control of teenage faith. You knew better. But is it not glorious, giving in to it? Is it not release? We know what it is to surrender and be made well again. See: a tunnel, a storm, an earth on our knees, letting the mountain remake.

Alone, you stood before mirrors, tracing the paths where you let him touch forbidden skin. You stared at your reflection as though you expected to find something monstrous there, because you wanted him too. You looked at yourself in fear and hate, and for the first time, your ache called at the wind. Because he touched you, and after that, it is as though everyone you pass sees right inside you. They see that you have been changed.

You know what all your elders would say: Girls like you do not want; girls like you are in control; girls like you cannot make mistakes; girls like you are precious, sacred, pure. Girls like you do not find pleasure in being none of the above. So you are no longer her. You are simply a lie in the shape of her. You love a devil's boy and you let him inside you. You let him ruin you.

And then whispers arrive, but not the ones you feared. They are about a boy who does not deserve God at his funeral, and they are about your friend. And in grief, the boy you made love you becomes someone you cannot reach, and it crosses your mind as suddenly as an instinct that Mason Kane and Zachary Tai were never just friends. Suspicion starts as a seed that becomes knowledge over a night. So, wonder: Did he ever really love you? Were you simply the safer option? Have you spoilt yourself only to be the villain in their story?

You cannot look at him now. Everything is dirtied. Everything but you and me.

BUT WHAT'S THIS? You sit at the piano, as you always do. Only now something makes you pause. One hand rests on the keys, while the other searches for your pencil and begins to write, face twisted in concentration and confusion. It is only when you look up and seem to see me that I realize you are attempting to write my voice.

I have erred, I have erred, I have erred. I have learned, in all these years, how much presence to exert so as to remain safely behind a veil. But something in the songs you play brings me closer to you than I intend.

You will not see me like this. I have made that mistake before. So, if you are hearing me, Wren Carver, hear this:

You know the rules. Hang a chime in the east and let the irises grow. Do not answer to the dark. Do not topple the cairns. Only light a night fire with water or walls nearby. To grieve a sinner is always a sin. A son will become a man and become a father. A daughter will become a woman to become a mother, but only in time. *Only in time.*

You do not break the rules, so why do you let him touch you? What comes next, Wren Carver? You may break the rules of your town, but you cannot control the laws of nature. He has been inside you, so what follows?

Child, oh child, child, child.

YOU LIKE THE ROCK IRIS BLOOMS, but you like their winter roots too, the way they last through the cold and survive the cracks of a barren surface.

Think now, however, about the way they spread and latch feelers on to their host. There may very well be a child in you now. Does it braid into your blood, take your tissue for eyes? What else will you lose? Your body, their love. You have always wanted children, but what kind of mother would you be now? You let a devil's boy ruin you. You have ruined yourself. You are sick at his touch. He cannot come near you any longer. You can only wait for blood and pray, but you will not be waiting so long.

I hear your prayer first. I know how prayers echo when they are screamed. How it sounds coming from a collapsed lung, through broken teeth. The earth absorbs it, you see, seals us off from God's ear. So I hear you before God ever does. After all, I stand over your dead. I am the sieve through which your worship must first pass.

Your mother wishes you would never grow up. She knows what awaits girls once they grow, and she is so afraid of watching it happen that she has never told you a thing, hoping to prevent speaking it into existence. *You're too young,* she has said all the time, kissing your forehead; *when you're older.* You are old enough for rules but not old enough to be told why you must follow them, only that you must.

So how could you tell her anything now, about your desires and fears and these sins you have committed? No mistake will feel worse than killing the image of the little girl your mother loves. She does not know this side of you. She will not love you any longer once she does. You grow and grow in the skin of your younger self. When will you run out of space? Do you already begin to suffocate, turn into something twisted?

So anger at what they expect of you. Anger at how they deny grief. Anger at the way in which your body is created to betray you. They did not tell you what a baby could do to a body, even as they grew you to be a mother. The boy said he loved you, then left you. Fear what anger twists you into, yet wind it up your veins all the same. Crush it against your lungs. Let it drag you to the floor, where you watch dreams turn dark. You think to know me, but do you recognize yourself any longer? Feel a kick with every bump into a cabinet. You have always been so good at laying plans, but you cannot control the way a body forms or breaks. Like our elders, our bodies betray us. Lungs flat when we wish to scream. Limbs crushed when we wish to crawl. Womb swelling when you wish to stay small.

Imagine what they will say. Feign sickness for some time; anemia, perhaps, or plague returned. How long do you have left before they know what you have become?

I am not our town's only story. There are tales of witches in the deep valleys that the mountains coil over, witches who only wretched girls go to. So you can dream of the world you might build, the children you might teach—but dream, too, of escape. Dream of stealing away, of finding the place where the cliff heads touch. In only a night, you could return whole. You could be worthy of their love again. The fairy princess. The child. Perfect. Pure.

And here, when the first thing you lose is your mind, I will show you the way: across the lower roof and down the tree, across town and up to the pond. I promise, I promise, I promise: the witches' path waits beneath the water. It waits for you.

Don't you wish to be cleansed?

We will be quiet, Wren Carver. Girls like you know better. I do not like it, but I will teach you to be better.

What they do not tell you is that the wretched girls become witches in turn. And witches prove innocent when they drown.

22

IN THE RED HOUSE, WE HAVE TO GET PAST A horrified nurse, but Trish plays it off as her own mistake. Except for a boy getting casts on his legs, there's no one else in the other rooms. There's a mournfulness in the hallways, like the manor misses death.

Mom jumps at us when we enter the room, gripping Trish's shoulders and shaking her until I yell, and she yells, but I can tell she's just been scared out of her mind. Eventually she says she has to go back home, to clean up, and I promise to stay with Trish. None of us tell her about the accident. I'm still too shaken by it myself.

Once Trish is settled back in, she says we should get food. "I'm not hungry," I say, but she says, "Yes you are."

I stare at her. She stares back. Mason hovers. He's never had siblings. He started cooking for himself in third grade because Sharlene sometimes forgot to prepare anything for him. "We shouldn't be alone," I remind him. "And I'm not leaving Trish."

He takes his phone from his pocket. A moment later mine vibrates, miraculously still intact after the crash. He's requesting a video call. I accept grudgingly and he smirks, leaving for the nearest shop while my screen confirms his safety in the form of a blurry rectangle. Smart-ass.

Trish drifts off into another nap. While waiting, my subconscious is aflame, nerves prickling for a fight I can't anticipate. Being in the Red House doesn't help. Because it was once also a manor, it's furnished more like a hospice than a clinic. The standard white bed is stark against the rich dark walls and stone finishings. The bedside table is antique wood. The art is less gruesome here—a painting of the cliffs in summer hangs in an old frame. The presence of its history gives me the creeps, like Cecily Vandersteen is still roaming the halls with the kids she drowned, trying to turn mine-blackened lungs red again.

I prop Mason up on the side table, glancing occasionally at his head. I run a pen over someone's leftover napkin, trying to coax something out, but it doesn't come. I'd never wanted the visions and now suddenly I'm upset they're not coming, because there *was* a power there. Now there's only a void.

I end up starting to draw Trish as she sleeps. I hate that we're wasting another night, but the dark falls so quick in winter, and the last thing I want to do is be out in it.

I glance up at Trish, trying to catch how her hair falls. Something about her feels off, though, and I can't at first tell what it is. Her chest rises and falls peacefully.

But then I don't hear her breathing.

"Trish?" I reach over to her. My fingers, extended to her face, touch her exhaled breath. I'm about to pull back when I realize the exhalation isn't ending. Her chest is still rising and falling, but she's breathing out without breathing in.

"—shouldn't have chased you away."

THE DARK WE KNOW

On my phone, the screen is a slant of tiles and dark fabric. I can't see Mason's face anymore. He's holding his phone slack by his side. I tap to unmute. "Mason?"

I taste acid. Trish's breath trails over her, lengthwise down the bed, out over the floor. Toward the door, where there's just the low sound of Mason's voice outside, a half second ahead of the relay on my phone.

I snatch the phone off the table and practically skid out the door. He's standing in the hallway, back turned. There's someone with him.

Around the edges of his body, I see white skirts and a flash of curly hair. As he says, "I'm sorry, I'm so sorry," I step to my left and see Wren.

The sight of her here, in person, knocks my breath out of me. She looks just like I remember; sixteen going on seventeen, with butterflies clipped to her curls, a white dress, muddy sneakers, and a smile that lights me up. Mason managed to call her? Here? Why didn't he wait for me?

"Wren," I get out thickly. Then I realize I can see her, and I shouldn't be able to see her without touching Mason. I stumble. She smiles and reaches into his pocket, draws out the piece of sheet music folded there. All those faces, plucked from the Angel's gallery. We never thought to guess if it could manifest with just one.

"Mason, that's not—"

He turns around, eyes shining. Behind him, Wren lifts onto her toes like a ballerina and hooks her chin over his shoulder, nestling her head in the crook of his neck. With one hand, she strokes his cheek gently. With the other, even as I lunge toward him, she puts a pipe to her lips and blows.

For the first time I can remember, my mind goes still. I hadn't noticed how much stormed inside me until everything goes light and silent beneath the music. *Oh*, I think, *is this how other people live?*

Seconds slow to eternity, and Wren is no longer Wren. She's Zach instead, arms around Mason, mouth pressed to the hollow of his jaw. I feel hot and cold, a strange dark shape fluttering before my eyes. Then the song turns into gurgling water, and I'm in our house's kitchen.

The tap is running into the sink, rapidly filling it. The oven is on, although there's nothing inside. The window is open. Outside is night. Where the table should be is instead a pit of earth. Somewhere in the far distance I can feel my feet moving on the ground, but the sensation slips away as quickly as it came.

A voice I somehow know gasps, *Save her.*

Then the knob turns and my father walks in the door.

PEOPLE USED TO COMMENT how much I look like my father. Now it's like seeing myself warp. I'm frozen as he stops next to me around the pit of earth. "Go on," he says. "Haven't you always wanted to know what's under this house? Dig, then."

I shake my head. I don't want whatever's in there. He grips my arm, twists it behind me until a hiss escapes my mouth and my knees buckle into the soil. *"Dig."* The pit shouldn't be here. The floorboards just disintegrate into rich earth. Even as I stare at it, it seems to shift, something moving under its surface.

A rat's nose pops out. It wriggles onto the topsoil and scampers toward me. Dad makes an annoyed sound at the back of his throat that makes my nerves spark. His shadow falls over me. "Did you not hear me?"

In a trance, I dig. As my hands move through soil, I dislodge more and more of the rats. They burst through the gaps my hands are creating, running over my knees. Where are they coming from? Are they ever going to stop? They're coming for me, me, me, twisting in the dip between my knees, rubbing against my ankles, climbing over one another. I move soil faster and faster, reaching deeper and deeper. Every time I look at Dad he shakes his head. *Not yet.*

My fingers hit something solid. There's a weathered root at the bottom. The skin is leathery, but it looks like a face. My face. Only where my mouth should be, a baby pink rat crawls out and grows fur.

This is what lies beneath the house. Me. And around me, rotten, are other buried figures: Wren, Zach, Trish, Paige, Otto, Mom, Matthew. I couldn't step in. I couldn't move. I let it go on and on. I chose myself instead. I abandoned them again and again. Selfish. Uncaring. Inconsequential. Invisible. "You did this to yourself," Dad says. "Aren't you tired? Aren't you sick of it? Aren't you lonely? Aren't you sick of yourself?" *Yes, yes, yes, yes, stop, please, stop.* But he never stopped. "You tell yourself you push people away because you fear losing them. The truth is you're just saving them the time of trying to love you. You're pathetic. You're alone. You're *just like me.*"

Over his shoulder, a long, gray arm comes through the window, beckoning for me to take it. It's familiar. It's here to take me away from him. I reach for it.

A hinge creaks. Over by the sink, which has overflowed, one of the cabinet doors swings open and two kids peek out. They're squeezed inside with the pots, water from the sink streaming in front of them. A girl and a boy, somehow familiar, too.

The girl catches my eye and holds up something that ripples between the water. A wedding ring. She flicks it through the air. It enters the back of his head and drops neatly from his forehead onto the soil, red specks clinging to it.

As he collapses, the hand in the window slowly closes into a fist.

A second hand comes through, hooks slender fingers onto the sill, and starts pushing the window upward.

The kids in the cabinet are gesturing urgently now, mouthing words I can't hear and don't understand, but I know suddenly that I want to listen to them and not to the thing coming through the window. As a gray head slides under the sill, I launch myself across the kitchen toward them. The girl reaches out for me— *Wren*—and our hands touch.

Dreams split around me and I fall right through them. Zach swinging off a tree branch. Zach on the Ridge, clutching Mason's collar. Zach saying, *Hi, Isa.* Zach saying, *I think I love him*, and in this dream I tell him, *I know*, because I did, in some deep corner. I saw the way he looked at Mason and I recognized a part of myself I wasn't ready to recognize, so I just chose not to see it.

I fall further and everything is Wren like I'm fifteen again: Wren working out a song, Wren cutting out paper tiaras, Wren playing with Danny and the kids because she's always wanted her own family; and I wish I knew how to dream like her and not be afraid of messing it all up. Instead I dream of Wren breaking the glass baubles her mother hung on their Christmas tree, cutting open her palm and smearing the blood across her face, saying, *Don't you only want the pretty parts of me?* She says, *After he died I looked for you, and you wouldn't look back.*

Somewhere above an angel slides through the kitchen window and turns into Dad but they can't find me in these crumbling dreams of my friends, no one can. Flashes of stone and little feet and darkness cut through the images as I'm pulled deeper and deeper. Then the flashes grow longer, and the darkness solidifies, and I'm in a stretching dark tunnel that smells like deep earth. A hazy light drifts from an unseen source, enough to illuminate the bodies tucked into the walls.

23

"ISA," WREN SAYS, AND I WHIRL AROUND. SHE'S not there, but her voice hangs in the air.

"*Isa*," Zach's voice comes next, and then I see them both carved into the wall.

They're folded neatly into it, hands folded over their chests in the exact same way. Their proportions are perfect, the detail exquisite. They don't have faces; they've been sanded away, or just never bothered to be replicated, and the longer I look the less I know why I recognized them.

I feel like I'm supposed to remember something important, something urgent about how I got here. I remember Zach and Wren dragging me downward, away from Dad and the thing coming through the window. Falling through layers of dreams. Pulled like a beacon toward them.

I've been here before. The memory comes back: slipping beyond the stream of Enoch Kane's brushes with the Angel, into a tunnel where the Angel found me. This is where it keeps its children. I've somehow fallen back here. Into earth so deep it's removed from laws and time.

There's movement in the corner of my eye. I whirl around and find Otto's upper body dangling from the ceiling, pale arms covered with dirt. "Jesus—*fuck*—" Even as I stumble away, though, he flops right through the hole and lands with a hard thump on the floor, where he miraculously stirs. "Otto?"

But he doesn't hear me. Instead, he wanders to a blank space in the wall and presses an ear to it, scratching with one fingernail. "Paige?" he murmurs. "Show me where you are." Then, somehow, the wall in front of him crumbles into a hole. He falls in, and it seals him up.

I'm being messed with by another illusion. But strangely I think I can still hear him: a light skritching just behind the wall, starting to move down the tunnel. Some instinct tugs at me to go after it. I glance back at Zach and Wren's carvings, and then I notice something. In the time between first seeing them and Otto cracking the wall, their hands have changed. Instead of curled fists, both of them point a single finger in Otto's fading direction.

"Damn," I whisper, and follow.

The ground curves steeply downward, flush with gradients of shadow. Space collapses and expands between carvings that become increasingly unrecognizable as their features are stolen away. Somehow, I begin to find them sadder than anything. I pass one figure and suddenly I hear, right from it, *Isadora*. Then, from my other side, higher and more girlish, *Isadora*.

As I go deeper, still following the scampering behind the wall, they continue calling to me. Unlike the first time, where the Angel's voice seemed to radiate from every corner, these pipe up distinctly from the carvings I pass. They linger in the air after me, though, echoes blending into what sounds much more like the song. Oh, I think. They *are* the song. Their voices, layer after layer. Woven into a weapon by their keeper. Except I can tell them apart.

Don't call for me, I think. *Tell me who you are.*

There's a pause, in which I realize I've almost lost Otto's footsteps and have to pick up the pace to catch him skittering right along a junction. Then the silhouette that's tucked into the bend says, *Luke Lawton*. His voice is scratchy, as though underused. Farther down, someone else says, *Melisandra Ruben*. And then: *Lucy May Brandenburg*. And then, more clearly than any of the others: *Paige Anna Vandersteen*.

The light flickers. When it solidifies again, Otto is standing in front of Paige's carving. Her tilted face and Otto's are exactly the same height, eye to shut stone eye. Beside her, though, there's another human shape outlined in the rock. Light lines scored in the surface in preparation for the chisel strike. Like the Angel has prepared for someone else.

As though hearing me, Otto reaches for it. "Waiting for me?" he murmurs. I see then, immediately, that the outline is exactly his. Am I traced out into these tunnels somewhere too? How many of us does the Angel study, gliding from one window to another? How many of us has it prepared for?

With a feral scream, Otto smashes his outline's face. His knuckles crack and bleed over his wrist. The wall remains blank and untouched . . . but then something in the stone rumbles, like it's awakening. He pants. Then with another cry, he slams the side of his fist into his outline's heart.

The stone floor upends itself. I trip, landing on my back, and scream as the tunnel crashes down on me, pinning me under.

When the dust clears, I realize I'm not alone. Five faces stare at me from the rubble. My stifled second scream is quickly swallowed by the realization that it's not rubble at all that's surrounding me. I can still twitch, squirm a little to get a better look. No, the rock around me isn't broken pieces from the tunnel, like I thought, but a jagged single mass.

Which means these five . . . are the kids who died in the collapse. The original heart of the Angel. For some reason, unlike the carvings outside, their faces are perfectly preserved, just twisted. As though despite the landslide fusing them together, the original kids are still there in the Angel somewhere, nestled in its core.

"Tell me your names," I whisper.

They simply bear down, mouths wide, arms tangled in one another. It feels like they're tightening around me. I can't move. I can't breathe. "Help," I croak. I can feel my chest tightening, about to start gasping for air. I can't panic. This isn't real. Is it? Deep breaths. *Deep breaths.* More skritches overhead, and deliriously, I swivel my head toward them. Rats, or Otto, I don't know. "Help! Please!"

The scampering fades away, and no one comes. I clench my fists, squeeze my eyes, and focus on the only thing I can: their faces. Just like a still life drawing, I think. I feel insane, but my mind is already clicking neatly into its automatic track, pushing away the urge to scream and heave and zeroing in on the lines and contours.

The more I study them, the more my racing pulse calms. They are, in fact, just kids, with crooked teeth and the ghost of a dimple and uneven bangs plastered to their foreheads. Kids that killed my friends; kids that, unknown to them when they entered the mine that morning, would become a monster unrecognizable to themselves. This place and all those carvings I passed are still a gallery of its crimes. But seeing them up close like this, I feel like

I know better the thing they've become. Which means it can't scare me quite as much. There's power in being able to name something, I think, but sometimes all you need to do is see it. To know it's there. And here the Angel's bodies are, still buried at the heart of it. I lock on to one of the boys, the one with the dimple. I don't know how I know it's him, but his name slips onto my tongue. "Stanley."

As the second syllable leaves my mouth, there's a crack. Dirt pours over me as light opens up above. A sliver of Wren's face, and then Zach's lean strong arm reaching down, grabbing my hand, and yanking me back up into the tunnels.

"Run," Wren says. A root bursts from the corner of her lip as her skin goes gray. *"Run!"*

Zach snatches my hand. His skin is already going cold. But we tear down the tunnel, the outstretched hands of the statues now grabbing at us. Something's awakening. The tunnel thins and curves like a rib, veers sharply, and curves again. He's too fast and I almost can't keep up. He never loosens his grip, hauling me to my feet again and again as I stumble. The roof cracks and collapses. A wind fills the tunnel, shrieking as we dash through it, against it, despite it.

Then the walls fall away and bristling spires erupt from the ground, trees piercing the now-open air. A forest. I recognize this place, don't I?

Zach twists around and pulls me into a crushing hug. "The sound of the sky," he whispers.

WHEN I OPEN MY EYES, I'm curled up on the soil, gasping through the tears that have suddenly burst free. I can still feel the phantom weight of his arms around me. I can almost feel his chin resting on the top of my head. But he's gone.

Evening is falling fast. I sit up and realize I'm in the middle of the forest. Ahead, the lip of the quarry bisects the horizon.

Oh shit. Oh shit oh shit oh shit. Zach is dead. Wren is dead. Dad is dead. The Angel played a song and sent me here. At the heart of the forest, in the mouth of Slater. Where just yesterday, we turned up bodies upon bodies.

Mason.

Save her, he said. Somehow Wren and Zach broke through to me, when they never should have been able to. But if they were with me, then who was with him?

I don't see him anywhere around me. He might have been faster than me. I hurtle to the edge of the quarry and before I can stop myself, I look down. My legs nearly give way with relief when I see nothing there.

But then where is he?

Slater is small but not small enough. Now it spirals and spirals. Too many roads, too many doorways, too many cliffs, too many buildings, too many trees, too wide a river to reach him anywhere. Panic threatens to overtake me. Not again. I can't be too late again.

A hum stirs the air, along with the dry leaves and a voice in my head that sounds like both the Angel's and the chief's all at once.

Please state your name for the record.

To my right, Mason emerges from the trees. In my mind, I hear his reply.

Mason Kane.

I shout his name, and when he doesn't respond, tackle him to the ground. We hit the hard earth and roll, pain shooting through my body. He's taller and stronger, but I'm fighting harder. When I've locked him tight, he stares at me, shadows in his eyes. I can't tell if he's lucid or not.

What was your relationship to Wren Carver?

She's my girlfriend.

"It's all my fault," he says, and the worst thing is that he seems to know what he's saying. His heartbeat pulses through his ribs, slow, sinking, resolute. The interrogation continues, whether in his head or in the currents around us, I don't know.

Did you know that Wren was pregnant?

"It's not your fault," I say out loud, struggling to keep the two strands apart. "You know it's not."

No.

"I turned them away when they needed me the most."

To your knowledge, were you the father?

I suppose I would have to be.

These messages were found on her phone, on an anonymous account.

"This isn't you talking, Mason. This is the Angel. Wake up. *Wake up.*" I look around desperately, as though Wren and Zach will appear and help me drag him off the edge. But they're not here. We're alone. And if he dies, I'll be the only one left.

I hold tighter, and I think he's still talking, but the sounds here and the sounds in my head are all blurring together.

Did you write these messages?

"Listen to me."

Did you tell her these things?

"There's nothing you could've done."

"I've never paid any consequence." His voice, not his voice at all, makes my muscles lock. Far away and right here, the chief

267

asks, *Aloud for the record. Did you write all this?* "My existence has only left bodies in my wake. Everyone in this town despises me." *Yes, I did,* comes the reply. "This is all my life will ever be. Why stay? Why not atone at last?" My eyes are inches from his lips—*All right. And did you kill her?*—and so I see them when they stretch, when they curve, when they fix into a smile. *Did you kill her?*

"I can go to them now. I can make it up to them. Who'll care? Teddy will bury me, and they'll only thank God. See, the path is so easy."

Did you kill her?

I'm so fixated on his smile, I don't see him move. His knee slams into my stomach. As I jerk away, Mason heaves himself to his feet and leaps off the edge of the quarry.

24

"NO!"

I grab at Mason's arm, but his weight carries us forward and I slam into the ground as he goes over the cliff. My arm jerks and blazing pain explodes across my chest. I clamp a hand around his forearm, the other tangled in his sweater. In the haze of shock and pain I think, *Thank God he's not Zach, I would never have been able to hold on to Zach*, and then I'm almost laughing through the tears because Mason is dangling over the edge of the cliff I once tried to jump off and I'm making *jokes*, but he's *So. Fucking. Heavy.*

"Let me go." He smiles faintly, and I almost drop him in revulsion. But the smile is less possessed than tired. There's a drifting haze over his eyes. "Let me go, Isa."

"No. *I'll* care, you asshole! The Angel is trying to tell you death is a better option than fighting it, but when the fuck have you ever done what anyone wants?" The gravel rakes through my ribs into my lungs, every breath like inhaling blood. "This isn't how you make things right! You fucked up! So did I! Life fucked us up! Zach and Wren didn't get a chance to find out what might have been. You gonna let it take that from you too? You think they're going to be happy to see you? *You* want to let the Angel win? Then let go! I fucking dare you!" My throat is scraped raw. I don't know how I'm holding on, but he's not responding anymore, his sleeve is slipping beneath my hand, and as much as I refuse to lose to the Angel, I refuse even more to lose to Mason Kane.

"Listen—*listen to me*—it is going to screw me up forever that I spent so long running that I forgot how to stop. There are so many things I didn't tell you guys because I knew you'd care too much and that scared me more than anything. I hated that suddenly we flipped a switch and Wren loved you, and I couldn't stand to be around you, and Zach couldn't stand not being around you, and it was all so pathetic and I thought love was fucking rotten. All it had ever done was ruin people's lives and mess good things up and let people do horrible things with an excuse. I thought, what a stupid thing for us to die for. So I left or I was gonna die too.

"But you stayed, and I see them every time I look at you. You make my dreams full of them. You refused to let this go, you chose the fucking harder path like you always do, and I started remembering that before being stupid fifteen-year-olds who didn't know what to do with big feelings, we were stupid ten-year-olds, and it was so easy, and I loved all of you like I didn't even have to think about what love meant, or whether I could ever have it. I wasn't afraid of myself. I think we were born knowing what love is, and I can find my way back to it. But not if you fucking let go. You asked me to come back, so I did. And now I am asking you to stay, for a while longer, or I will drag your spirit back from wherever the hell it goes anyway. I am not letting you have peace like this, Mason, *I refuse to lose you too!*"

His eyes snap wide. He's heard me. *Really* heard me. It's only the barest shift, but it's enough.

He gasps. His feet scrabble at the cliff. I pull and he climbs, and in a great, straining tangle of limbs, he lurches over the edge and we both collapse to the ground, lying at the edge of the earth, staring up at the sky.

ROBERT MAYER had a little pedal boat he'd let kids take out onto the pond.

The last time we did, we decided to rig a pirate ship. The bedsheet sail had rabbits on it and the crossbones we drew with a marker were uneven, but there had never been a more terrifying vessel than the *Jolly Slater*. We mapped our travels on Mason's journal and battled enemies with sticks. We collected our treasure—plastic rings, Zach's hat, Wren's butterfly clips—feasted on sandwiches and broken-up chocolate, and toasted to the fortune of the *Jolly Slater* with apple juice. It was victory, until it started to rain.

One moment it was mild and gray-blue, and the next the sky tore and wind ripped away our sail. As rain pooled at our feet and we tried to row against the choppy waves, we hit a hidden rock and the boat sprung a leak. Zach and I couldn't swim, and Mason and Wren didn't want to leave us behind. We clung to one another screaming for help as the boat sank lower and lower, unable to fight the storm.

Then Robert Mayer's motorboat puttered through the water and the grumpy old man himself pulled us one by one into the hull. By the time we were bundled up, it all became the most exciting time we'd ever had—nearly drowning in a storm! We were giggling by the time the Carvers and Tais came. Nothing could stop us, not even their lecture, or Mrs. Carver's remarks that Wren and I were getting too grown to be going around in wet shirts.

Zach and Wren should have made it here with us. Hell or high water like we promised as kids. But it turns out sometimes hell is too real and there are things worse than high water that you can't sail a boat through. And that's not *fair*. They should have had the chance to fight through it. Instead there's only Mason and me, and we hold on to each other like the ship is going down again.

Maybe we don't deserve to be saviors. But we deserve to be saved.

I TELL HIM about art school. The ground is cold and the dampness seeps into my back, but I tell him about the projects I did, the food I got to try, the worst tattoos people have gotten, the time someone painted all the windows of our dorm a different color of the rainbow overnight, the time someone's bird got loose and pooped all over the easels. The funny, stupid, little things that seem inconsequential until you're lying in the forest in the dark with your body wrung out. Suddenly the stupid things are candles in the dark.

In return, he tells me about the first time he tried to do a séance by himself. How he'd always seen ghosts as the things trapping his mother here, but when he summoned a belligerent great-aunt who proceeded to lay into him about her flower garden, he found they were still just human. He tells me about grave-yard shifts, talking to ghosts who just wanted a bit of company: the old man who missed his morning coffee, the woman who wondered how her cat was doing, the miner who moaned about missing the lottery drawing the week he died.

As the sky starts to lighten, we tell each other about the past two years, finding the good parts. It hurts every time there's a silence while we dig for more—Mason's end has particularly long stretches of quiet while he thinks. Darkness hangs over it all, the only true constant, and somehow it takes effort to remember that that wasn't all there was. It doesn't seem fair, that grief is so everlasting, while the happiness seems to fade as the moment does.

"We used to dream about being pirates, and knights, and adventurers. Now we dream about dead friends and mistakes and the things the world is missing rather than the ways the world could be." I exhale, watch my breath cloud. "I think we should get to dream of beautiful things again, you know?"

"One can hope."

"We should. They're not always easy to find, especially in a place like this, but you do find them." I mean the stories, but I happen to glance at him. He must see my head move in the corner of his eye, because he turns, and for a suspended moment I understand why, when we were all just children, we decided to follow him anywhere.

His mouth curves. "Are you implying something, Isadora Chang?"

"You? No. You're the easiest person in the world to find."

"I'm glad your dad died," he says.

"Well, me too—"

"If it brought you back here. Even if just for a little while."

"Don't count on me staying, Mr. Vandersteen."

"God," he says, like he's just remembering. "I reject that. I don't want to be defined by a name that doesn't care about me and that's hurt so many people, just because we happen to share a bloodline. I'm my mother's son, and there are other people I care more to define myself by."

A beat, the kind that lingers.

But then he holds up his hand between us, inviting me to take it, and the space fills. I grab his hand with the arm that doesn't hurt. He pulls me to my feet. His gaze flicks over me and I can't tell what he's thinking, only that my palm fits into his like a homecoming.

It occurs to me that if we both stay in this town, we would be each other's easiest option. Maybe it's not even entirely out of the cards. But I've spent too long with options that bury parts of themselves to leave the surface smooth. I hate that genuine feelings could ever feel like surrender. Like we'd given in, become proper, when all we would've done is chosen one of various paths.

I don't feel powerful. I don't know how to fight the Angel and save everyone, or even save ourselves. But in this moment, I think maybe just being here, together, is the most revolutionary thing of all.

I let go, or he lets go, and it's only then that sense jolts back into me. "*Trish.*"

25

IT TAKES US ALMOST AN HOUR TO GET BACK
on foot and I spend the whole way imagining different ways Trish
could be dead right now. But when I burst into her room, Trish is
still in bed, asleep. Only now, Mom is sitting beside the bed, and
Pastor Charles is standing beside her. Mom jumps up as we enter.
We look like we got dragged through the dirt and I expect disap-
proval, more accusations, questions about what happened, but
instead her expression darkens. Oh shit, I realize. She knows. She
gives the tiniest, sharp shake of her head.

"Pastor," Mason says behind me. I step on his foot before he
can say anything else.

"Isa," the pastor greets me, blatantly ignoring him. "The doctor called me because Trisha was calling to an angel in her sleep."

Shit. Behind him, Mom's eyes widen slightly. No, I got it the
first time. She's asking me not to tell him the truth. As if I'd be
that naive.

"Do you remember what I said about the Angel, that it will
return?" the pastor continues.

I exchange a glance with Mason. "Is that what you think Trish
is talking about?"

"It has always been watching. Those who are willing will heed its warnings." Mom's eyes darken further and I know Mason was right about who made her paranoid. "But now the Angel is returning. We are all due a lesson. We've gone too far astray and the earth does not bless us the way it once did. What is coming may not be easy, but it will be necessary. Think about your actions now, Isa. There is still time to come back."

I've never seen the pastor like this, and it unsettles me as much as the mention of the Angel does. He doesn't look like he's been sleeping; sallow-skinned with a hungry look, too narrow yet eager, anticipating.

"No invitation for me?" Mason remarks. "I can speed it up for you, since that's clearly what you're implying. I'll cut my wrists, stab myself in the side, whatever—"

"I'm not coming back," I interrupt. "I don't know anything about the Angel," I lie, "but I'm also not giving myself for this town to relive its glory days. I don't want to be a martyr. I don't want to be what you want me to be either."

Now the pastor looks at Mason, and it's clear who he thinks is at fault. It pisses me off that he thinks I must be the victim here, but he crosses the line when he says to Mom, "You should have kept her home."

"How many children would be an acceptable sacrifice for you this time, Pastor?" I snap. "Fifty? A hundred? All of us? How many of us do you think need to be purged away?"

Somewhere in his whittled gaze there's a haunting. Does he dream of omens when he sleeps too? Does he dream of revelation?

"They can still be saved," he says, "if you would just listen."

"And if we don't, then you told us so?" I glance past him, through the window, outside somewhere. "If the Angel's here, let it come."

He mutters a prayer, and abandons us, thankfully. And now, with him gone, I turn my focus onto Mom.

"You've heard the Angel. You went to the pastor for help, and he said you just needed to be better. What happened when you heard it, Mom? And *don't* lie to me this time." I point at Trish, prepared to make a big statement, but instead my voice cracks. "Please."

Her face blanks. "I heard it after I got pregnant, and your father had to marry me."

It's the way she says *got pregnant, had to marry*; the way that, Angel or not, having us as good as ended her life. Didn't I wonder why I was able to sense the Angel even before I survived it? Why the rats and her obsession with the windows had always been there? The moment I realized I was being watched, didn't I want to board up the grotto too? We know it's passed down. From Enoch Kane to Sharlene to Mason, a family that sees the ghosts for what they are. And now from my mother to me. "But how did you snap out of it?"

She's quiet for a moment. "The first few months after the birth were hard," she says finally. "One day I was so tired, and I hear a voice telling me to follow it and it will take away my sadness . . . it was so easy, but then your sister cried so loudly that I wake up and realize I'm holding the knife."

"Why didn't you say anything?"

"They would call me crazy, or bad mother. Why don't you say anything?"

"It's not my fault I can't tell you things, *Mom*." But the anger I've always kept for her has suddenly been dulled. Maybe I'm still soft from having lain there on the ground with Mason talking about good memories, letting our own voices fall over us. I'm glad I came back to town and had a friend; I'm glad that even though we've lost them now, we had Zach and Wren once too. Meanwhile, Mom's never really had friends, that I know of. She was friendly with some of the other mothers, but she mostly kept to herself. When she came here and had Trish, had to figure out how to make a life not just in the town but this country, she would've been younger than I am now.

Fuck. Learning to sympathize with my mother will definitely, completely make the rest of my life more complicated. But maybe she deserves that just like my friends and I do. To be seen as a whole person instead of one story, one label, one past wrong.

The whole day has been too much all at once. Unfortunately, Mom's not done—she squeezes her fists and whispers, "I killed him."

My mind goes blank, convinced I heard wrong. "You what?"

"I bought a gun. But I was too afraid to use it. In the end he was making dough, and I switched it with almond flour. I only find him later, when they already found him first." A shadow of a memory flicks across Mom's face. It turns her alien and haunted and—

Vicious.

All this time I thought she was terrified by the state of the body. No—she just didn't want to be caught for killing him. The scene paints itself in my head, and I wonder how long she watched the rats eat my father's corpse. When did she decide that it was enough, that she should call the doctor, sobbing like a panicked widow? Before they chewed off his ring finger, or after? When did she call Trish, who clearly knew—*I would've if she hadn't*, Trish had said, without me understanding. Mom and Trish. Trish and Mom. And now, finally, me.

She leans forward and I almost don't recognize her with this hardness in her eyes. "I didn't do the wrong thing. Because the Angel never come back for me. Instead it comes for you and Trisha."

"More than once," I say tersely, not knowing how to handle where this conversation is going.

"Yes," she says fiercely. "And then I know that when they say it is to punish, they are wrong. Or otherwise I will not accept they are right. Because there is nothing my daughters do that you should die for. Nothing, *nothing* that you should hurt yourself for. I am the one who give it to you. If the Angel only want you, then it is wrong too."

When she tries to touch my arm I let her pull me into a stiff, awkward hug with arms that don't know how to position themselves around my teenage body, and then even though I swore I'd run out of tears, I'm choking into her shoulder. The smell of her hair, the way I'm a couple inches taller than her in these boots, feels like bleeding and bleeding. But it's a good thing. For the longest time, I thought that nothing can hurt you if it can't get to you. But the things that hurt leave their bruises. Healing is stopping the knife, but it's also tending to the wound. It's letting the disinfectant sting. It's wrapping it in gauze, even if it shows you're fragile. It's giving it time and care until it closes over itself.

"Stop it—stop it—God—I'm glad he's dead—" Through thick gulps, I bat her away, weakly and then harder. "I—we're trying to stop it, okay, we have a plan."

She finally pulls back from me, gripping my wrists. "The Angel?"

"Yes, it can be hurt. We're going to summon it and then destroy it."

There's that unfamiliar look in her eyes again, the one I can only imagine she was wearing when she was watching the rats. "You need help?"

Before I can reply, a loud voice bursts from outside.

"What room are they in? Do you want to call my parents? No, I didn't think so—it's *Mr.* Vandersteen—we *own* this estate—"

In the hallway, Mason jolts aside to let Otto Vandersteen march through the door, followed closely by Sharlene. Otto is feverish and the sleeves of his oversized sweater are muddied. His hands, balled up, are covered in dirt. "What did you do?" he demands.

"His parents called me," Sharlene explains hurriedly. "He was in some kind of trance, trying to dig out the garden with his bare hands, saying his sister was under there. I snapped him out of it, and he—"

"The Angel had me, pretty strong," Otto interrupts. I notice that the dirt on his hands isn't just dirt. His nails are cracked, stained red. "Stronger than I've felt in a while, and it caught me at a bad time." He blinks away again. "It's angry, really angry. There was no pity in it this time; it was just trying to claim me, like I owed it. I was fighting it, but it was like my brain getting smothered, and I thought I heard . . . Paige."

Mason grimaces. "You might have. We saw Wren just outside; I think the Angel can borrow the form of the kids it's taken. It's starting to lose patience, so it's manifesting here so it can use more power against the few of us who are aware of it."

280

"It's only appearing for moments at a time, though," I point out.

"That's long enough to stop it if we're ready, but that means once we call it, we'll need to draw its focus and keep it around long enough to destroy it. I think we might need your help to pull us out," he adds reluctantly to his mother.

"Of course," Sharlene says, surprised. "Here?"

"The cemetery. The old quarry foreman said the kids from the collapse were buried on the far lot. That should be a good enough anchor to pull the Angel to us."

"Mom—" I turn to her, the place we left off still hanging, not sure how to pick it back up. "You want to help? Keep Trish safe."

She doesn't even balk at this. "What about you?"

"Mom," Trish murmurs. We all jerk around, but she's not entirely conscious. She mumbles through stiff lips: "The Angel can be hurt." Lips pinching and opening soundlessly. Then: "I found your box."

Mom stares at her. "Yes," she murmurs. Then, louder, to me, "Yes. Safe. And you stay safe too."

"I will." I wonder what afterimage the Angel left on her. Why I've never felt it in her before. I got the walls from her too, but they're breaking now. I've always been afraid of my instincts—the anger, the attractions, the hauntings—and of giving in to them. But how did Mason describe it—a prism? I think it's starting to feel more like that, these days. I'm not some wild thing that needs strict lines to be presentable. I'm taking an undercurrent of the world and opening it up into something clearer. I'm a conduit, not an omen.

"You *destroy* it."

"I will."

"Shall we?" Otto says. I almost forgot he was there. He's studying something in the grain of the wall. The Red House has stood since before the Angel; it will stand after. I remember what he said about the Purple House keeping its children, and wonder if this manor is the same. Another pair of Vandersteen twins. He looks around at us. "It's light out. Dreams are ending."

26

IN THE PREDAWN, THE CEMETERY IS A FIELD
of long shadows. The wind whistles through the headstones, a
different pitch in every direction. It feels impossible that it was
only a few days ago that we were last here for Dad's funeral. Now
every statue makes my nerves flare, expecting any one of them to
turn into the real thing when we're not looking. Sharlene trails
behind. Otto is restless beside us, playing with the stone crucifix
at his throat. He washed the grime off, but his nails are still
cracked and encased with dried blood. One of the angel statues
clasps its hands over its skirts. It casts a dim shadow toward us,
even with the overcast sky. The rock irises have found it.
Desiccated creepers thread outward from its uneven eyes, trail
down like tears.

The wash of sky flickers a memory. "The sound of the sky," I
say to Mason. "Something Zach said. Does that mean anything
to you?"

He frowns. "It does, actually. On those hiking trips with his
dad and brother, he always said that the best time they ever spent
together was just sitting around the fire playing his dad's

harmonica. He said there was this lookout you could actually hear birds, in the distance, and his dad could name them all. He said he never saw the birds, but that was what he thought the sky sounded like. Why?"

It's maybe the softest story I've ever heard about Zach and his dad. It makes me think on the flip side of Wren running into abandoned houses, of Wren squeezing glass shards.

We first make a stop at the groundskeeper's, where Mason and I grab shovels as possible weapons. I feel stupid holding mine, but it's got a sharp edge and good weight, and I've seen the Angel lose to a fire poker. Otto turns a third one down, but makes us break into the church one more time, where he goes straight to the back and finds an old rifle hanging in the store. "You know how to use a rifle?" I ask incredulously, as he roots for bullets in a drawer.

He blinks at me. "My ancestors are old rich Europeans."

"There isn't even anything to hunt around here."

He peers through the scope. "Well, now there is."

Even with a direction from the foreman, we find the unmarked grave faster than we should. Gut instinct pulls me through the oldest parts of the cemetery, coming to a clearing behind withered bushes that looks like it's been abandoned for a long time. In a few months, it would've been covered by grass, but for once winter does us a favor: the bare ground reveals a single plaque, inscribed with a verse:

Psalm 69:15
Let not the waterflood overwhelm me,
Neither let the deep swallow me up;
And let not the pit shut its mouth upon me.

"Is that being in denial, or being morbid?" Otto muses.

"It's like saying no homo," I suggest.

"'No mine collapse.'" Mason motions for us to gather around the plot. He and Otto settle on either side of me, with Sharlene just behind. Otto lays the rifle across his lap.

My spine prickles looking at the pressed earth, knowing what lies beneath it. Boys who were crushed and, somewhere in three nights of flood, became a reaper. They were even younger than Wren and Zach. I understand exactly how that kind of loss and anger can demand extremes for coping. But understanding doesn't mean forgiveness, or permission. Understanding doesn't mean it gets to hurt everyone else. My forgiveness stopped exactly when it decided to use its death as an excuse to kill me and my friends.

"Ready?" Mason asks. I nod. Sharlene won't officially be a part of the séance, since she's pulling us out. But we'll draw on her energy, whatever sliver of the Angel's shadow still infuses us, either by inheriting it or surviving it. She turned down a weapon too; I guess she has her own ways. She might have to, since she's also our watcher if something goes wrong.

Mason lays his hand on the grave, just below the cairn. I put mine over his, and Otto puts his hand over ours. Once more, Mason pulls out the chime. "Stanley McLean," he says, still the only name we have. Even as he gives the first ring and we echo it, I can feel the chime's power, already starting to draw currents toward it like a line of magnets.

I let the undercurrents vibrate into shape, directing them for the first time around an image of a boy. A dimple in his cheek, bristle brows. He's in a dirty shirt.

Ding. The air grows humid, whistling with an underground draft. My mind easily fills in the world around him: Maybe it's summer, and the quarry wasn't surrounded by a forest yet. It's the end of the work day. He's mopping his forehead, streaked with dust. Workers move behind him. A voice comes from out of frame. *Hey, Stan.* A friend, I think. Then I'm sure—not just a friend. One of the other boys.

Corey, Stan replies. *Rain's looking bad tonight.*

Pain flares in the back of my skull. Something snapped toward us, fearful and furious. I recognize the prickle of its attention now, less like a weight and more like static—hundreds of pinprick eyes clustered amidst the low hum of its hive. In one part of my mind, Stan's voice is still in the middle of breaking, still warm and tumbleweed. In the other, though, the Angel has noticed what we're doing—and it's noticed what we know.

It might not want to come, but we'll make it. The thread I have of it is strong enough to tug, pulling more and more of Stanley through: Grinding equipment, heavy dragging. Feet pattering across gravel. Buzz of lamps. Earth falling. Thunder. A hum coming through the debris, reaching for the children crying.

Every tendon in my body feels stretched out. The effort makes me feel raw and breathless, opening me up from the inside. Those we've known become parts of us, and they're not the haunting I've been trying to bury. They're just what's made me, and right now, it's a power. These threads of people stretching through space and time, living new lives in memory and in creation. We embed them, extend from them. And it's not something I should be afraid of. They will come through me from now to always. They are in everything I draw, every stroke I paint, every song I hear.

The Angel might know me, but I know it too, now. I know where it comes from. The Angel is the song, is the pieces of my friends it's claimed and taken; the Angel itself is a composite. It's made itself out of all these spirits, but that also means I have that many more places to pull it out from itself. "Stanley McLean," I whisper as a wind rises. "Wren Carver. Zachary Tai. Paige Vandersteen. Matthew Accetta."

I don't know if Mason and Otto are doubling my connections, but the trickle becomes a flood and the breeze turns into a roar. I pull on the threads it's stolen, as many as I can think to hold—not just Wren's warmth but her drive, her anger; not just Zach's strength but also his softness, the way he could make you laugh—and I find I can hold all of them and more; I am not suffocating under their memory, actually, I am infinite with space for them, and who they were, and who they wanted to be, and who they might have been. They're so solid I can close my fist around them and pull, and—

Someone's tugging at my coat sleeve. Almost gasping, ears drowned with noise, I turn to find Trish smiling at me, hair tangled. Behind her, Sharlene's slumped on the ground.

I jolt, but Trish doesn't let go, and my coat is yanked off my shoulder.

Mason catches her around the waist as she raises the bloody rock in her hand, and they both tumble to the ground.

"Otto!" I shout, struggling to keep Trish's flailing arms from hitting either of us in the face while the song continues to get louder. "*Not like that*," I yell, as he goes for the gun in obvious confusion.

"What am I supposed to do?" Otto yells back.

But then Sharlene pushes herself up on her elbows, dazed but conscious. Her attention snaps into focus when she realizes what's going on, and she rummages in her pockets as she runs over. "Where's your mother?" she exclaims.

"I don't know." That new panic threatens to take over, but Mom can fend for herself. "Can you keep Trish out of it?"

"Oh, sure." I can barely hear her. She dabs a cloth with a cloudy liquid from a bottle. "Sorry, Trisha." She clamps it over Trish's face. Instantly, Trish goes still. I almost fall over as she turns to deadweight.

"Why do you carry that around?" Mason demands, as I roll Trish over. Her eyes are glassy, but she's no longer looking murderous.

"Maybe if you spent more time letting me teach you, you'd know!" Sharlene takes Trish from me, and I grab the rock she'd been holding and throw it as far as I can. Sharlene is bleeding from the temple, but she seems more or less fine.

"Is that stuff legal? What's even in it?"

"Ask me later," Sharlene says, just as Otto, Mason, and I double over with the sound that slams into our heads. The song rises, too loud, too big, like a tunnel collapsing, like a storm front crashing down, like earth being shoveled into the pit, like water rushing over our heads. *Follow,* I think, *follow.*

"It's near." Mason gasps.

"No!" Otto and I say at the same time. Sharlene stares at us, completely unaffected, and I realize she can't hear it. The Angel only wants us. Otto squeezes his hands over his ears. "It's not coming here. It's pulling us toward it."

"To *where*?"

I just shake my head. The Angel is stronger than it's ever been, but I don't see it around us; I don't feel it around us, so why can I *hear* it like this?

Somehow, though, through the song comes sobbing.

On the path outside the cemetery, a boy is crawling past. His mouth moves soundlessly, but he keeps reaching forward, as though he's chasing someone. I match the words to his lips. *Wait for me.* He drags himself along, revealing one leg in a cast and then another. Tears streaming down his face. *Wait for me.*

Are we not the only ones hearing the song?

Mason grips my arm, pointing beyond the cemetery. The suffocating music in my head fades enough to let the final piece through: in the distance, the faint echo of a crowd. "I think we got its attention."

"Go," Sharlene says. She winces; maybe she isn't doing that well after all. When we don't move, she gestures harder. "Go! I'll take your sister and try to find your mother."

I only hesitate for a second longer, staring at Trish. It's enough, however, for a blur to dash past me. "Otto!" But he's too far ahead, and he's left the rifle behind. "Shit." Can't tell if he's possessed or just reckless. There's no point bringing it if it'll just slow us down. "Car?"

But we took Sharlene's, and she needs to move Trish. Mason comes to the same conclusion. "Run," he says. Sometimes to live is to run *towards*, and to fight for something, I think, and so I do.

We rush to the gates. The boy continues to crawl after us, still sobbing. I look over my shoulder to see Sharlene run out and pull him off the road. His kneecaps are bloody, and he flails before she knocks him out too.

I shake the sight from my head and turn back to the road, only to find Mason has disappeared.

"Mason?" A sick feeling rises in me, even as the song presses ever downward on the base of my skull. I swing around. Don't see him in the trees, or by the church. The wind whistles. The pressure in my ears builds and builds.

My heart skips. I feel something fracture—feel my guard slip—and darkness descends.

When the darkness lifts, the song soars. A girl catches me by the waist and swings me, laughing, into the arms of a tall boy, who hooks his arm into mine and pulls me into a march. Light and color expand: dozens of kids around me, moving so quickly forward that I'm forced to move with them. Half of them are wearing pajamas, no coat, no shoes. They're laughing, a blur of faces and voices.

"Stop," I say, but no one can hear me. I can barely hear myself; there's only the song in my head that sounds like the universe, and love, and the mountains, and myself. It's beautiful, so *beautiful*, and it makes my insides quiet, and—

I blink, and we're in the woods, still moving. The parade floods through the trees. Where are we going? How did we get here? How much time just passed? A girl's sleeve catches on a tree branch and tears. Somewhere below, one of the pale bare feet comes down on sharp bark and tears too, blood flowing as the heel lifts.

"Mason!" I manage. "Otto?"

Darkness presses closer, wanting me to just fall into it again, but I push back. My vision expands, sharpens. Yes, the woods. Where? I struggle to form my thoughts. I know this place. Know this path.

"Isa," Zach shouts, and without meaning to, I turn around.

This time, I punch through the numbness even as it descends, but I still lose time. When the sensation lifts again, we're in a completely different place. I'm almost running now, as the song strings through the firs and bursts underfoot. My legs ache. More kids are bleeding around me; the forest isn't friendly to dancers, but they dance anyway. Their mouths stretch like they're not used to such big grins and their eyes shine like lamps. My cheeks hurt. We are the creatures of the forest. We are the strange things in the dark. Limbs tangle, torn sleeves and red, scraped necks. We are little rats and fluttering moths, streaming back to where we came from, our home, our origin—

"*Isa*," Wren calls, but this time I'm ready for it. This time I don't listen, and I see as the trail breaks into a familiar road headed for a tunnel, headed down.

"Mason," I shout louder. "Otto!"

Ahead, blonde hair whips around. I catch Otto's eye before he vanishes again behind someone taller. I try and push toward him, but the people are all knotted. I can't fight the current. It pins me even as it pushes me along. How long have we been running? Surely parents must have noticed by now. Surely they must be coming after us. They have to come. The mouth of the tunnel emerges, the head of the parade already disappearing inside. The song amplifies in its throat, voices both dead and living rising and rising and rising.

"Isa!"

No, it's still a trick, I'll just lose myself again.

"*Isadora!*"

That's Mom.

I whirl around, slamming into the boy behind me. His shoulder catches me between the ribs and shoves me back into the crowd's momentum. Mom is running after me, car stalled behind her, a box outstretched. She's not going to catch up and I can't get to her through the clot of people surging into the tunnel—but then she throws it.

I snatch the box from the air and feel something rattle as I'm pushed inside. Her face is the last thing I see before the entrance seals, swallowing us in darkness with only one way forward.

we

I ASK AND YOU FOLLOW. I SHOW MY HAND
and you take it. This has been my purpose; this has been my offering. But you refuse to see what I offer. Instead you demand of me,
and spit in my grace, and so I will make you listen.

I have a mission. I am deliverance, and they will know gratitude. All of you, you say, all of you.

27

MY FEET KNOW THE WAY DOWN THIS PATH, even in the dark, but with all these people, the tunnel is suddenly alive. Echoes fill it, their speakers melting into one mass. I shout, but my voice is instantly swallowed. The tunnel seems longer than I remember, swelling as we flow through it, constricting again behind us. Are we still moving forward? Are we still moving at all? Where's the end? I keep hearing familiar voices. They seem to call my name from every direction. I fumble blindly with Mom's box, lose the lid to someone's swinging arm, close my hand around the shape of a revolver inside.

I bought a weapon, Mom said, *but I was too afraid to use it.*

It wouldn't be the first time someone's shot their husband, I think, but I press it flat against my chest, finger off the trigger, hugging it as tight as I dare so it doesn't get knocked away from me. Someone slams into my spine. Someone else tucks an elbow into mine and leans their head on my shoulder before slipping away. All the while the voices and the song, one and the same, sing my name and push us along. I stumble and stumble, not sure if I'm moving so I don't get crushed, or moving because I'm being told to.

Then light hazes the tops of heads, revealing Mason ahead of me. I shout his name, afraid it'll get lost in the echoes.

He whips around, locks eyes with me, and then we're all spat out into the light.

I stumble onto the Ridge, almost tripping at the sudden lack of someone to press against. "At the end!" Mason shouts. We push past the kids as they twirl into lines. Four a row, then three, then pairs, and then a trail of one by ones. At the far end, on the jutting rock where another twin once jumped into the channel, Paige Vandersteen stands playing a silver pipe. Otto takes her hand as, beside them, another girl steps lightly off the rock and into the water. I muffle a shriek.

"Why?" Otto is saying. "What were you thinking? What could I have done?" I know it's the Angel, borrowing Paige's form like it did Wren's, but even as I raise the gun, I can't bring myself to fire. She locks eyes with me, and one of the gray Vandersteen irises switches to blue. As it does, Danny Carver dances to the edge.

I'm watching Paige so closely I notice too late. I shout as he steps out and falls in violent slow motion. He's been so lonely, I think suddenly, he's been just as sad, and none of us really saw it. Then I swing back toward the Angel and pull the trigger.

The shot goes wide, but the ricochet splits the air and as the Angel jerks back, Mason sprints past me and dives into the water. All around me the children freeze, eyes going glassy over wretched smiles.

My hair whips as the falsely resurrected Paige Vandersteen lowers the pipe and turns, brushing Otto aside. The Angel's features jerk and bubble like a baby moving under the skin of a belly, and when it faces me again, it's not Paige any longer.

"Isadora," Zach says. "Hello."

· · ·

WE'RE HERE AGAIN. Me, him, the water rushing by.

But it's not him. It's not Zach. And this time, I'm holding the gun.

I force myself to look past the veneer. It still has Zach's face, Zach's body, but it doesn't stand the way he did, broad-shouldered but slightly hunched, like he couldn't quite take up the space he was meant to. Zach was always restless, and the Angel is simply still. It hums, like a swarm, with the ancient energy of something that does not obey our laws. And there's absolutely nothing of Zach in its eyes, which are his dark brown but lack the warmth, lack the feeling that they could make you laugh.

Those eyes flick toward Mason as he surfaces in the river, dragging Danny with him, and I know I need to keep the Angel's attention.

"Hey!" My heart is pounding, everything about this going against my better instincts, but I keep the gun pointed at its chest. This close, I could take it and it knows it. "Look at me," I rasp. Then, "*Look at me!*"

And when it does, with the exact tilt of Zach's head, my hands shake and I can't bring myself to shoot. Not when it's Zach, not when I'm the one person who might have been able to save him the first time around.

No. It's *not* Zach. Still, it regards me with his face. It's wearing his jacket. "The world is unkind to you," it says softly. It's Zach's voice, weighted and layered with sympathy and familiarity, maybe the kind we both wanted more of from each other when he was alive. Zach's voice if he wasn't holding anything back; if we were willing to really talk to each other. I miss him sounding like that. Did he ever sound like that? Or is my memory now just taking this version I prefer and replacing it?

Would that be so bad?

Despite myself, my own voice is drawn from me. "Yes."

"The world is unfair."

"Yes."

"You are a beautiful, shattered thing," he—it—goes on. "I can make you whole again, Isadora. That is the promise I was born again to fulfill. I have never wanted anything less. I have never wanted anything more."

The Angel's voice once reached the hollowest parts of me and filled them, showed me how I could be whole. In person, lips to ear, the Angel seeps into me and prizes me open, bares my soul and cradles it gently, tenderly. The Angel says, it is not your fault. It says, you do not have to choose to hurt. It says, I can take away that guilt. I know what it's doing now, but I still have to drag myself from the enchantment, and the effort contracts my ribs with a scream of pain.

"But maybe we want more."

"Fleeting things. Are you happy, Isadora? All the time? Tell me the world isn't worse than this town. I, too, see the wars. The systems break, the forests burn, the debts are never paid. They are everywhere, over and over. This world does not deserve its children." Something twitches in its face, the first time its façade has come loose. "Does not deserve us."

I glance toward Mason. He's kneeling over Danny, pumping his chest. Where did he learn that? It doesn't matter. The Angel and I are not an *us*. We are not the same. I focus on the way it says my name, the way a stranger would. Not the way Zach would have. It might know me better, but it has never loved me, not really. The two things aren't the same.

I focus on my fury: that it dares to claim to save and then uses their faces this way, puppets them for its own ends. Zach didn't die for this. It's not Zach. It's *not* Zach.

"No," I struggle out, "but you don't get to decide that. We deserve the chance to see the world get better. We deserve the chance to *make* the world better. To do better than was done to us."

"Lie and tell me they'd ever listen then." I almost recoil, because for just a moment, that *is* Zach. But the Angel can't keep it up. It falters, and when it speaks again, its voice is once more dusk and echoes. "Say history learns from its mistakes. Say the world is worth it."

"You don't have to fix the whole world for life to be worth living. You don't weigh your life against the world. You weigh it in seconds, minutes, moments that make it worth it. I claim the right to survive. I claim the right to get to the other side. I claim the right to exist on our own terms."

Its lip curls, but I'm looking at these kids around me, who have everything left to find, and I'm rambling now, hot and furious. "What makes it worth it? I woke up one day and saw the sun break over the city, and it was so big and gold at once. I looked in a mirror and recognized myself for the first time. I kissed a girl in a crowded room and everyone was dancing and I didn't feel afraid. I see the flowers bud in spring. I see the streets glitter after the rain. I know the world can be kind, that people can be kind, that it isn't something you just have to lose when you grow up." Mason tilts Danny's head back and presses air into his mouth.

The things that keep us living are so fragile and so small, but they can be everywhere. You find what you can, give what you can. "They deserve to know it's okay if all you are for now is alive," I say.

We deserve to dream of beautiful things again.

As if it hears my thoughts, and maybe it does, the Angel replies, lifting the pipe to its mouth, "Child, dreams are the biggest delusion the world ever sold you."

I think of a forever calm, where nothing hurts and nothing exists, where I am simply sunk in and erased. And then I think of the past two years, where everything hurts a lot of the time, but there are moments where nothing hurts at all, and those moments have stretched longer and longer. I want to finish things. I want to start things. There are things I want to try, places I want to go, people I want to make things up to. On bad days I might take a forever calm, but on the good days I can look ahead at forever and see something solid and real on the horizon. And how, in those moments, I feel intensely proud I've made it far enough to see it.

"No," I say. "You are." As Danny gasps and Mason yanks the kid to his chest, sobbing, I close my eyes and pull the trigger.

28

THE AIR SHATTERS. I OPEN MY EYES TO SEE
Zach vanish and a bullet wound appear in the Angel's side, gravel
and water pouring from its veined skin.

The Angel falls to its knees and the entire illusion vanishes.
Underneath it is a multicolored mirage thing with sinews of grass
and tendons of lightning, silkworm intestines and striated bones,
meteorite teeth and copper veins, ten mismatched human eyes.
It struggles upright, eyes pinning me, and for a moment, it's ach-
ingly beautiful—silhouetted in pre-dusk gold, its smile beatific,
its skin dewy and glowing, like spring come again.

Then it falls onto its hands and shrieks.

"Isa!" Mason bellows. The two sounds together split my skull.
As I drop the gun, the Angel bursts into motion and slams Mason
off Danny, into the ground.

Danny screams, but before it can go for him I yell, "Corey!"

I don't know what made me say it—Stanley, in the memory,
saying his friend's name—but the Angel jerks violently. When it
whirls around, something's fractured in its façade, a million tiny
wrongs shattered and pieced jaggedly back together with none of
the seams quite matching up. Its movements are too human, too

physical and gangly, like it doesn't know how to use its own body, a many-limbed child with too many eyes casting around. Despite the pouring wound, it closes the distance like the wind and then closes its hands around my throat.

My spine hits the ground, but I feel no pain. Up close the eons turn in its eyes. In the jigsaw of its face I almost recognize its pieces: Zach's cheek cracks into Wren's lips split into Paige's throat opens into different shoulders and different hands, all these dead and kept kids. Then spots fractal in my vision. Its torn face blurs and all those shreds become my own. Older, younger all at once, a patchwork of Isadoras with all the despair in my many eyes flaring. It's so bright I almost look away but I don't do that anymore, I'm not afraid of that anymore. I stare right back at it, at myself.

So instead, her mouth leans in, and her song leans with it. "Follow me," she whispers.

"No," I choke out. I try to remember what I said just now that made it react like that, but its voice has swept into my mind and the part of me that dreams is already slipping. The Angel brushes against my cheek, a stone-cold butterfly kiss.

"Come with me," Wren's voice says.

Something bright flutters; something iridescent folds; the trees turn green. The four of us are in the grotto with our feet wet from the creek, the wonky arch of the entrance looking out to rustling trees and the blue summer sky. Irises twinkle around us. We're laughing. She's holding my hand. Somewhere else my fingers are scrabbling against the ground, but here there's a beautiful memory I could live in forever and ever. It would all be okay, and nothing outside this cave matters.

No, something's wrong, I think desperately. I have to squeeze the words between the seams of the vision and even as I do they're pushed back out. *This isn't real!*

And then I see it—like gauze tacked back just a little wrong—Wren's daisy crown has the black tinge of rot. Zach's too tall for this memory. As Mason bites into a cookie, it scatters on his lap, and the crumbs start crawling.

This isn't real. The Angel's whispers have built this dream, but what it thinks it has for me is a thing pinned back just an inch out of place.

Something hums. Harmony and melody drawing together into one single, stunningly clear sound.

Sensation clicks back in. My hand catches on something hard and I swing it around, smashing the stone into the Angel's temple.

It howls as earth sprays and slams me down again. This time it's my head that cracks. Wetness seeps through my hair. I'm not going to be able to hurt it badly enough like this.

Wren, what would you have actually written, if you had the choice? Zach, what did you hear out there? When was the last time we spoke? Properly? I have loved you every day the way a kid loves wholeheartedly but I feel like we didn't know each other at all, and I'll spend the rest of my life trading little pieces of you with other people to fill out your edges.

The Angel pulls at my hair, gouging my scalp. It's going to smash me open on the rocks. The song's not coming through. I'm reaching and reaching but I can't get a hold. And why should I? I've never been able to hold on to what really matters. I've never been able to open myself up. Useless, useless, useless.

But then over the Angel's shoulder, the real Mason struggles to his hands and knees. He's bleeding from the mouth, but his chime's slipped free from around his neck. He grabs it and as his eyes lock with mine, the fog in them clears. I feel the force between us tug like we're touching. We're tipping on the edge of the answer and all we need is one more key.

He wipes the blood off his chin and scrapes the chime over the metal button of his coat.

As the metal screeches, vibrations unravel in my mind, between my ribs, in a sensation both in and out of me at once. I watch his mouth move, and though I hear no sound, a voice comes into my head with it anyway. "Matthew Accetta," we say. "Paige Vandersteen. Wren Carver. Zachary Tai. George Mayer. Anne Wheeler." He's memorized all their names. He mouths them, and I hear him somehow and say them with him, and in answer, they all hear me.

THE SOUND OF THE SKY. The song of the mountains. The voice of the buried. It's right there and it feels like it's tearing me apart—but I let it, and it bursts right through me. Suddenly I hear every voice in the song so clearly.

"MY NAME IS ANNE WHEELER. Annie, Mama called me. I've never been sick like this before; I think I see birds—"

"My name is Ella Williams, and I was never even there like they said—"

"My name is Sammy Vandersteen and don't you remember, Ides, chasing you around this place, getting our knees all torn up from falling? And Theo was watching and he wasn't such a stuck-up—"

"My name is Matthew Accetta, fuck, we missed him something insane, you know, but no one would say they would—"

"My name is Zachary Tai, and I will never be my father, but the sky is so loud out there; it feels like it has the space for my heart—"

"My name is Paige Vandersteen, and I will kill you if you touch him—"

"My name is Wren Carver, and I am not an angel and *I AM NOT JUST ANOTHER DEAD GIRL EITHER.*"

A thousand ghosts are screaming. It is not a beautiful sound at all, but it is a sound after all those years of silence, voices and contradictions spinning together to one singular shrieking tone going right through my spine, splitting every cell in my body. At some point, words fail, but I hear them anyway. The voices are enough to make me feel like I could hold them, reach them, and where I need to, *break it free—*

I wrench free a hand and drag my nails across the Angel's face.

Its skin tears like a chrysalis, and ghosts and earth pour out. I scream and the Angel screams back, one calloused hand after another digging into my arms and throat and face. I look at its torn face and I see it, I see it, I see you, I was abandoned once too, over and over again, but I will not become this, I don't think we have to become this, I think we can choose not to become what hurt us because that's how you know the world is chooseable and if it is chooseable then it is makeable and if it is makeable then we can make something better of it. Then people will *have* made something better of it, are *already* making something better of it, every day in little touches, little kindnesses: a teenage girl breaking into a shop only to be given chocolate and a blanket. Mason, me, Trish—Mom, Sharlene, Sarai, Enoch Kane—perhaps we become what hurt us, take on its curses. But we get to choose what to do with the hurt.

The Angel comes apart.

Layer by layer peels off, fluttering sheets that twist into ghosts. I gasp as its grip loosens enough for cold breath to flood back in and kick it hard off me. It shrieks, but it's eroding so quickly its jaw turns to soil. Wind erupts from it and spins. I stagger away as it consumes itself, slamming into a girl in her pajamas.

"Isa," Mason croaks behind me. His actual voice jars me, and the saturation in my head fades as he squeezes my shoulder, reminding me it's there, that I'm present. The muffled pain finally sparks up my shoulders and back.

All the while the screams fade away, falling back to a chant in five alternating voices.

"Stanley McLean," I whisper.

"What did you say?"

But the voices flow through me from the ether and I let them block him out with the final names, the only ones he never knew. *Stanley McLean. Gilbert Campbell. Thaddeus Fay. Selwyn Roussel. Corey Fisher.*

I know immediately it's the Angel boys. And they are only boys, half their voices not even broken. So I almost know, when the wind dies down, what dark shape is left.

A newborn angel is curled in the crook of the cliff. It's no longer anything quite human-shaped—a clot of twitching rock slabs jutting in every direction, and then, within that, the contours of individual arms and legs grotesque in the opening daylight. Somewhere near the ground, a lone eye weeps.

Stanley McLean. Gilbert Campbell. Thaddeus Fay. Selwyn Roussel. Corey Fisher.

"Wait." Mason looks around like he's just realized that the air is thick with freed ghosts. He must have gotten hit pretty hard; that head wound has bled down the side of his face, but his eyes are flicking through the crowd now, the Angel forgotten.

I can't let it go just yet. I can feel the tugging that recognizes my friends somewhere out there, but a louder sound still drowns that beating out. I walk toward what's left of the Angel, hearing its lost names echo insistently. I don't know why this final layer won't come apart, though. I guess while I was only freeing spirits before, this original fusing was caused by something different. It needs something different to undo it.

"You said—Stanley McLean?" Otto struggles up from where he'd collapsed and clambers toward me.

Oh. Original release for the original sin. He's now the sole heir to the Vandersteen legacy, the last one left who can talk to the stones. I nod.

As I recite the names again, he tilts his head, listening for the right shapes. Then he nods and lays a hand on the Angel, which shudders as a mass. When his fingertips touch the rock, it starts to fall away. One chunk after another, coming loose and rolling downslope into the water, revealing more and more of the bodies between them, enough to tell them apart. Stanley, Gilbert, Thaddeus, Selwyn, Corey. Then those, too, crumble into dust that the wind picks up with a slanted sigh, lifting the ashes through the ghosts and making them ripple at the edges.

_we_

ONE: THE WINDOW IN THE CHURCH, STAINED

with an angel, shatters, and

Two: In the cemetery, the statues fall, break apart on the cold ground, and

Three: The fountain cleaves in half, releasing wishes over the cobblestones, and

Four: In the Purple House, the bust of William Vandersteen collapses, followed by Beatrice, and Jakob, and Theodore, and Cecily, and

Five: on, and on, and on, and

Otto Vandersteen puts his lips to the ground, and for once the earth is the listener: "It ends with me," he says.

29

AS THE GHOSTS SWIRL AROUND US, THE LIVING
kids finish waking. Blinking, curling and uncurling fingers that
then touch the places they're bleeding. They're all dazed and wide-
eyed, awful relief dawning on their faces. I feel it too, the hush of
a shared truth. It's out in the open now; this one we can't deny.

Flashes of the ghosts trickle in as I duck through them,
looking for where Mason's disappeared to. A flowery dress, a
lopsided smile, mismatched socks, ribboned braids, dangling
earrings, an airplane figurine, an old camera, flaking nail polish,
a music box, freshly baked bread, spilled paint, frying onions,
glistening honey, crayons, an orange cat, a black dog, freckles
like stars, a scar on an elbow. The images filter into the edges of
my mind; they ask to settle and I let them, breathing in the little
pieces of dozens of strangers' lives. I'll remember them, in bits
and pieces, a stray memory surfacing when I'm in a bakery or in
front of a flash, or looking in the mirror putting my earrings in.
But for the first time that idea doesn't terrify me. If I let them
rest there, I think it'll be okay.

They're fading, anyway, dissipating like summer rain to wherever they go next. My heartbeat picks up as I look for the two

people I want to see—surely I haven't missed them, surely they'd stick around—and just as the last of the ghosts seems to disappear I see Mason at the end of the Ridge still staring into the air. A tear trickles down his cheek. And I know without knowing who's left behind.

"Mason," I say softly, walking slowly toward him. I don't know if startling him will ruin everything. But he doesn't seem to hear me. His lips move soundlessly, and he's crying silently, cheeks glistening in the sun.

I reach out and touch his shoulder.

"—Isa."

And they're there. Not shrouded this time, or entombed, but silhouetted in soft morning light, standing on the surface of the water.

"Hey, Isa," Zach says, and my name no longer echoes in his mouth.

Wren cups my face and I choke back the sob that comes from nowhere. Her touch is incandescent. "It's been a while."

What do you say, to friends you had and then lost before you could know one another again? "Hi," I manage, and Wren laughs, a sound like spring. "You're okay."

"We are now."

"What's . . . ahead?"

Zach grins. "I guess we'll find out."

"*No.*" The word strangles in Mason's throat. "No, I—I haven't had enough time. Please. I'm not done."

"We're always with you, Mason. Here." Wren brushes a thumb over his temple and his head tilts back, follows the curve of her hand desperately. "Here." She touches his throat, her fingers dipping as he swallows. "Here." She takes Zach's hand and lays it over his heart. Both of them, fingers interlacing, folded into one. The air thrums softly with a pulse. "But we can't stay."

"I'm sorry," he whispers.

Zach looks at me, and I know what I have to do. "Mason."

They pull back. He reaches up toward their withdrawing hands, grasps onto their wrists. "Mason," I whisper, and now it's hard for me to get the words out. Everything tastes like salt. "I know you're willing to hold on, and that changed everything. But now it's about whether you're willing to let go." Gently, I put my hand over his. *"Let go."*

He shuts his eyes and sobs. But there's a sigh in the air and Wren and Zach melt away into sunlight, leaving me grasping his shoulder by the rippling channel, and him, arms extended and palms facing the sky, as though in prayer.

30

AFTER THE FUNERALS, AFTER THE CLEANUPS,
Otto Vandersteen asks Trish and me to come to the cemetery. Or
specifically, he asked Mason to ask me.

what so you're like best friends now that you're cousins, I
texted.

Second cousins, came the reply.

And no I just happen to have a key

Otto's been holed up in the cemetery since Paige's funeral.
Mason's refused to tell me what he's been up to. "He's crazy," is
all he'll say as Trish and I get out of the car and he takes us
through the cemetery gates. "You'll love it."

I've spent the past few days drawing and painting in a mad
whirlwind, suddenly too full of ideas to get them all down, but
I managed to narrow it down to four. I'll write the statement
tonight, Trish will drive me back to school tomorrow, and I'll
turn them in a day ahead of time. I already emailed Professor
Rodriguez just to let her know I'm still alive and planning on
graduating. After this stop, I asked Mason to come see the
pieces.

I also finally apologized to Olivia and Yara. I told Olivia I was on the way back and I'd love to get a chance to talk. We have ice cream planned for tomorrow night, when I return.

The cemetery feels oddly empty without the angel statues, which we returned to find had simply collapsed into piles of stone chips. They'll be taken to the workshop to be reused eventually, but for now the mounds still stand where they fell. Across the slopes and graves, though, I spot one statue still standing. It doesn't look like an angel. "Oh, shit. That's new. Did he—"

Mason rubs his temples. "I think he sleeps less than I do."

Trish squints. "Where is he?"

We cross a few columns of headstones, into the Vandersteen plot, to find that Otto is, in fact, curled up on the ground beside the statue. "Is he *napping*?" I say, even as Mason nudges Otto's knees with the tip of his shoe.

"Hey! Don't sleep in my graveyard!"

Otto cracks open an eye and squints back at us. "What time is it?"

As he gets up, I'm already staring at the brand-new sculpture beside Paige's grave. Remade from the pieces of one of the angels is a girl with her head tilted to the sky. It's his sister, unmistakably, and I have to turn aside for a bit before I start crying. I guess that's the prophecy of the Vandersteen twins—one of them dies and the other loses a part of themselves. We'll never know, exactly, what threads of Paige's fears the Angel tugged on to bring her to the edge of the quarry. What, in the end, consumed her. We can still only guess at Wren and Zach. That question is a ghost in and of itself. But we don't have to stay with the ghosts. We hold them long enough to tell each other we were both there, and then we move on.

Most kinds of sculptures are a process of carving something beautiful from a whole. I decide the thing I like about sculpting from slate is that already broken pieces can still be shaped into something beautiful.

We have brunch at The Court and talk about our plans. Trish will be here for a while longer, but she and Mom are talking about options. Yesterday, Mom disappeared with a phone call for a long time. We heard her talking, to our huge surprise, in Mandarin. Then she came out and asked us whether, on my spring break, we wanted to meet our grandmother.

Otto's looking at colleges. "I thought my parents would be thrilled to get me out of their sight, but now they're asking for my help to rebuild the stupid family busts."

"Are you going to do it?"

"To give Theodore a third eye, sure. I'll do Sammy and Ida too while I'm at it."

Mason's also decided to apply for college after all. We're planning to be in the same city, so we can find a place to be roommates. Neither of us know completely what we're doing, but we'll figure it out as we go along, sharing shitty furniture and instant ramen.

It's not entirely over. The truth is that it's never truly over; that for all the supernatural monsters, there are plenty of human ones too. But the ones that save us are so often human, too, and hanging on to them keeps us alive long enough to outlast everything else. To see the seasons change. Right now, it feels like it could be okay.

"Watch me come back with industrial piercings," Mason remarks. Our plan isn't a miracle solution, and there's about a thousand things to figure out, but just having a destination in mind makes all the difference. For the first time, it feels like we're all looking ahead to living.

"My piercings are *helixes*, amateur."

And in the meantime, we can try to enjoy the world even if we don't understand it.

WE LEAVE OTTO so I can go back and pack. Even from a distance the house looks cleaner, excavated. The empty flowerpots outside look less like urns and more like pods waiting for warmer weather to unfold. As we head up to the door, Mason glances at the Carvers' house. From the window, Danny waves. For a moment it looks like Mason's going to go over, but he just waves back and follows me inside.

My room is still a mess of paints and drying papers.

"Oh," he says. I've drawn the four of us in pencil, exactly the same in the center of each canvas while the watercolor background shifts between frames: The pond in spring, glittering. An open cave blooming in summer, the sky around us patterned with birds and stars. A diner booth in fall, yellow and orange tiling the glass window. A campfire by the water in winter. A kaleidoscope world turning around us. *Forgotten Places* sounds like abandonment, overgrowth, but I've spent too long forgetting the good things.

Mason touches the paper, traces our faces. "I'm glad you're still doing this."

"Yeah. It's nice to have something to hold on to." The grief will always be there but so will we, sitting with it, letting it rest, carrying on. Now begins the hard part of figuring out who we are without it defining us. But whoever we are, at the end of the day, we're still *something*. We've been bound together by those we've known and those we've loved. We exist in each other's gravity. For now, that's good enough.

I put the pieces away, brush flecks off the floor.

"Isa." Mason's voice sounds slightly odd, and I whip around, but he's just leaning out the window, reaching for something up the wall. He withdraws a second later and walks toward me with something cupped in his hand.

A purple flower, still dewy.

He extends it questioningly. Confused, I nod, and ever so gently, he tucks it behind my ear. "For good omens," he says.

A clean wind lifts the curtains, sending them fluttering like wings.

acknowledgments

The original title for this book was *Those You've Known*, and while we ended up with something a little spookier (still a homage!), I like to think that it's still a great title for this section specifically. I wrote this during pandemic isolation, and that song, that theme, and this book, ultimately, are about being a consolidation of the people you've known and been known by; about those who've shaped you, the grief of what once felt like a whole life coming to an end, the yearning for its return—but perhaps more healthily, owning that their power and presence within you never fades, even if time has moved you past it. Yes, *Past Lives* made me cry a little bit. Anyway:

This is not a book about theater, but in my heart it's a theater book. Sam Heg, I said, "Do you want to direct a show about repressed horny German schoolchildren?" and you said, "Bet"; sharing *Spring Awakening* with you imprinted it on my heart. Haya, fellow clown, with me in the wings, here's a book for your cake. I think of you when I drink apple tea. Rolfe, I wish I'd gotten to do this with you bitching about my onstage band but killing it anyway. Estelle, these aren't film credits, but maybe it's something. Jaeho, I hope to see you flying one day. Cowan, you are steadfast. Lorelei, stressed designer extraordinaire. Nathan, who would've killed it on lights. Dave on the barbie. Lydia and Yaning, who would've made the music. Joey, who read the show's synopsis and went, "Wen, what the fuck?" (valid), and the larger world of UCL theater. I am a better artist for having shared space with you, for learning to build time around creating things together, to believe we could do pretty much anything, turning up over and over instead of doing our degrees. I had the time of my life with you. I watch where you are now with such joy.

I've been lucky enough to support and be supported by so many in the long lead-up to debut. Of course, Isabel Kaufman: cat mom, always champion, who once called this "tis the damn season but horror" and made me so mad I didn't think of that first. The publishing team: Tiffany Liao, for challenging me to whittle this book out; Gillian Flynn, for giving it a home, and for all the messy women; Lexy Cassola for picking up the reins and TJ Ohler for holding the fort down throughout; Rachel Kowal, Anna Hall, Chloe Texier-Rose, Emily Morris, Nathalie Ramirez, Natalie Ullman, and everyone else at Zando; Karina Granda and Anders Rokkum for the haunting cover; various readers for the insightful comments in honing this book and spot-checking me down to the commas. The odds of getting two Tiffany Ls from Taiwan on the same book are low but never zero: thanks also to Tiffany Liu, who saw me in the group chat trying to draw badly and immediately whipped up a hair motif for the inner pages.

Then, for once it was done, thank you to all the authors I admire so much who also took the time to read and say such kind things about this book: Allison Saft, Andrew Joseph White, Courtney Gould, Courtney Summers, Kerstin Hall. And Trang

ACKNOWLEDGMENTS

Thanh Tran, keeper of my sanity—I would haunt any house with you too.

All the 2024 publishing children, especially Trinity Nguyen—PJ to my Josie, Barbie to my Oppenheimer, Vietnamese roommate to fake Singapore study abroad—and Ann Zhao, purveyor of common sense. Maddie Martinez, Sophia Hannan, Birdie Schae, Tiff again, truly Losing It. The large and noncomprehensive host of people that propped me up along the time this took to be published: Alex Brown, Amber Chen, Amy Leow, Aliyah Fong, Auden Patrick, Cath Liao, Chiara Situmorang, Camille Chong, Clare Osongco, De Elizabeth, Gabrielle Bonifacio, Hannah Wastyk, Jennifer Carnelian, Jen St. Jude, Kyla Zhao, Layla Noor, Mary Joy Kawano, Nadia Noor, Sai Tsaika, Sabrina Lunavong, SJ Whitby, Sophie Wan, Sujin Witherspoon, Sydney Langford, Ysabelle Suarez. Clarion West '22: Ana Hurtado, Kerstin Hall, Varsha Dinesh, Naomi Day, Steph Kwiatkowski, Kel Coleman, Yvette Lisa Ndlovu, Issa Marc Shulman, Alex Cruz, Takim Williams, Jonathan Kincade, Sam Davis, Subraj Singh, Louis Evans, PH Lee, Sloane Leong, Tania Fordwalker. Cossette, my target demographic. Isa joins the trench coat loner theater girlies (Ilse, Eurydice, Eponine). To Nicole and Juliana for the gorgeous commissions that brought my children to life as I was writing, and to everyone who's ever told me they were excited about the book, or posted about it—thank you.

Kimberley Chia, Christian Yeo, Laetitia Keok, with whom I've convened through various chances; light, and kind grief, and holding space, and yes, tenderness; who write vignettes from lives made in different spots of the world and figure out where is home. The epigraph is all yours, because you all shared it to your stories on the same day. That's what I get for being

323

friends with poets. Siken and too many people telling me to read Bluets.

Felicia Low, as of me writing this, we still haven't gotten coffee, but thank you for the kaypoh help and gossiping. Tze, Nic, Mimi, Max; Beth and Dani, earliest readers who I promised to dedicate my first book to (okay, it's not the dedication, but close enough). To James, for the flowers, way back when—it meant more than you know.

To family, who grew me with the capacity and the privilege to write. My mom introduced me to musicals (the *Les Misérables* tenth anniversary recording shaped me as a person); my dad took me to bind my first books. To Min: tell your stories; your horizons are never too small to build a life around creating. To my grandparents, who I wish I had the language to know before it was too late.

To me at sixteen, nineteen, twenty-one: it'll be okay.

And finally: Deaf West's *Spring Awakening*, the piece of theater that made this, and Taylor Swift, for asking, "Are there still beautiful things?"

about the author

WEN-YI LEE is a Clarion West alum from Singapore who likes writing about girls with bite, feral nature, and ghosts. Her speculative fiction has appeared in venues such as *Lightspeed*, *Strange Horizons*, and *Uncanny*, as well as in various anthologies. *The Dark We Know* is her debut novel. Find her on social media at @wenyilee_ and otherwise at wenyileewrites.com.